CUG0878357

Do You Want to Live Forever?

by

R N Stephenson

ISBN: 978-0-244-45798-3

First published in 2019

This edition published in 2019 by Altair Australia Pty Ltd

Do You Want to Live Forever?

By

R N Stephenson

Published by
Altair Australia Pty Ltd

Thank you to Alice, Emma and Joshua,
for helping to make all this possible.

Prologue

The Prelüstitel

His fingers pushed through my skull, holding me to the wall. The cold was crushing, freezing all thought as he stopped time. I couldn't move, couldn't breathe. The room black-iced over; crackling over the bone covered floor. The walls, the ceiling became an impenetrable night sky. Bones turned onyx. Aza'zel wanted information. We were in a secret room, a killing room long forgotten to history.

"Who has it?"

"The icon?"

"No. The book."

"I haven't found it yet." His snake-like fingers dug deeper, searching for the truth. I could hide things in my mind, but not everything.

It was a mistake to write the book. A mistake to entrust it to Uri. Aza'zel had made me, that should have been enough.

"Do a casting, find this book or you will be flung like a stone into the *Abad*. And bring me that urn!"

He withdrew, and I collapsed forward. On hands and knees, I fought for breath. He fractured and dropped into the bones, a crash like glass on stone. The cold lifted, I drew back as a shadow shifts across a wall. I had followed Sarina since the day I was resurrected into the dark, but now I had her and the book to act upon. Castings were not perfect, nor were they ideal; too much could go wrong or be misleading. I had little choice. He knew of the book; he was not patient.

Pacing the room I built a dream, thick with promise, glowing with light. It would find who I wanted, but it would not lead me to them. I cast, let it flow into the skeins of night. It would take time, perhaps more time than I deserved.

Chapter 1

Cassandra

I'd showered and tried to wash the invisible blood from my hands — Mariz's blood. Three months of scrubbing could not wash away the stain.

I was one of America's top-selling Gothic author, and twice New York Times best-selling author; I should have been the happiest writer in Santa Monica. I wasn't. All my life I had lived in the place of writers and artists, walked in the footsteps of Andrews and Aya, lived in Dogtown for cred for a year and I had achieved great things with my writing, only now it meant nothing. I'd become part of Santa Monica history but for all the wrong reasons.

Tonight, I was breaking out of my enforced hiding, not an easy or comfortable task, and I was going to face my accusers. I stared into the bedroom mirror; a murderer stared back. I hadn't shot, stabbed or poisoned my victim. No, my weapons were a computer keyboard and a single email. Mariz Sanchez was dead because of me, because of what I'd discovered. He'd driven into Beverly Hills after being stripped of his award and branded a fraud by the media. The police found him a day later, in his car; a vacuum cleaner hose ran from the exhaust and had been pushed in through the rear window. Suicide, the police said. The coroner's confirmation made it clear, but I knew I had killed him. Now all I wanted was for him to be out of my life out of my house. And I didn't want to die to get him to leave me alone.

His ghost stalked the rooms, thudded down the hallway every morning towards my bedroom. He'd sit on the end of my bed, staring, saying nothing. I'd scream; throw pillows. He didn't budge, didn't flinch. Then he'd say, "Follow". Mariz had become a glowing blue apparition of a man I'd driven to death.

It's true I'd wanted to destroy Mariz, bring him down, ruin him; all because I wanted Samantha's love. I wanted to take her from him. After the brief inquest, she never spoke to me again. In a way, I'd murdered my chances at love as well. I considered calling her a few times to explain, to find out if she'd got my calling card. She wouldn't tell me if she had, not after what I'd done, and what it meant. The one-time fashion model, the woman who'd captured my heart was forever out of reach — our one moment together a joy and yet sadness at the same time. Her hatred of me hard to deal with.

The haunting started soon after Mariz's death three months ago. I'd thought of them as drunken visions; the visits were every day, the same in some way. "Follow," he'd always say. I might have had the tendency; it was just committing suicide to atone for my sins wasn't on the cards. Not yet anyway. My home became a haunted house, a place of restless sleep, and there was plenty to be haunted by. Mariz's ghost had taken up permanent residence, a punishment I guess, his revenge. I'd thought about moving. Would he follow me? I thought he would. My memories were in the house, my life; the room where the first three bestsellers were written. I couldn't just walk away, ghost or not.

The tight little clique of writers in the people's republic turned their backs on me once they'd put all the questions and answers together, working out it had been me who'd set the ball rolling towards Mariz's end. Though they all knew he had taken his own life: I was still blamed. They would never forgive me for that. Could I ever forgive myself? Somehow, I doubted it, doubted anything could undo the past.

The Santa Monica and the Venice Beach area might have been one of the brightest places in American literature in its time, but it was also the darkest hole on Earth if you stepped outside of the expected etiquette. I'd taken that step. I'd done nothing wrong; I should have been the hero, and in many parts of the literary world I was, but not in my back yard. My connections were under question, my motives less than pure. Beware of the truth; it isn't always the right thing to do.

Three months on the outside was a long time in this business. Three months locked away with his ghost an ever increasing well that drew on my already shaky, depressive moods. Regardless, this town was where I was born, and nothing was going to drive me out, not even Mariz. Tonight, happened to be the Writers' Fellowship's annual general meeting. I was a fully paid up, voting member, and I had every right to attend. The group hadn't asked me to leave. Even so, they'd stopped inviting me to functions and my space at the Writer's Junction didn't feel comfortable anymore. I couldn't ignore their motives; tonight, it was time to face them head-on. I finished my glass of George T, my fifth, and sighed with the thought of coming out of my seclusion, out of the darkness.

I adjusted my jacket. The denim, worn and frayed on the shoulders and elbows, it set off the Black Sabbath T nicely. In the mirror I looked more like a rock fiend than a writer, then I did live a partly Goth life. They were the only people who accepted me for what and who I was. True I had to go to LA to fit in, and the strip wasn't always ideal, but I belonged, and the way things were at the moment I needed to fit in somewhere. The jacket I'd chosen would do little for the chilliness of October and next to nothing if it rained, which didn't seem likely. It was my look and who I wanted to show at the meeting. With thick, black eye makeup and bright red lipstick, I was ready. A leather jacket might have completed the picture, though that wasn't my thing.

"Follow," Mariz said.

I ignored him. Not tonight, I didn't have the time.

"Follow."

I grabbed my bag and keys off the hall table, flicked on the outside light and slammed the front door after me. Pressing back against the rough wood, resolve a little shaken, I slowed my breathing and let the cool night air settle a head full of doubts. Not tonight I thought, as I walked to the car and climbed in. It had been raining early in the day, and the air still had that clean, fresh smell. I lowered the window, taking in the scent of eucalyptus trees, I had some of the remaining trees on 9th street; their oils released because of the downpour. I needed as much friendly support as possible, even if it was just the aroma of my garden.

The drive was free flowing down Nielson Highway to Pacific Ave, the night dark, the cold keeping people indoors. The silent journey, through romantic restaurants and closed shops, led me into the low light Abbott Kinney Ave. The whole time I thought how Santa Monica held more lost souls than hell itself. The one-time hive of artistic types had become the world capital for weirdos and those who had nowhere else to go. Even with its nastiness, I loved the place, the people, the casual living; the Goths and their isolated ways. I'd lived in New York, and it harried me with its ever-rushing, fast lifestyle. Here, no one rushed, or could even be bothered to rush. The place housed a world that would pause if you let it. It wasn't backwards, or slow thinking, it was just focused on what seemed more important. Living, and enjoying the time you had.

I parked near the French restaurant, the old Volvo not a real target for car thieves and I hated parking on the street by the Fellowship Meeting, too many opportunities for someone to stop me for a talk. I didn't want to talk. The car locked, my nerve set, and with several deep breaths, the time had arrived to face a part of this world that contained more bitterness than a cup of lime juice.

A brisk walk across the parking lot to Electric Ave, through grey barrenness in feeble light, frightened many in the group, but my look had always given me street protection; a 'one of us' look that kept me in touch with most of the locals and touch with my readers. I hesitated. I should have called into O'Brian's for a quick drink on the way. A whiskey would have been appropriate about now. I wouldn't be able to stop at one and turning up smashed would cause more problems than I could deal with. I paused at the door of the building, the next block up. Cars passed by. Electric Ave was a mix of life going somewhere, and right now I wished I was going somewhere else.

Despite determination, a sweaty nervousness began to take hold. I checked my makeup in a reflection of the building glass frontage, pushed long, black hair off my shoulders and offered a forced smile. It would have to do. The climb up the stairs became a slow immersion into the growing hubbub above, the voices of those who'd chosen to shun me. It was hurtful, giving in to it would hurt more; self-esteem had been weakened, my usual positive nature gone. My shoulder bag felt heavy, and my stomach dragged with a flow I hated, had always hated. I stepped into the room and the pervading smells of coffee and wine. The wooden floor echoed firm clicks as I walked; my high heels showing beneath the ragged hems of jeans. Instantly, the mood changed.

Conversation stopped as stares tried to snap every bone in my body. I remembered stares like that; my father's stares. He'd wanted me to marry, have children and give him grandchildren. I wanted to please him, make him proud. I'd tried. I couldn't be what he wanted. My first girlfriend was only for show, and I still feel some regret for it. My father's face reddened when I introduced her. He'd already become defensive when he'd seen her tattoos and piercings.

"Meet Star, my girlfriend," I'd said. He sat at the table reading the Observer. As soon as he frowned, I knew his love had slipped away. "We're living together."

"Room-mates?" He clutched the paper in his white-knuckled fists; his meagre hope.

I laughed, trying to lighten his shock. "She's my lover."

That's how I felt now, the reception, cold and reproachful. The gathering returned to their chatter and pretended they hadn't seen me, the tension worse than the drag in my stomach. They stood in their little groups, each group closing ranks to keep me out. Samantha, wearing black slacks and jacket to match her blonde hair, looked up and then deliberately away. She talked earnestly with Amanda Debbs from the Santa Monica Artists Fellowship; a rather fat woman with a less than merry view of the world. The Fellowship had rejected my last grant application. Was it because of what had become known as the "Sanchez Incident" or because my last novel showed the local writing world up for what it was; an insecure shadow of its former self? My book outsold all the books the authors in the room had produced, and a New York top 10 set it up for Best Seller status. Before Mariz's death I would have been the toast of the town, the celebrated author with homegrown talent, but now I bore the mark of Kain; unjustly so I thought in my better moments, rightly so at other times.

Amanda sucked up to writers, fed on their egos. She couldn't feed on everyone's though, maybe that also had something to do with the grant process?

I purposefully walked by them and offered a nod of recognition, then helped myself to a glass of cheap red wine. The drink helped; the pressure to be bold and confident draining.

Be strong. Ignore them. Be yourself.

The small groups talked of writing and the business, about the only thing they could find common ground on. I wanted to talk about movies, fast cars, sexy women or vacations. I wanted to talk about the ghost in my house; the man who refused to let me rest. I heard the snickers, the short laughs coming at some lesbian joke. I knew how to live with it, pity they hadn't.

"Fuck off." I gave one group the finger. They turned their backs. I sipped wine. Being strong is one thing, being demure and polite another. I should have stayed away. Mariz's presence had shortened my temper, made me edgy.

9

A newcomer, unaware of how I was supposed to be treated, introduced himself and then rambled on and on about his 'what if' dreams. I'd heard all the woes before, so I knew when to nod and agree. His eyes kept drifting to my breasts, a typical male action. Even when I told the guys I was gay, their focus of desire remained. Men didn't get it. Not *hetero* men, anyway.

"Are you always a dickhead?" I wished he'd avoided me like the others.

"No, no," he stammered.

I wanted to be seen, not bored to death. "Then I suggest you shut up and piss off somewhere else." I suppose living with a ghost changes you. I never used to be rude. Never.

"Sorry." He took his bottle and joined one of the groups. They closed in around him, voices whispered, eyes flashed reproachful stares. I should have stayed home; I didn't need to do this.

I was standing alone by the hired room's entry someone caught my eye. A tall, attractive woman, another stranger; she looked a little out of place; an oddity in this collection of misfits and wannabes. I felt a sense of relief as our eyes met. She smiled. I returned the gesture. A good feeling, a warm acceptance, which I hadn't felt in years, seeped through me.

After five minutes of meet and greet the meeting was declared open and we took our places, me at the back; the pariah and unclean. General business was discussed; soft applause went up for someone's book being published. I didn't clap, couldn't be bothered; didn't care. The meeting closed as all meetings do, and the dragging sensation returned. With bag under arm, I escaped to the toilet to take care of an urgent matter. Later, joining the flow of members to the supper tables and drinks, I wondered if I should eat something. I hadn't eaten all day. The groups reformed and once more I was shut out. The bore had been absorbed by the others: Amanda whispered in his ear; no doubt he wouldn't speak to me again. The thought gave me no sense of loss, more acceptance. Exiled, I washed down cheese cubes with glasses of wine, lots of wine. Feeling a little numb, I turned to leave; there seemed no point in staying, I could be equally alone by myself. The attractive woman blocked my path.

"You're Cassandra Whitehall." Eyes hard and determined, a brilliant blue, peered from a slender, angular face. "I've always wanted to meet you." Black lipstick parted slightly over the words. Her black hair and pale skin attracted me; she looked like she just stepped out of one of my books. She projected an aura I couldn't or didn't want to resist. Being celibate for a while makes you needy.

"And you are?" I was polite but neutral.

This woman wore a mannish black suit, black blouse and an onyx brooch; the lines of the suit emphasized her trim figure. Her voice, soft, accented, and old, far older than the twenty-five she looked, reminded me of eastern Europe.

"I am Sarina Jeppe." She offered her hand. "I've read all your books."

I liked her look. I'd visited Romania for a book signing tour a few years back; a gimmick trip as the book had been set in that part of the world. This woman had that same look only the eastern regions could produce. High cheekbones and strong features.

"I hope they were as enjoyable to read as they were to write." I liked fans.

"I recognised you from the photo on a book jacket." She still held my hand. "You look very pretty."

She, too, was ignorant of my pariah status - or didn't care what others thought. I ignored the comment about my looks. If believing it, I would have thanked her. "Are you going to join the fellowship?" Her touch felt soft, warm. "The fees are reasonable."

"I might join, though I do tend to speak my mind, does it trouble you?"

I became wary. "You can say anything you like, no skin off my nose." I scanned the room, was this a setup. No one looked my way. "Just don't get personal."

"I won't, well I will try." She didn't lose the smile. "I read 'The Stainless Hammer of God' when it was released. It moved me. I was very taken by your dark touch, the humanness you injected into the fantasy."

The Stainless Hammer of God was one of my better books, and I liked praise just like any writer. I'd written it when I was twenty, twelve years ago, and I knew my drug related concepts were way above teenage readers.

"Thank you." What would she have gotten from such a dark and brooding tale? "Didn't you find it a bit challenging? I mean, you must have read it when you were, what? thirteen, it would have been difficult to understand, surely?"

"You would be surprised." Sarina moved in close. Her perfume subtle, spicy. My skin tingled with her closeness. I felt strangely excited. "I came here looking for a writer," she whispered. I could smell wine on her breath.

"Anyone, I know?" She occupied my space, yet it didn't feel intrusive.

"I came looking for one writer. You, Ms Whitehall." She touched my waist. I didn't pull away; warmth radiated from her hand. "I want to tell you a story," her voice so soft I struggled to hear. "My life is quite interesting."

I'd heard this line at least a hundred times and should have expected it from someone who knew my work. The excitement faded.

"I've written some notes, and I need help to make sense of it all."

My first reaction was to excuse myself and leave. As soon as people learn I am a writer, they try to convince me the world is waiting to read their stories. It's an affliction of the profession. But she was speaking to me, in front of the others. I wanted to be seen with someone intelligent and willing to speak to me, being beautiful and young came as a bonus. I'd been single for years and had a yearning for good female company; perhaps she would ease away the ache I felt for Samantha. I didn't need love or understanding. I didn't even need emotional commitment. I needed someone to hold me, to listen.

11

Remaining polite, "I'm certain your story is interesting, but I don't ghost write or work with others wanting help with their stories," which wasn't true. I had offered to write Lindsay Lohan's story some years back. She had problems, and her agent baulked at the idea. I still think I could have done an excellent job for her. Now there was a person's story that needed telling.

She took my hand again, squeezed gently. I felt a tingle, my energy waned. "Please, will you help me?" Her eyes softened, the blue penetrating, alive, calling to me. "I mean it when I say I have had an interesting life."

She captured me like any woman is captured by the attentions of another. I didn't want to fight against the feeling; I liked the deep warmth of her touch, the slight draining sensation at her touch. The book might be interesting. What in this woman's life could be worth telling? She looked like a model, tall, leggy; perhaps a story on behind the scenes of the catwalk: bitch talk and bad mouthing. I'd settle for a few drinks and a kiss now; the pariah status isn't all that enjoyable. I could tell her about my ghost, maybe she'd run away from me, not sure what to make of the mad woman, or she might have an idea of how to get rid of him.

"Perhaps." I didn't completely back away. "We would need to talk about it first."

"Call me." She scribbled her number on the back of a business card. "I need to leave; my energy is a bit low this evening. Please call." She handed me the card and headed for the door. I liked the way she walked.

I examined the card. Blank on both sides with just the hand-written number in black ink. Odd having a blank card as a business card, then I'd met quite a lot of odd people over the years. I drank some more wine before leaving. I would certainly call her, even if there weren't a story to tell.

The first time I'd seen Mariz's ghost I thought I was dreaming; I'd been recovering from a hard night at the Goth Club at the time. I'd been drinking for about a week, trying to drive away the images of the funeral and the animosity towards me. He'd appeared sitting at the dining table, looking sad and downtrodden; his usual pose. I rubbed my eyes and then he was gone. The second time I'd just stepped from the shower, walking through the living room drying my hair. He was sitting on the sofa, a book in his hands, reading. I screamed, made a poor attempt at covering myself until I realised the man on the couch was indeed Mariz Sanchez. I screamed again, wrapping the towel around myself and tried to get my boozy body to react.

"Follow?" he said, though the voice seemed to come from within my head.

At first, I didn't know what to do. I froze and just stared. He was there in front of me, yet not there. The blue glow about him telling me something wasn't right.

"What the hell is this?" I said, eventually finding my voice.

"Follow."

"Who are you? What do you want?" I blinked a few times, but he remained. It looked like Mariz, only he was dead. This time he gazed straight at me. It was definitely him ... well, the ghost of him. I went from fear to confusion in a matter of seconds, from there, guilt settled deep in my stomach. It was a drawing down feeling; like a period. I thought about running into the bedroom, but the whole situation, a surreal memory now, kind of galvanised my mind. It was though I stepped back and watched myself talking to the ghost and knowing what was going on.

"Follow."

I didn't know what he was talking about. And being naked I wasn't going anywhere.

"Where?"

He grinned like he knew something I didn't. "You must follow." Then he was gone. Just like that, vanished. Of course, I questioned whether I'd seen him at all, then I saw the book he'd been reading lying on the couch. Something had happened. He'd been reading his book, *Me and Him*. Did he recognise his fraud? I didn't like ghosts, not that I'd seen them before, just the thought of them gave me the creeps, and I felt creeped-out. I shook from far more than the cold. I stood in the middle of the room and stared at the couch. Inexplicably, I felt ashamed. I had been arrogant enough to even go to the man's funeral. Later in the day, I realised what I'd done. I'd played with the lives of real people, caused a real death and even shed some false tears as the eulogies had been given. The tears didn't start until I sat in my dining room hours later. At the time, it had been as if Mariz and Samantha were just characters in one of my stories. That night it rained; heavy, heartfelt rain.

The lights in my home dulled to a melancholy yellow, and unusual for October, a thick fog had settled over the streets. A grey halo surrounded my home, clung to the garden. As I thought about the suicide and the single email to Mariz's publisher, I emptied the contents of a bottle of George T Stagg. The bite didn't bite after the first two glasses. Mariz's wasn't the only death on my mind. I thought of the old man who died on the side of a road; Uri. Could I be responsible for his demise as well? In a way, he'd helped me bring Mariz down.

I spent most of the next two days in bed; ill in so many ways. Mariz wanted me to follow him in death. I was sure of it, and I was determined not to if it could be avoided.

Chapter 2

The Prelŭstitel

Uri had taken the book. I know who he gave it to, but they were now both dead. My casting led me to Mariz, only I forgot caution, and Mariz Sanchez's darkness and life was sucked dry before I could question him fully. He had used the book to create another, one that was accepted as fiction and not of real concern. So great were the changes, so comical the new renditions of the old ways. His mind, filled with darkness, was like grabbing at information through the crisscrossed mesh of a cage, his thoughts cloudy and troubled. I took him too fast, his hold on life too weak and he emptied before I could find where he had put the book and who else had seen it. I did find another connection, weak and indirect; it came from his darkness, a fear that had driven him to seek death. The man's spirit was now mine; to control a ghost isn't a difficult task, trying to trace it to its place of haunting impossible. I could send commands and only hope what I wanted would come to me. He had to lead this person to me, along with the book.

Aza'zel wanted the urn; I owed him that much. I owed him my very existence. I stared up at the window, Sarina's apartment; the cold winter air of the sea kept the beach deserted. No one could see me unless I wanted them to; still, I hid beneath the jetty. She could see me; she has part of what made me, only more light than dark, more alive than dead. She protected the urn, and in a way, I protected as well as hunted her. It wasn't natural to find nurture in my state, and it would have troubled me if I could have found why I truly cared for her and despite the influences of Aza'zel, I found I could not move against her. Not yet anyway.

The window stared back, empty, a sheet of glass like all the others in the wall — clouds, heavy and ready for storming, reflected in their surface; a mosaic of the sky.

I am a Prelŭstitel, a hunter, a creature of darkness who can hold onto light when I have the need; it allowed me a presence in the world of sun and artificial light. I cannot enter close to Sarina's world, because of what she is, or more to the point, what I am not. Her kind, bright with light, are also alive with the energy, and glimmering light of the living. In some ways she was human. To stand before her would be like standing within the heart of a sun. To get the urn I must find a way into her realm, and she is too old to fall for simple tricks.

The wind whipped around me, through me, it's cold like the outer darkness, the stuff that keeps me in the world. Rain would fall soon, wet the glass and fracture the view. She would wake, look down and know I watched and waited like I have always watched and waited. She would not give it up easily. Aza'zel understood the importance and the heritage that reached back through time, all the way back to the primaeval. A test of Godness which created something that could draw on light more powerful than any void created by humans. I know it now, wished I'd known it a long time before. I cannot change my decision, nor would she accept me if I could. He wanted me to watch her, look for a weakness to exploit. Aza'zel saw no need for light and Sarina was light; it was s simple matter to him to remove it so darkness could be complete. I could not delay the inevitable forever; I only hoped that Sarina had used my delays wisely. Within the cold, I thought of old Paslenov, his dedication, the hardships of living and assisting something beyond his full comprehension. I didn't need companionship but at times living in the human world served *Him* better than drifting in and out like a spirit. There were parts of the world I could not have fed without the covering protection of my companion. I knew he had wanted to help, he might have even thought his actions would please me, perhaps honour me. Instead, he released a secret into the light, one I must get back; no human could know the truth that lurked beneath their legends. I understood the need for human mythology to Aza'zel, the murkiness between truth and reality, the hidden powers that had kept our presence protected since the dawn of all time. Aza'zel didn't fear what the book disclosed, his darkness fed on the legends created around him, to diminish such legends would lessen the darkness of desire. Legends helped create a dark well within humans and make them an easier target for his Prelůstitel. The book must be found; found and destroyed.

If I could mourn death, I would possibly mourn for Uri. Only my feelings as a Prelůstitel are strange, often disconnected images of times past and random events jumbled together like a child's puzzle. I remembered the sea, the spray in my face and the sounds of cannon fire and screaming men. I remembered the face of a promise, the eyes of salvation and the denial I exchanged for eternity.

Uri was gone, and I thought I missed the old man's company. Paslenov deserved better than what he got. Those responsible would be punished by a hand only he would appreciate, and it would be difficult to revenge in a manner befitting the old human; human ways are hard to manage - complex. As I waited, watched, let the rain blanket me, I let the darkness I'd taken from a family on the beach bleed from me. To confront such a being as Sarina I would need more darkness than I could possibly hold and survive, only Aza'zel could easily stand before her.

Sarina appeared at the window, skin pale. She stared down on me; I resisted the urge to tilt my head in acknowledgement. We would have to meet, eventually, and I, for one, wasn't looking forward to the occasion, but I must protect the internal night - no one must learn about the darkness.

Chapter 3

Cassandra

Mariz had at one time been brilliant, a creative force into his prime. I saw his fine-boned face, his curly, brown hair, his dark eyes that, more and more, had expressed pain. In the years before his suicide his writing fell into decline, his confidence slipped from under him, and he quickly became a man of desperation. His last contracted book fell through because he couldn't meet the ever-extended deadline. Then he had gone into hiding. Samantha, the fair-haired fashion queen who stumbled into his life, gave occasional word of his progress on a new project. "The best thing he has ever written," she would gush. During this time Samantha and I had slept together. I took advantage of her drunken state and emotional turmoil. Mariz was in Chicago for the weekend, and I'd taken her back to my place to sleep off our girls' night binge. When she woke the next morning, laying naked in my arms, she wasn't shocked or concerned.

"I needed that," she said, touching my face. I kissed her. She kissed back.

"I've always wanted you." I felt at peace with her, the touch of her lips against mine a pleasure I had longed for. I'd watched her face, touched her hair and became lost in desire as we made love. I felt it was meant to be. I had found someone to love and perhaps love me.

"I know, but you know it can't be anything else." She sat up, the sheets falling from her to reveal small breasts, pert. Fair skin, alive with youth and dotted with a few brown moles teased me and drew me further into her aura. Her presence cried out to me. I wanted her; I loved her. "Last night felt wonderful, Cassandra." She climbed out of bed. "I'd never been with a woman before …" She hesitated. "I love Mariz; he is who I am meant to be with. He needs me to help finish this book."

I watched her dress. Words failed me for the first time in years. Tears dribbled down my cheeks. What could be expected from one night of sex? As she left the bedroom, I listened to her footfalls down the hall and then the click of the front door. Why didn't I say anything? Why didn't I stop her from leaving? Staring at my dressing table, the clutter of perfume bottles and hand creams, I felt the hesitation my depression brings when faced with a difficult issue. I thought I had a chance with her. That night had shown me the way. I had to get Mariz out of the picture.

To me Mariz was washed up, falling further and further into his emotional black hole. I just had to be there when Samantha also realised the futility of her love. A shoulder for tears, a word and ear, a hand of reassurance and the embrace of care. All mine to offer. Time would bring her to me.

Then Mariz's new book came out. It was brilliant, dark, full of shifting shadows and secrets. It was truly one of the best books I'd read in the last ten years. Mariz had somehow found a new voice from which to write, and I was jealous, concerned and highly suspicious – it wasn't his book. I hated him even more, and I set out to undo the fraud he perpetrated. Six months later he won the 'Southern Pen Award', then a World Fantasy Award for best fantasy novel. Samantha slipped from my world, became further and further out of reach.

I'd never won an 'SPA', although I had been short-listed twice. You have to be part of the clique or scene to get nominated down South. Mariz had family down there, so it made sense. Since his death I became the outsider, the unwanted and no longer part of the considerations of the scene, they frowned heavily on anyone who stands against one of their own. The big-name authors still respected me, spoke to me in public and private, it was only the fellowship, the local scene, the little whispers amongst friends, that undermined parts of my career.

Coupled with guilt, past issues and loneliness I dropped deeper and deeper into depression. Being down in mood was normal, the drop further created a well deeper than even I could imagine. Heavy medication kept much of the black dog at bay and visits to Dr Sholan always helped monitor my feelings, though I didn't always go where he wanted me to.

I'd get so down on myself the doubts would swallow me like I gulped whiskey. My ghost seemed to take joy in this decline. Every day I'd see my face in the mirror, try and fathom what was behind the blue of my eyes. I was considered beautiful and intelligent by women and men I knew; I'd been told often enough. Knowing isn't the same as feeling though. In the mirror, something dreadful always stared back. The cold hard face of a killer; a very unbeautiful person examined me coldly. I deserved the haunting. Mariz had every right to be angry with me; I was angry with myself. Each day in the house with him helped keep me in touch with the vile soul I'd become. Late at night, him sitting at the dining table, me with a packet of peanuts and a bottle of George T. on the couch, I'd slip further and further into the same embracing shadow that Winston Churchill had named during his own darkest hours. The yapping of his black dog persisted at my back door. The drugs helped me get through the days, helped me meet the deadlines for my work, it was they could do little to blanket memories, or drive away my ghost.

Most of the time I felt old and haggard, so I stopped venturing out during the day, preferring to stay in bed and read, and write a little in the afternoon; drink a bottle or two of wine, dampen the spirits. Then after the sun had set, take to the night, the dull illumination of city back-streets and the strange characters that flowed along them. Goth Club, on the Strip, became a second home. The music, the clothes, the scene, the views of the world matched with how I felt and looked at myself; I grew into the darkness, and it took root in me. In three months, I'd gone from outwardly forward to inwardly sullen.

These days I was usually so drunk I didn't care what others thought of me, the only thing that remained constant was Mariz. More than once I wondered if he also felt depressed about being dead; would he have a ghost dog on his back?

Fortunately, the Goths had accepted me with open arms after my book, 'Deep Blood, Black Lips', a novel about a young couple dealing with the ever presence of evil beings that ruled their waking moments. I couldn't shake the depression out of my life even then, and it showed in everything I wrote. Like David Bowie's Ziggy Stardust, I had inadvertently become the principal character from my work - 'Amalia', the paranormal sleuth who had it all, magic powers, dark lust, and the whole Goth world at her feet. Unlike Amalia I didn't go too deep into the culture; Goth in spirit, if not in look. They became my tiny lights in the murkiness; it is how I thought of them — small glimmers of hope that kept me attached to life.

A bottle of twelve five-year-old whiskey, George T Stagg, always waited behind the bar of the club. I'd been told, as remembering nights at the club was difficult, I would never leave until the bottle was empty and a new one had been ordered. He didn't visit me when I was soaking up the strobing shadows of the club, soaking in the grey stink of cigarettes and booze. Here I'd let the shadows consume me, drown me in hazy recollections and shifting faces. Only until I could no longer lift the glass to my lips did I stop drinking. I'd always wake up home and in bed. A rescuer would deliver me from evil, return me to safety. I never knew who it was, and for a short time I questioned the bar staff about it, they'd just shrug and put a whiskey in front of me. Now I didn't care, what was the point? A dark angel watched over me, and one day I'd be taken for good.

The memory of Samantha's night of lust haunted me just as much as Mariz. The thought that I'd lost her to truth was difficult to accept. It had been another troubled sleep, another drinking binge combined with pills that should have driven the pain from my mind. The only way I got a good sleep these days was with sleeping pills; they didn't always work. I forewent the morning shower, dressed in a paint-stained tracksuit – from the days when I thought I'd be an artist as well as an author - ate some muesli, then grabbed a bottle of wine from the rack. I'd work at the dining table, the mess of the office too reminiscent of my troubles.

I checked my morning email, head aching, and saw I'd picked up a nomination for Best Fantasy with, 'Eyes of Darkness' the follow-up book to 'Deep Blood, Black Lips'. The idea of winning an award made me feel better. An email, from my publisher, wanted another book to make a series, to capitalise on the nomination. The small joy washed away as I looked over the top of the laptop's screen and saw him staring at me from the kitchen, the waist-high room divider hiding his legs. He hadn't said anything for days, though the look in his eyes said he was about to. I always waited for him to say 'Follow'.

"And?" I said, sipping wine straight from the bottle.

Nothing but the same old doleful stare.

"If you don't talk to me, I won't know what you want."

He tilted his head, an inquisitive gesture like a dog questions its master. Today, did he want to say something different. I needed to know what it was; hear the words. Even after two Valium, I was on edge. Couldn't sleep, couldn't think. The Effexor for my depression worked well enough, not enough to deal with him. I wondered if being bipolar had anything to do with the ghost. I'd told the shrink about Mariz. He wrote some notes and said this was normal with grief. A strange comment I thought, but then again, Doctor Sholan was a little strange.

"You know I don't want to follow you."

He smiled, brief and definite.

"Doesn't hanging about here get kinda boring?" I'd get bored just haunting someone. "Look, I know you want to say something, it's written all over your face, so why not say it and get this over and done with."

He stared, and I stared back. I knew the look, he got it every time he wanted to ask someone something or break into a conversation. Still, he didn't speak.

"Get lost," I said, the words offering a minute element of control. I looked back at the screen, sipped my white wine, and tried to think of where I'd take the next book. Mariz vanished after about an hour; saying nothing. When you're drinking it is easy to ignore a ghost, after a while, the blurred vision helped hide him amongst the furniture.

After a full day of writing and several bottles of wine, I collapsed into bed. The firm mattress, good for my back, wasn't a soft welcoming; the smell of old perfume and musty clothes waiting to be washed didn't conjure good thoughts.

I lay awake, staring at the shadows on the ceiling; the low watt bedside lamp bathed me in a dull pool of light, hiding the mess of the room. Wind rattled the windows, the sound of leaves rustling like a dry sea tried in vain to lead me into dreams. Then he sat on the end of my bed.

"For God's sake." I felt the need to vent, hadn't for a while. "Go away." I threw a pillow; it passed straight through him and clattered on the dressing table. He shook his head.

I felt the power of his eyes. Felt like yelling, felt like screaming at him to leave me alone. I dropped back into the pillows, mindful of his stare.

"Please leave me alone." I was tired. "You've had your revenge. I'm sorry, I'm truly sorry."

Nothing.

More nothing.

I waited and waited.

I tilted my head up. He still sat there staring at me, a dumb expression on his face, the one he always wore around women; how did Samantha ever fall for such a sap? He frowned.

"What more do you want? I can't change what's happened." I pushed up on my elbows, the room became chill, and the wind ceased.

"Follow."

"No!" I dragged the quilt over me, the cold increased, pushed through the down. A smell of roses pervaded the old perfume stink; sometimes his visits would bring the smell. I hated roses, did he like roses? Though meeting the man on a few occasions, I'd never really got to know him, and as a ghost, I felt even less inclined to get to know him better.

"Follow."

Always the same old crap. I wasn't going to follow a ghost; no way, not ever.

He didn't move.

"Just go away."

He stood and walked from the room. I threw back the quilt, ready to follow him into the hallway. I'd had enough, confronting him might prove better than waiting. The bedroom door slammed shut, the bedside lamp blinked out, and the wind began its buffeting against the window. I felt hot, sweaty; the cold lifted as soon as he had left. There'd never been any chill in his presence before. The door stared at me, a silk robe, a yellow shimmer, hung on a hook. It was clear he didn't mean follow immediatly. I dropped back on the bed and let the darkness and wind take me. How much longer would this go on?

"Fuck you, too," I whispered.

My fingers wouldn't deliver the words to the computer; I'd given up sleep at about 5 am and thought writing would help pass the time. Like Mariz, I ended up with an annoying nothing. Heavy with a boozy head, not the best way to start a day, I went to the toilet; the flush sounding like the rushing away of my existence. Face washed, and teeth brushed with tangy mint paste I decided keeping busy seemed like a good thing to do. There were some deadlines to meet, calls to make. The laptop stared, the phone stared; it wasn't going to happen; even after a good crap, I wasn't going to get anything done.

A few hours of shuffling papers in my office proved even more pointless than writing, with a swoosh I pushed a pile of old manuscript drafts onto the floor; messy, but it felt good. I readied for another shove, this time books when I noticed Sarina's card staring up at me from a pile of notes by the keyboard. It had been a week since the meeting. It was clear what was needed. I needed company, live company.

Chapter 4

The Prelŭstitel

I watched as he moved about the room, candles fluttering with the motion. He avoided candles, didn't do well with the light; why were they here? I stood by the door, its peeling paint adding to how I felt about the last few years in Australia. I'd followed Sarina as instructed. Found her; watched, planned and delayed where I could. The fact he made a point of taking human form meant he had concerns that ran deeper than I understood.

"Are you sure she still has it?" His lack of light swallowed a bank of candles as he spoke. Part of the room became him.

"It was with her in Spain, like I said, I followed its essence here. You must have felt it?"

"They can mask well. I must be sure, it is vital we get it."

The darkness increased, the candles above an empty fireplace dulled. He lifted one to his face; its light absorbed into his form. He could snuff out the flame as easily as water. He didn't. He stared into the flicker of yellow. Thinking. It was dangerous when he paused for thought.

"I have a spirit, the ghost of a man close to the book. A connection made through Uri."

"Has it found the book?"

"No." I didn't tell him I'd taken his light before getting all he knew. "The link is fragile."

"Maybe you need better skills to manipulate a spirit."

"I have skill enough." I accepted his rebuke. "He was close to the book; time will bring it to me."

I collapsed against the wall. His black rush crushing me, pressing me into the old brick. He knew of my mistake. I should have told him. He pressed, invaded, pressed again. Then release, welcoming release.

"Get it. Cast again if you must. I want that book." The tone was final.

I eased from the floor and sat on a chair by the wall; the paper floral, old. The chair creaked. My legs felt weak; it would take a moments recovery before I could stand. This house, which had sat in ruin for many years, its darkness resolute and firm, welcomed us. Darkness always knows who we are, for we are the darkness. The last of the candles went out.

"I will bring it back. I will bring both items back". It was time to leave, time to feed. I needed some dark energy so I could continue my watching during the day.

"Make sure you do. A human cannot know what it is."

"No one can know the existence of my book," I said, equally definite.

"More is at stake, Prelŭstitel."

He dissolved into the air, while I sat staring into the ruins. I knew there was something at stake; he just wouldn't tell me what it was if I had to, I would caste again. Would I find another? Could I use it better than the ghost I already had? I decided to wait. The ghost of Mariz Sanchez would bring it to me, I was sure of it.

Chapter 5

Cassandra

Sarina lived in an apartment near Venice Beach not far from the Venice Beach Pier. A late-night dinner at the Waterfront Cafe had been arranged. Well priced and romantic after the sun had set. This time of year, finding a car park wasn't a difficulty. The wind off the sea was cool and penetrated my thin coat and the light dinner dress I'd chosen. Tonight, looking pretty seemed important. The smell of seaweed, strong in the air, reminded me of coming down to the beach as a kid — good and bad memories. I checked my watch as I crossed the road; it had just gone eight thirty. Pavement leading to the cafe held a few desperate young people trying to be a gang; their flimsy streetwear wasn't up to the task. I guess it was the look that mattered.

Once inside the relative warmth of the cafe; my anxiety, heightened by touch of cool air, eased a little. I had my laptop, the battery fully charged, and a small pad and pen in the front pocket of the bag. I hoped it wasn't going to be all work.

"Cassandra," Sarina called from a table on the patio. She wore an LBD; hair pulled back. A waiter took directed me through the tables towards her.

"You look nice," she said as I sat opposite. Funny, now sitting outside it didn't feel as cool.

"Why, thank you." I put the computer bag by the leg of the table. "You too."

"Forgive me, but I have already ordered wine." Sarina's skin looked pale under the soft lighting. Lips glittering with a metallic black gloss showed off the whiteness of her perfect teeth. The smile looked expensive.

"I'm driving, so I shouldn't drink too much." I often drove intoxicated; it just sounded better if you suggested constraint. A waiter brought over a bottle of Californian red, Echo Falls, showed Sarina the label then poured a sample in the glass, waiting for her to taste. She waved him away, refusing to taste or to let him fill our glasses.

"Relax." Her voice calm, reassuring. "Enjoy the night; you can stay with me if you drink too much."

"We'll see!" The idea did meet with some expectation. I didn't want to sound too eager. She poured two glasses, raised hers to me.

"To the start of something special."

We clinked glasses. "To your story." Regardless of what the story entailed, I already had a comfortable feeling with her. I decided to drink too much.

Dinner was all minimal eating and three bottles of wine, of which I drank the majority. Sarina asked about my work, how many books I had written as opposed to how many were published. She expressed interest in me. And me? Well, the wine, her looks and my libido were keenly interested in her. She originally came from Austria, had moved around a bit over the years, owned several companies, though she didn't say which ones and decided the USA would be nice to live in for a while. Santa Monica especially. Sarina no longer had to work for a living. I was amazed at this young woman's total independence; I would have expected this from a much older woman. She had only ever been in one real relationship, stressing it had been one-sided, her side — unrequited love. We talked about love, her finding it difficult being beautiful, and me being famous. Many women wanted to be with her. Many women just wanted her money. I didn't mention Samantha; the evening was working out well; to spoil it with tales of my unrequited love would serve no purpose. We were asked to leave so the cafe could close, and neither of us liked drinking in bars, so to her place we headed.

With a little swaying, and Sarina carrying my computer, we braved the walk down Palisades, the night and made it to her apartment on the second floor of the nearby apartments. The building, brand new and well appointed, seemed like the right place for such a successful single woman. I'd walked along Oceanfront many a time, and I couldn't remember seeing the building. We laughed all the way up in the elevator, her touching my shoulder now and again. I liked the contact. She used three separate keys to open the door to the apartment, and quickly bolted it once we were inside, including a large slide-bolt. It was a problem the beach had drawn undesirable, but it always paid to be cautious these days.

Sarina flicked a few switches by the door, and the place came mutely alive with copper down-lights. She led me into the large, front room and helped me onto the three-seater, black leather sofa. The cool touch of the leather pressed through my off-the-shoulder dress. It was then I noticed the walls were also black, the ceiling, the doors, the carpet, every piece of modern looking furniture, black. The copper lighting, reflecting off some of the highly polished surfaces set up not only an unusual effect but also created a deep, oddly comfortable mood.

"I like black," Sarina said, noticing my frown.

"Obviously." I felt more than a little drunk. "What's with the lights?"

"A taste thing." She touched a switch on the wall, and two more copper lights came on over the floor-to-ceiling window, immediately turning it into a wall of black glass. "Just relax I have to prepare." Sarina left, more copper lights came on in an adjoining room.

I could smell age in the place, strange considering the newness of the furniture and the recent construction of the building. I got to my feet and ventured to the wall-sized window. My reflection stared back. The blue of my dress looked odd, wrong somehow, colour didn't have a place here. I touched a black, stone statue of a horse on a stand beside the window, one of the room's few personal decorations. It felt warm, excessively warm. The smoothness of its surface said this wasn't the work of mass production; the statue showed true craftsmanship, time-learned skill. Under the smell of age, I detected a new fragrance; sandalwood, subtle; more a hint of perfume, a suggestion rather than the scent itself. I took in the rest of the room, a low cabinet, doors concealed, the black sofa and two wide, square chairs. The coffee table looked to be a solid block of black stone. A tall black vase stood in one corner; black twisted sticks reached towards one of the lights. On the walls hung three, black paintings in shiny black frames. Except for the lighting the entire place was black, not a single colour.

"Cassandra," Sarina called from the other room. "I'm ready."

I left the window and walked into the room. Sarina lay naked on a massive bed; her white body in stark contrast to the black sheets and pillows. This room wasn't totally black, around the walls hung large black and white photographs of a movie star. Bela Lugosi. I knew the old films; they often played them at Goth parties. What was going on?

"You a Goth?" I asked, torn between two immediate desires.

"In a way, you couldn't imagine." Sarina slid one hand over her modest breasts. "Now to cap off a perfect evening."

"You don't happen to have *Bela Lugosi is Dead*, by Bauhaus?" I'd heard it once or twice during some of my underground sojourns. Considering the moment, it would have been a kinky twist to what was running through my thoughts.

"No, but I have heard it." She looked a little anxious. "Please, join me."

I looked at her naked form. The evening had been more than I had expected and there was certainly a need. I wanted to say something, question the suddenness, only the spell would have been broken, the moment lost. I wanted her skin against mine.

"It has been awhile," she said. Simple statement, and one I understood. Sarina's black hair spread across the pillow like a high lustre shadow. Black pubic hair, in the classical V, was an invitation hard to ignore, not that I was doing any ignoring. I undressed. She watched. I sat beside her on the bed feeling self-conscious in my nudity. Sarina eased up towards me, cradled my head in her hands, a gentle gesture that took my breath away. We kissed. I closed my eyes. We kissed again, and again, our hunger growing with each touch of our lips. She broke away and kissed my neck, the caress, the closeness, the intimacy I'd failed to find for so long released from me with a sigh. Yes, this is what I wanted.

After making love several times, I lay exhausted beside her, letting my breathing settle. It was unusual for me to climax on a first date; I didn't trust easily, this just felt right. Staring into one of the copper lights over the bed the total release began to abate as the creeping darkness of depression closed about the room. I closed my eyes and let the sensations do what it always had done.

Snuff out the light of hope. In the miasma of cascading emotions, I kept playing over the press of Sarina's flesh against mine, the hardness of nipples, the heavy breathing of satisfaction. It was an effort to regain the joy of those moments.

Sarina kissed my neck, softer this time, no frenetic desire or lust. She pressed her hand against my brow, a firm, dry touch tingling with heat. Then euphoria. The world sparked with a high that made me gasp and gasp again. A deep comfort pushed back the blackness of despair, and I surrendered to wave after wave of ever-heightening euphoria. I opened my eyes and looked up at her; her eyes were closed, a bright light ringed her wrist and the hand against my head.

"What are you doing?" It was hard to speak.

"Giving you something no one could ever give you." Sarina opened her eyes; a blinding white light pierced the balloon of depression.

Tiredness, a heavy, all-pervading weariness took me. I wanted to question; the word wouldn't form my eyes could maintain their vigil of wonder. A well of lightness called and into it, I fell willingly.

Sunlight streamed through a small window above the bed, the black of the room absorbed its light, magnified its warmth. I lay naked; my head ached slightly. Had a dreamed the light, the draining contact? I eased into a sitting position, legs over the side of the bed. My dress and underwear were gone. On the end of the bed was a tracksuit, in black. I pulled it on, a little too long. I felt less exposed dressed.

"Sarina," I called, walking into the front room, the window now alive with the scene of breaking waves on the white sands of the beach. The vision, coupled with the clear sky, created a sense of summer warmth. Unlike previous times the scene created a sense of joy. It was strange to feel that way, very strange.

"In the kitchen. Down the hall, first on the right."

In the day the black looked sad, heavy and depressive. It had lost its emotional appeal. As I walked the joy faded and how I usually felt washed back like a wave over a sandcastle. By the time I'd left the front room I felt – down, defeated. Sarina had done something to me last night, but what? The realisation, mixed with emotional instability, made me angry. Even knowing there had been moments of euphoria, there was also the realisation of violation; somehow Sarina had forced me to feel happy. How dare she?

I entered the kitchen and came face to face with Sarina, sitting at a small table. She wore a black pantsuit. I rubbed at my temples, easing the ache a little. She stared me in the eyes. "What did you do to me?"

"I knew you'd feel better?"

"What the fuck did you do to me?" It wasn't the answer I wanted. I crossed my arms. I knew I blushed, and it became difficult to keep in check a sense of anger. Depression made me unreasonable and right now I wanted to be unreasonable until I knew what was going on.

"Sit down, Cassandra, there is something you need to know." Sarina gave off a calmness that annoyed me; her eyes displayed impatience.

"What did you do last night?" I didn't want to sit.

"Sit down, and I'll explain. Please." She pushed out one of the four chairs with her foot.

I sat, tense and confused. I didn't dream the light or the sensations of extreme peace. I knew this woman had done something. Was it drugs? A hallucinogen?

Sarina placed her hands on the table, long fingers spread, nails painted black. She sighed, weariness obvious in her body language. "This is going to be hard for you to understand," she said, looking into the glossy surface. "I am not quite what I seem, well, I am a lot more than what I seem."

I unfolded my arms, the ache in my head had subsided. What I'd seen last night looked... hell I didn't know what I'd seen or how it looked. "You some kind of spiritualist or something?" I waved my hands in front of her face. "A voodoo woman and what I saw last night some weird magic?"

"Nothing spiritual I'm afraid and voodoo has been practised by my kind over the years, just not this time. Cassandra, whole religions have started up around what I am." She stared at the table top, Fingers pressing down on the surface so hard I thought she was going to break her nails. "I am an Uttuku." Sarina looked up, face unlined, young, eyes old. She spoke with a slowness that indicated time meant very little to her. "In some cultures, I am a demon."

"Yeah, right, and I'm the tooth fairy." I wasn't amused.

"You saw what I could do, experienced it."

"What was last night? Besides the sex?" I felt my brow, "and what the fuck is a ooba boo?" I resisted folding my arms, and gently interlaced my fingers on the table. Remain calm, I thought, everything will have a logical explanation. I counted to my first ten.

In the darkness of the kitchen, the blackness of the small world around Sarina, only the slow tapping of her fingernails on the table made a sound. Silence hung heavy for several minutes. Her stare seemed to lose focus, disconnect from me. Like the cold from Mariz's last visit, I shivered, goosebumps prickling my skin.

"I took from you, what religious folk might call a small piece of your soul." Her words were measured, careful.

"I'm not religious and don't have a soul."

"I took a small piece of your life light, the energy that gives you life." She was serious.

"And the glowing shit?"

"You weren't harmed in any way. Uttuku do not harm humans. Your light, the energy which is your life, the thing that makes you who you are is all we need. I need this to survive. Not much, just a little every day or so."

"You take souls?" I was incredulous.

"Yes, I suppose." She reached across the table and took my hand. "I would need to do this again in a few days, if you let me, of course."

"You want to do this again?" I had to admit to feeling a little shocked, and drained, which made me laugh. "You want to do your oody doody stuff on me again? What am I? Do I have idiot tattooed on my forehead?"

"I am an Uttuku." She ignored me. "Since the time of Lilith we have walked the Earth with Gods, Pharaohs, and Kings. Cassandra, I'm over five hundred years old."

"Bullshit!" I laughed. I had never heard so much crap in all my life. Sarina sat back, face neutral. I'd done the drug thing in my teens. 'The Stainless Hammer of God' was about my needle using days. A five-hundred-year-old woman who didn't look a day over twenty-five, get real. I laughed again, this time maliciously.

"You're one fucked up chick." I'd believed in a lot of weird stuff until I turned to writing. Hell, I'd made up enough weird stories about alien invasions and the world of darkness to almost have me certified. I stood. "You drugged me, simple and I don't care why, but you're spinning me rubbish and that I do care about. You just turned a good night into a fucking joke."

"I have no reason to lie to you." She sat impassive; eyes fixed on mine.

Sarina must be twisted to believe her own story so seriously. Last night had been great, enjoyable, and Sarina did make me feel good. I didn't want to deal with anyone else's mental problems though, too many of my own to worry about.

"I think I'd better leave." A freak I didn't need right now. "You can keep the weird shit to yourself."

Sarina stood, the chair scraping across the black tiled floor. She walked past me and out of the room. I followed, still needed my clothes and the computer. This was a story I had no intention of writing. She stood before the lounge room window looking down on the beach. I joined her, but the view wasn't of interest. I wanted my stuff. She handed me some binoculars.

"See that man just under the pier?"

It took some time to focus on the distant pier, but I managed. A man dressed in a black suit stood close to one of the pylons. A couple walking a dog were heading his way, and a jogger ran by. "So, he's a booga booga as well?"

"You can see him, that is important."

"Oh, he's supposed to be an invisible man?" Things were getting worse. "Why are you doing this?"

29

"You can see him because for a short time after me taking some of your light. He becomes visible to you; he also becomes visible when he wants you to see him."

"Invisible people and Booga loos" This was just too much with an aching head. "You're nuts!"

"I am an Uttuku, and the man down there is Orlando." She hugged herself. "He followed me here; he's been following me for over fifty years. He is a Prelŭstitel, a hunter of us."

"And what the hell is that supposed to mean?"

"It is a Romanian term; it's what his kind prefer. He follows me everywhere."

"A stalker." Crazy or not, a stalker is always bad news. There were plenty of those between here and Santa Monica. "Call the cops, there are laws to protect you." It was time to leave.

"He wants something from me, Cassandra."

"That's your problem." I didn't want to get involved. I had a ghost to worry about. And whatever a Pissy pants cat was I didn't want to know.

"He knows you stayed the night. He might come after you; a Prelŭstitel will kill anyone to get to me. It is their way."

"If he follows me, I'll call the cops. Simple."

Sarina turned on me, her eyes piercing. I couldn't read her face or judge her mood. I felt uncomfortable. This woman was weirding me out, and I could feel my anger towards her growing. Easy girl count to ten, and ten again. She reached for me. I jumped back; she was quick. Her hands gripped my shoulders. I struggled. Grabbed her wrists; too strong.

"Let me go. Fucking let me go, bitch!" Struggling was getting me nowhere. "Fuck you!" I screamed, trying to pull free.

"If he thinks you're with me; If you want to stay alive, Cassandra." Sarina gripped me harder. It hurt. "You might need my help."

I slapped at her hands, once, twice. She let go, and I staggered away.

"If you think I'm fucking believing in this shit then you're crazier than I thought!" I was yelling. I wanted to run, get out of the place. "Where are my things?"

Sarina pointed to one of the living room chairs. My bag, coat, dress and shoes were in a neat pile. I grabbed them and ran for the door. I shouldn't have called. Story or no story, this was a situation I didn't want to deal with. I threw the locks and pulled on the door, twisted the handle, it wouldn't open. Sarina slowly walked towards me. I pulled and pulled. Panic. She came closer. I felt like crying. I was crying. I didn't want to die. I didn't want to be killed by some crazy voodoo bitch. Sarina reached passed me and threw back the slide-bolt. The door opened, and I rushed into the hallway. Lift or stairs? Lift or stairs?

"If he follows you, come back tomorrow." She closed the door.

I shook so much I could barely walk. I pressed the lift button and waited, tears streaming. *Tomorrow*. Not fucking likely.

Chapter 6

The Prelŭstitel

"How much do you know?"

"About what?" He'd summoned me to this place.

"The icon." His voice crammed into my ears.

"That its representation is important to them." I knew more. Could he feel my lie?

He moved between the graves like smoke over flames. The night unusually clear, the moon, a half crescent, cast a silver light over the old, white headstones. He was searching again, stepping back and forward through the realm. Dipping into graves now and then. Aza'zel, if anything, relied on completeness. Human death wasn't final death. Only he could deliver that. The remnant energy of life-light lingered in the dead, he took it and cast it to the *Abad*.

"Your ghost may not be worth controlling any more. Whoever has your, our, work isn't following." He stood before a monument of an angel.

"My mistake can be undone. I am sure of it."

"I want his darkness." His voice slapped at me. "He knew nothing of worth."

"Give me more time; he will bring the book to me." There was more. "If I get the icon, will you forget about her?"

His eyes, blue in the night, glowed brighter. He was considering. I could no more tell him what to do than I could resurrect myself from the dead. I had interests of my own, and if I could, I would protect them.

"Perhaps, but you must return the words."

"Can you influence the ghost?" He was the darkness after all. "It could hasten the retrieval."

"No, your casting has blocked him from me. Just do as I ask, do what you promised me."

"The icon is one thing; the book is mine."

"And my existence!" His voice resounded around the cemetery.

He drifted over the wet grass to a plaque on the ground. He'd discovered something. His darkness was a hole in the shadows that fluttered around the graveyard; his presence a coldness outside of the weather. He knelt on the plaque and placed his hand above the inscription.

"Leave me."

I couldn't tell what he was thinking; he had no features to read. Beneath the black hair was little more than black lines holding the blueness of his eyes.

He was a walking shadow cast by the world, a representation of all humankind's fear. A fear made by men.

"I will find it." I looked for my own shadow to disappear into.

"Our presence must not be known." The intent obvious. "If you can't get it back, then trick, make her taste the night."

He slid into the grave like a shadow vanishes under light. He had found his feed for the night. I looked to the stars, thought of her. There had to be another way. To trick an Uttuku took planning. I could do it with someone else, but not Sarina. I also believed he knew more than he was telling. His influence was everywhere; he had to know more. He could easily get what he wanted, why use me at all? The way of the darkness should not have been strange to me, but he was doing something, and it did not include his Prelüstitel.

I had found one of the book's thieves, not the book itself. The ghost must lead it to me, must.

Chapter 7

Cassandra

I watched TV and managed to write a new chapter; the morning's strangeness pervaded my words. Demons and devils littered the prose, something I had avoided in all my works. The day's writing was wasted. I'd edit everything out eventually only to be left with a workable paragraph. I sat in the darkness letting the colour of the TV throw shapes over the walls and ceiling. The colour reached into me, helped me feel alive after a night within a black apartment, and what was it with the copper lighting? Sarina was insane, which saddened me as much as it surprised. Deep down I'd hoped something good might have come from the night. I poured another whiskey and sipped through a commercial break; a tampon ad. All light and fresh, a woman's new freedom fluttered about the room. I hated the ads. They always looked like they'd been written by men. There's not much freedom in cramps and pain; a bloody tampon couldn't fix that. Whiskey helped. I couldn't judge my cycle, even if it ended last week I still never knew when the mess would begin, and constantly wearing panty liners just in case was a real drag. The ad changed. I drank some more.

Something smashed against the wall above the TV. I dropped my glass. It thudded on the floor. The TV blinked off, plunging me into darkness. Mariz. I rolled from the chair and onto the mat. I couldn't see him, but there was the coldness of his presence. My thoughts struggled. What to do? What to do?

"Follow."

Follow? I could barely move. Breathing hard, and trying not to, created an ache in my chest. I crawled around the chair and looked towards the doorway. He was standing there, a non-casting light in the room. He held a vase in his hand.

"Follow!" he yelled. One fist clenched at his side.

I ducked back. The vase smashed against the wall; breaking glass, the slosh of water on the floor. He'd never shown violence before. What had changed?

"I'm sorry," I yelled from my hiding place. "I didn't want you to die."

"Follow." His voice had changed, become firm, urgent. "What have you done with it?"

That was new. I looked to him again, both hands at his sides. "Done with what?"

"Does she know?"

"Does who know? Who are you talking about?" I dropped out of sight again. Would he attack? Could a ghost kill a living being? He blocked the doorway. I couldn't escape. It would take too long to open the window and

34

make a break for it across the garden. Crouching lower, hiding on the floor in front of the chair, I tried to concentrate. What to do? How do you escape a ghost?

"Follow!" The scream forced my hands to my ears.

Then silence. The cold lifted. He'd gone. The smell of roses the strongest it had ever been.

I didn't know what he wanted, what he was talking about. I grabbed a cushion off the sofa and held it close, trying to will comfort out of it. The TV came back on, an old black and white film, a horror movie. I gulped and thought of Sarina. I felt like crap. At least he was gone. I sat on the floor, knees drawn up. I couldn't move, the smell of my body thick. Fear, real fear. Who was he talking about? Who was she? The only *she* I knew was Samantha, and we hadn't spoken since his death. Sarina? That was last night and this morning. How could Mariz know about her? The man under the pier? Orlando? But what would he know about Mariz? He wanted something, something I had. I didn't have anything of his. I got up and looked out the front window. Was he waiting for me? Should I follow him? Standing across the street, under the single street light, I saw the man in black. I escaped to my spot on the floor. Fuck, fuck, fuck. I grabbed the phone off the lounge and called the police. I went back to the window; they'd want a description. He'd gone. The phone answered.

"911," a female voice answered.

"Sorry," I said. "I saw someone and panicked. It's nothing, sorry to bother you."

"Are you sure, miss?"

"Yes, yes, I'm sorry. Just a bit edgy, everything's okay." I hung up. No one in their right mind would believe me. I didn't believe me.

I switched the TV off station and stared at the snow between channels for hours, my backside aching from sitting on the hard floor. I wanted to go to bed, to sleep away the nightmare; couldn't, would he be waiting for me in the bedroom? My smell grew stronger. I didn't want to move. Too many questions, and not a single answer. I wished I'd never uncovered his fraud or gone to Sarina's place. I should have just been happy in my depression; it was what I knew best, I was safe when I felt bad, safer than I felt now.

As soon as the sun streamed through my front window, I felt the grime of a sleepless night clinging to my skin like grease.

"To hell with it all." I headed for the shower. "Could it get any worse?" Under the hot water, I scrubbed and scrubbed until my skin stung with redness. The fear clung to me, penetrated my core. If I stayed in the water any longer, I think I would have drowned.

Showered and looking at the rings under my eyes in the bathroom mirror, I knew I had to go back. As screwed up as Sarina was, she'd probably be the only one who'd understand. She was the one who pointed out the man under the pier, and now he was following me. I didn't like it, but that crazy bitch knew whats- what was and if I had to smack her over the head to get the truth, I was just in the right mood to do it.

I ate some toast, washed down with two half coffee cups of whiskey. Still, the nerves, settle the stomach. The drive to the beach was as uneventful and boring as always. I paid the on-street parking fee and headed towards the ritzy apartment. The wind, blustery, wasn't as chill as two nights ago, but it still managed to get my hair in a tangle before I entered the building.

Standing outside Sarina's door, leaning on the wall beside the lifts for what felt like an hour, the effort to ring the doorbell wouldn't come. Would she be home? Would she attack me? Go crazy and do that light thing with her hand? I didn't know what was worse, Mariz, the guy watching me last night or the idea of visiting a booga loo or whatever she was. I pressed the button, the doorbell rang, a dull tune of deep notes. My jaw tightened. The door opened. She said nothing, just stepped aside and let me in. So far, so good.

Sarina sat at the kitchen table. I told her about Mariz and his visits, about his visit last night. Sarina had been right. Orlando did follow me, and I needed to know what it meant. Had she known about him? After an emotional outpouring, punctuated with my most used words, she left the room for a moment and returned with a book. She slid the photo album across the table, the cover old, tattered black leather with a faded embossed symbol. My hands shook. Last night didn't leave me with too many choices. I opened the first page. A hand-drawn picture of a long-haired man with one eye closed, it looked seventeenth century.

"Don Blas de Lezo," Sarina said, quickly turning the page. "A longer story than I wish to tell."

"Everything." I turned the page back. "I want to know everything."

"He was a Spanish sea captain, a great man. I knew him, but we parted... he is dead now." She turned the page again, this time I didn't interrupt.

A sepia photograph stared up at me. The image was of a tall man in military uniform with three stars on each collar and medal on the left shoulder. He wore an impressive handlebar moustache. Standing beside him was Sarina and another woman. Sarina wore a long, black evening dress. The backdrop was artificial, a staged picture.

"Archduke Franz Ferdinand," she said. "His death sent a friend to war, gave him the injuries which would later ruin him."

"Why are you showing me this?"

"You need to understand what I am before I can offer any help, Cassandra, and before I help you, there still needs to be something done for me. I need your help, and it is personal."

"This could have been photo-shopped." The picture didn't prove anything as far as I was concerned.

"There is a picture like this in the archives in Austria. This hasn't been altered, I can assure you."

She turned the page. More photos. Sarina in a black uniform beside a tank, then I saw it. Sarina standing beside Adolf Hitler. She looked the same as she did in the first pictures, exactly how she looked now. Her off the shoulder evening dress and necklace of black stones clashed with the greyness of Hitler's uniform. She towered over him with elegance as well as stature. Despite a deep reluctance, the belief in Sarina's age started to penetrate. My palms became sweaty, hands shaking even more.

"What's this to do with?"

"At the moment, nothing; you have to believe and trust in me if I'm going to help."

I looked at the photos again. "You're a Nazi?"

"Turn the page."

There was a photograph of her with Winston Churchill, his black suit fitting in well with her full formal dress. They were seated in a study, a wall of books behind them. A relationship with my depression almost had me knowing Churchill like a shadowy father. Another showed her with a man with braces on his legs, yet another with a small Japanese officer in a white uniform.

"I don't understand." I looked up and no longer saw the beautiful woman I'd had sex with or the crazy bitch who said was a demon. I saw someone else entirely, maybe even crazier.

"I couldn't stay in one place for too long, as you can appreciate." She touched the photographs with the tips of her fingers. "My obvious attributes were useful in creating protections others couldn't afford." She sounded weary. "I learned a few things about ghosts. Hitler had one, Winston had several. Franz, of course, became one."

"And you think you know what he wants?"

"I didn't say that. Only you know what he wants. What I do know is there are several kinds of ghost, and the one you have in your house sounds like the worst kind."

"Great. All I need."

"You have a puppet," she said, "Someone whose ghost is controlled by another, a specific other." She looked grave. "A Prelŭstitel is the only one with that kind of power. You said Mariz held a vase, a normal ghost couldn't do that. Knock one over, yes, but not pick it up and throw it."

"Orlando?" This was getting worse by the second. "He's controlling the ghost?"

Sarina shook her head. "I believe so."

"If he some kind evil spirit?"

"Not really." Sarina pushed hair out of her eyes, the movement simple yet graceful. "You know the religious meaning for devil?" I nodded. "Well, in that context Orlando would be the son of the devil or one of the sons of Aza'zel.

The night itself; a darkness as great as time and space. In my context, the one you should accept, Orlando hunts for him. He takes all the dark energy from his victims. It is what sustains him. Aza'zel seeks completeness in all things."

If not for the album I would have laughed. What had I become mixed up in?

"Which is?"

"Total darkness, the abolition of light. All light."

Not a good prospect to look forward to.

"I still don't know what this has to do with me."

"Tell me what happened with this dead author, inside you will hold the clue."

I told her how Mariz had died, and it was my fault and haunted me because of it. I explained how he wanted me to follow him into death, for me to take my own life like he had done and atone for my sins. Sarina thought on this.

"The question is how did the Prelŭstitel know to get this specific ghost? I had thought he followed you from here, but the haunting has been going on for months. What did he know that connects you to me through the hunter? I don't believe coincidence has brought us together." The way she spoke made everything sound so considered, well thought out.

"I don't know anything. He killed himself because I ratted him out to the literary community." I rubbed at the ache forming in the back of my head. "Maybe the Prelŭstitel is a critic?"

Sarina shook her head, obviously not getting the joke or seeing the funny side of things. I needed something funny right now, anything to ease away the sense of impending doom. I focused on Sarina's perfume, the subtle sandalwood fragrance from before, and for a time I was back in the throes of lovemaking, being transported out of the pit of self-loathing and hate. Again, I wished I didn't find Sarina's card and call.

"It is possible a Prelŭstitel, or even Aza'zel took him." She said, looking troubled. "He could have taken Mariz's darkness, or life energy, and put the empty, still alive, shell of the man into the car and set it up as a suicide."

"That's a lot to buy into." A lot of effort as well. "We don't even know why he'd do this."

"Everything is connected, Cassandra. I am glad you came to me with this." She touched the back of my hand. "The only way to know what the Prelŭstitel and Aza'zel want is to follow the ghost."

Following a very dead Mariz was not something I wanted to do. A new, and pleasing thought came to mind. I wasn't responsible for his death. I pondered this for a while. Could this *Dark One* have killed him? In my heart, I wanted to accept the explanation, needed to accept it — three months of beating myself up, suffering under the judgments of others; all for nothing. There was no way of proving such an outlandish situation and even if I could, who would believe it? So, despite me knowing what might have happened the rest of the local literati would still blame me. My guilt lifted a little, not much, just enough to ease back on my mental assault, self-flagellation. I still felt depressed. I wondered if I'd taken my pills this morning.

Of course, Sarina could still be a complete nut case, and I'd been drawn into her strange aberration of reality; depressive and a psychotic on a unified journey into madness. Not a healthy combination. What would Doctor Sholan make of it? And could I tell him? For now, I could live with not being responsible; the prospect would at least solve one of my problems. After an hour we were still no closer to knowing anything to help me, but I was feeling better through the sharing, as odd as that sounded.

"Did you know Aza'zel was looking for me?" I gave in a little to weariness. Learning about a whole new world existence was tough going. I needed a drink. "Is that why you approached me at the writers' centre?"

"No, not at all. I do want you to write my story, that's why I was there. I'd been to some other meetings you hadn't shown for, so I was surprised when you did walk through the door." It was hard reading the woman's emotions; her voice always had a neutral, well-balanced control. "Please don't think I know more than you, please."

"If this Dark One is all powerful why hasn't he come for me himself?" It was a fair question.

"It is strange he hasn't found you." She looked up to the ceiling, thinking perhaps. I felt pleased he hadn't. "Mariz has a psychic connection to you, Aza'zel or his Prelŭstitel would only need to follow this. The Prelŭstitel knows where you live." She stared at me. "None of this makes sense."

I didn't care if it didn't make sense, nothing made sense. I usually wrote fiction based around old mythology and legends; had larger than life characters hero their way throws difficult situations to eventually save the day and fall in love. Happy ending books with a wide readership and passionate fans. Would those reader believe this if I wrote it?

"Sarina, Mariz and I hardly spoke, we attended the same functions, only his circle wasn't my circle." I thought of Samantha. "We did have sex with the same woman."

Sarina crinkled her bottom lip, a funny look. "Maybe that's why he hasn't found you." She considered something, slid her fingers across the table as if ordering thoughts, switching the letters in a game of Scrabble. For a while, she started drifting away, became lost in the puzzle. She lifted her hands, slowly clasped them together then glanced at me. "The connection is secondary, a minor thread that leads your way, and it isn't strong enough to lead Aza'zel directly to you. I wonder if he is actually meant to be after this Samantha."

"That's good, right?" Samantha could have the ghost; he was her boyfriend after all.

"If I'm right, yes. I'm only guessing though, Cassandra. Orlando followed you because you spent the night with me unless he saw he ghost at your place, he wouldn't know you are the one he's looking for."

"I could call Samantha and ask if she's been contacted by Aza'zel or Orlando." I wouldn't mind shifting the madness on to her. I might have loved her once, maybe still did, it was just his death crushed that emotional state.

Sarina shook her head. "Aza'zel doesn't work like that; if he wants her, then she's already dead." I couldn't hide shock. "If she's in the death notices we'll know why. I don't want you to contact her because you might complete the connection with him." She hesitated.

"And?"

"It would be your name in the paper."

"Oh."

"Somehow we are all involved; we need to find out how."

"I don't like the sound of this."

"I'm sorry, it is just... just a lot to put together, and if Orlando is involved, then your life is in danger. We have to work together, do you understand?"

"No, I don't. Why don't I go down and ask him?" It was reasonable. "Instead of trying to guess what he wants let's just find out."

"I can't let you do that."

"Why it would solve our problems, won't it? Get me off the hook and maybe get rid of the ghost once and for all?" Why was she hesitant? The blackness of the room was making me miserable. I needed some light.

"Cassandra, he won't talk to you, he won't tell you what he wants."

"Why not? To me, it seems pretty bloody simple." I made to get up; she grabbed my hand.

"If you approach him you will die. A Prelŭstitel will strip what it wants from you, no questions asked."

She made a good argument. "Then you ask him; it's you he's been following, after all."

"Uttuku and Prelŭstitel do not speak. Never have, and I dare say, never will. It is just the way."

"Then do you know what he wants from you? It might help us work out my problem." Things just went from simple to nasty. I didn't like nasty.

"I know what he wants."

"And that is?"

"It isn't relevant to you; it won't help you."

"Great, that's just great. A ghost who won't talk to me, a pissy pants, whatever, who will kill me and a bloody mystery that doesn't want to get solved; not a good start in cooperation is it?"

Pulling from her touch I rubbed my eyes, pressed against the dull ache that developed behind them. Work with an Uttuku, a demon thing, this was something straight out of a Walmart horror book. I looked at her, the seriousness in her face. Did I have a choice?

"Can you protect me?" She looked away. In that moment I thought I understood the magnitude of what she'd just told me. The look-away giving me an answer I didn't want. I sucked in my lips, felt the pressure of my teeth and wished my bipolar depression was making me delusional, and any time soon I'd wake up in the hospital with a nice Doctor asking for my name.

"If you can't protect me who can?"

"I don't know." She looked worried for the briefest of moments. "I will make you a promise. I will do everything possible to keep you safe."

"Well, I hope so, Sarina, the idea of ending up dead isn't all that appealing." I sat back, folding my arms tight across my chest. "All I wanted was some company, now look what I've got. Fucking brilliant."

We sat, the quietness of the apartment affording us time to contemplate. Me thinking about all this shit and Sarina, well I'd no idea what crashed through her mind. She studied the table top, gently shifted her hands over its surface as if conjuring a spirit. Was she? The thought troubled me. What else could this woman do?

"Why did you approach me at the Writers' Centre?" I broke the silence, after all, it was her meeting that started the mess. "It wasn't really about a book, was it?"

"The book or story is true. I wanted you to write a book for me, a special book, it's for me to keep as a kind of memorium. I don't have many memories I want to keep, this one I want to treasure." Sarina showed the first signs of real emotion. A sadness turned her lips down, her eyes clouded. "I wouldn't have brought harm your way, Cassandra. The arrival of Aza'zel, your ghost... Orlando, it's all just come in a rush. I don't know what to make of it." She placed her hands one on top the other before her. "The book could help," she said, face brightening. "It might help solve what is going on, and at least the work would help us understand each other."

I wasn't sure. He haunted me real enough. I'd seen Orlando, his dark form on the beach, in front of my house. Thinking surrounded by black was difficult. Bad thoughts, negative thoughts flowed in and out of the walls, were framed by the black squares above the table. My reflection in the high gloss table-top offered respite with its shadowed coloured image only it wasn't enough. Could I believe Sarina? Trust her? She watched. I thought and tried to find answers amongst the lines of the kitchen cupboards, the gleam of the refrigerator. Black on black, thought on thought, nothing resolved itself, nothing was clear. Being with Sarina might keep me safe. My gut was rarely wrong. Within the black, the one deep and heavy in my bowels, the solution did seem to involve the both of us.

She reached for my hand caressed my knuckles. Fingers long, nails manicured and shiny.

"Will you still write it?"

"Is it about Orlando?" I didn't want to.

"I want you to write about a great man. I lost him many years ago. I loved him, and he didn't know I existed."

I frowned. How could she think of love? I'd also thought she was lesbian. I had good bisexual radar, this time I'd received no warning.

"I didn't always crave the affections of a woman," she said. "I fell in love with a man, a man who could have been more than he ended up as. Cassandra, please understand an Uttuku does not find love easily, or all too often. I have found it once and never want to forget it."

This was a plea, not a request. With all the happenings of the last three months, days even, I didn't think I could manage the task. Writing took a lot of work; a lot of me went into the words. Right now, there wasn't much to go around.

"And how do you think this is going to help me?"

"It will trust me. I know we can work this out together, and the book will keep us close; keep you within my protection."

"Who do you want me to write about?" I was short with her; if it was about Hitler – no way. The world knew a madman, making a lover out of him wouldn't wash.

"Bela Lugosi," Sarina said. "The man who strangely acted in horror roles through his stage and film career; he would be well suited to a role now, don't you think?"

"You're kidding me?" I couldn't contain the laugh. This was getting weirder.

"It's not funny."

"But he was a famous Hollywood star; it's a bit unreal to think of you and..."

"And what?"

"Sorry. All this stuff is creeping me out." Any time now I'd wake up in bed with a sore head. "You got any booze? I need a drink. This mystery is hard to get my head around."

"Talking to a human isn't easy for me either." She sounded hurt. I apologised again. "I loved Bela."

I thought of the photographs on her bedroom wall, the only images displayed in the whole apartment. He must have been at least thirty years older than her, in appearance anyway. I'd seen some of his films late at night when I developed insomnia after working on a novel chapter. I wouldn't have called him handsome or even mildly attractive.

"Were you married?" This time she laughed; a sad sound. Sarina opened a cupboard and lifted out a new bottle of whiskey, the good stuff; George T Stagg, my preferred brand. She put it on the table before me with a crystal tumbler; pure class and style. I tried not to spill any on the table as I poured myself a good measure.

"I wished for marriage, alas, no." Sarina remained standing by the cupboard, hands clasped in front and shoulders slightly stooped.

"How long were you together?" Funny how the writer kicks in. The whiskey too.

"We weren't ever together. I travelled after him from Austria – Hungary; he never knew who I was. It was hard watching him through all five of his marriages." She brightened at the memory. "I liked to think of myself as his black fox and he the lone wolf."

"I don't understand?"

"I loved him dearly and desperately. He loved others." She looked down at her feet. "I would have settled for friendship."

"Unrequited love." I couldn't hold my sigh. I knew the feeling well. "The pain of that must have been hard?"

"Love in any case. I still love the memory, the way it makes me feel. The times I spent near him."

"After all you have told me, why do you want me to write this, and why now? Don't we have a truckload of crap to work through already?" Sure, the love story would be interesting, and I was intrigued, but with something like the devil stalking us, and Mariz haunting my house, I wasn't convinced a book project required immediate attention. "Maybe after we sort this mess."

"Memories fade. I am afraid, more afraid now that there might not be another opportunity. I have taken an enormous risk in telling you who and what I am."

"Thanks for the encouragement."

For the first time, she cried. Not body wracking tears; small tears that clung to the corners of her eyes. "I wanted us to be together; I wanted to be around him forever. He didn't even know I was alive and because of what I am I dared not tell him, expose myself to the harshness of the Hollywood world."

"Yet, here you are, only a few miles away from that very world."

"Things have changed, Hollywood has moved on through numerous stars, I would be surprised if any current starlets would know who Bela was."

She took one stride and reached for the photo album, flipping to the back pages. There was Bela in a dark suit, smiling for the camera. There were other poses, restaurants, the front of theatres, sitting on a sofa, on a deck chair in a garden.

"He died of a heart attack." Sarina dabbed at her eyes with the back of her hands. "I don't think I will ever love another man. You have to understand this book is as much for him as it is for my memory."

"I want to help; I just don't think I can." Adding emotional baggage to my lot didn't thrill me. The idea of writing a book for her just felt too bizarre, too insane. Sarina also sounded a little obsessed. I'd been obsessed with Samantha, crazy obsessed and I did everything I could to win her. There was a story I didn't want to be reminded of.

Staring at her lovely face, the sadness that reddened her eyes, it was hard to resist. I'd known lost love. There was a never healed heartbreak in me to match the look on Sarina's face. From time to time I was overcome with similar sadness at not getting Samantha. Mariz's ghost had all but killed my desire for her. In a way, his ghost had helped me develop contempt. From love comes hate, passionate hate.

"Please, I will pay you well."

"I don't need money; I need a month in a psychiatric hospital." I didn't say this with any conviction. There wasn't a lot for us to do right at this moment. "I have to come to grips with all this ootidoo..."

"Uttuku; the name given to our race."

"Whatever, I still have to get to grips here." Sarina started to cry fully. Her shoulders shook, and tears flowed. I didn't know what to do. Feeling her pain, I reached across the table, offered reassurance, something I didn't even have for myself. Her hand, cool and dry, slipped into mine. "It is really important to you, isn't it?" Even as I said it the words sounded feeble and condescending.

"I sought you out because of *The Stainless Hammer of God*, and your understanding of what I want to tell you." She gazed into my eyes. The hardness had vanished, the intensity and age had slipped away to reveal a sad, young woman. "Bela died because of the needle, the drugs. I didn't want us to start like this, but here we are. Cassandra, please."

"What about Orlando, the ghost, all the Dark madness out there?" I pointed to the window.

"Let it come to us," she said; a quaver in her voice. Her cheeks were flushed, about the only time I'd seen colour in her face. "We will deal with it when it reveals itself, and in time it will. I need to get this out. I need us to work together; it is important to me that we work together. There is nothing more important than this to me."

All the craziness disappeared under the expression of raw emotion. I hadn't been close to anyone in an emotional state for two years, and it touched my heart far more than I expected. In moments I had agreed and joined her with my tears. We had a unity beyond the weird; we both knew loss and heartache. Only Sarina's five hundred years of life did challenge reason and logic and the threat of death complicated things a bit.

By dinner, I had several pages of notes, and Sarina felt better. She ordered takeaway Chinese and made sure my glass was never empty. This would be a necessity. Knowing her age, and how many partners Sarina would have had over the time, it felt odd that she attached herself so strongly to one person, and one that didn't even acknowledge her. She spoke about how brave Bela had been during World War One, his injuries, the sacrifices and death. She gushed about the handsome soldier she'd watch dancing and wrote about long conversations about life she would have had with him had she taken the chance. Love at first sight, she'd said. Bela didn't love her; his fondness for other beauties kept him busy. She said just being near was enough; I could see through the lie. I noted her emotions and considered how this could be worked into the story, though the point of view still wasn't clear. No matter how I wrote it, she would still come across as being crazy.

Sarina explained away Bela's first wife, Ilona Szmik as if she were mere fluff. Bela fell in love often and his many times down the aisle showed just how tumultuous those marriages had been. Sarina always lived in the background, doing extras work on movie sets, taking odd jobs so she could stay close to him. Such self-control, no matter the degree of love she bore, would have exhausted even the strongest of people. In a way, I developed a new respect for her.

Sarina had been right, the writing did take my mind off the present situation, only when I finished the notes there it was, and I knew, it wasn't about to go away.

In my own house, weary after the long day with Sarina, I felt the usual twinge of fear. Was he here? Maybe he had left, become sick of hanging around all day waiting for me. His presence couldn't be felt. The broken vase still lay on the floor; the flowers and water a mess waiting to be cleaned away. From room to room, I searched, hoping he wasn't around. Shadows followed me. Sounds were everywhere. The air smelt of bad cooking smells; each doorway a surprise waiting to leap out. Grab me, assault me.

I stood at the bedroom door; it was closed. Fighting fear my hand wrapped around the lever handle and eased it down, the soft action, a faint click as the tongue drew back from the jam. Breath held. Throat dry. Slowly, with a gentle push, the door eased inwards. Heart pounding, neck aching. Slowly, so slowly the door swung into the room. I closed my eyes, couldn't watch. Didn't want to see. Still gripping the handle, eyes shut, breathing ragged, the wait dragged on. Nothing happened. No cold, no shouts, no smell of roses. Taking a deep breath, I opened my eyes. The room was as it was left, trashed, the bed unmade and an empty wine bottle on the side table. He wasn't here.

Relief followed me into the dining area. At least, I had the place to myself. But he could materialise at any time. Only I now had an idea of who he was working for. I would have to be mindful of what he said, then call Sarina on her mobile and tell her. Sitting at the polished wood dining table the colours in the room, the distinct lack of black came vividly into focus. A chrome toaster and kettle sat on the white marble bench. The brushed steel refrigerator and dishwasher, the off-white cupboards with chrome handles; this was my world of light. Floral curtains, oak polished wooden floorboards, flower paintings on the walls and a cookbook rack stuffed with recipes. I relaxed, placed my head in my hands, closed my eyes and let my home wash the black from my mind.

45

On the way home I thought I'd seen the dark figure of Orlando in a car parked down the street; it was paranoia, had to be, did things like him even drive cars? I was weary from thinking, weary from a little too much drinking, and feeling lucky that I'd made it home without being picked up by the cops.

My mobile rang and vibrated in my jacket. I pulled it out and checked the number. It was Mariz's. Someone had his phone. I answered.

"Who is this?"

"Tonight," Mariz's voice.

I hung up, shaking, relaxation gone. Tension tightened in my jaw — neck tension. He was haunting my phone. How? Could ghosts haunt technology? I called Sarina; she had her phone switched to answer service. I knew she wouldn't call back until nightfall. She wasn't afraid of the daylight; shopping usually drew her out into the sun; she just liked the blackness of night more. *Always black*. I dropped the phone on the table. It was four in the afternoon, at least two hours before Sarina would call back. Could I last that long? What did he mean about tonight? Follow, obvious. I didn't want to follow, wasn't ready to face whatever it was he wanted to lead me to. Orlando? Aza'zel? What could such things want with me and why use Mariz? The only thing I could think of was his book. That didn't make sense.

Pouring a drink and dropping onto the couch, the afternoon confronted me. Eat? Sleep? Make the most of him not being around? Drink — a good option. The bottle sat on the floor to my right and the glass, filled halfway rested in the fingers. Drunk I could deal with just about anything.

I thought back to how things begun, hoping something would give me a clue, an answer.

"Mariz's won the SPA!" Samantha told me. She told me before I heard it on the local news. Had I not heard it from her, my reaction might have been different, less accepting or polite. Her excitement was proof that she cared for him more than ever. The moment I'd waited for faded. She'd never leave him now. He'd just given a radio interview on Charlotte's WPEG-FM, which was unusual given the listener mix, Samantha's media contacts would have him on stations across the country, and if the down South folks thought he was something, then the rest of the country will love him.

I drank myself to sleep that night. Mariz was a success again and my chance at getting Samantha gone like so many dreams in my life. I cried, and ranted, walked about the house knocking things over, swearing into mirrors, pushing all the papers from my desk, it didn't change anything. The woman I'd bedded and loved fell deeper into the arms of Mariz. Fucking hopeless, dull, and pathetic Mariz.

I bought the book the next afternoon. Head thick and eyes painful. *Him and Me*. His photograph, sepia, graced the dust jacket. He had been posed to look thoughtful and sensitive. I read the book through in one sitting, thought about it, drank some more. Something wasn't right. I flipped through the pages, one paragraph stood out, drew me to the words.

She moves. Shadow chasing shadow; not knowing I can see, feel her or sense her within the skeins of the world. There is blood on her lips, darkness in her eyes, in her clothes and light covers me as I seep through her world. She is the one time forgot, the one, the one…

It wasn't his style; I was sure I knew all his work, this wasn't his voice. I knew how he wrote, and I had seen the best and worst he could produce. I'd read all his books, his short experimental stories in magazines and even the turgid articles he wrote for Squire. This couldn't be is work. I did see touches of the man in places, but it looked obvious to me; he'd rewritten someone else's book. The book deserved the award; it was good, damn good. But whose book was it?

Did the original author know? Had they sold him the rights to the work and relinquished their claim to authorship? To accept the SPA under this type of circumstance was an act of literary fraud. The Southerners wouldn't take kindly to being had, and they'd lynch him on the spot. I could accept the loss of Samantha to him, but not like this. I poured blood and tears into my work, and like all writers around the country, we worked hard for our place in the literary world. I called Mariz; he was at first in full denial; the man was weak, and I knew how to get to him.

"Maybe I should call your mother?" When he said for the third time, he didn't know what I was talking about.

"Why?"

"You tell her everything, don't you?" This was true, he was a mummy's boy, and if anyone knew the truth, she would. She wouldn't tell me. He didn't know that.

He hesitated. "What do you want?"

"The truth."

"I can't. Di, I can't." I could hear defeat in his voice. "You won't understand."

"Try me."

"Even if you are right, it is too late to do anything about it, so just keep out of this, okay?" He was begging. His wimpy, light voice sounded on the edge of tears.

"And if I don't?" He hung up. I put the phone back on its base and sat back into the chair, the leather creaking. He as good as admitted it wasn't his book. Something could still be done, I knew.

I had to find out who had written the book. I needed proof before I could expose him. First, I went through the member list of the Fellowship, perhaps one of their books had been sold to him; it was a long shot, as I knew most of their styles and subject preferences and this didn't fit with any of them. Three days I spent chasing down dead ends, each and every contact made difficult by the fact I couldn't give away what I was doing. It became clear no one in the membership could have written the book. The next person to ask was Samantha, but if she were in on the scam, she wouldn't tell me. I decided to approach her as if I were writing a history piece on Mariz for the daily paper, which was partly true. I could earn some good money from such a story now he'd won the award. What I wanted was a list of his contacts; from there I would get the evidence.

Samantha told me nothing I didn't already know. She stood in her modern kitchen like a dutiful housewife. I sipped iced tea and tried to keep my mind away from her, thinking about her naked form in my arms. She looked good in jeans and printed logo T, her hair back, light makeup and soft pink lipstick. I wanted her so badly, loved her beyond reason. Even as I took notes lust crammed for attention. If I could only expose him, change the dynamic of this relationship, maybe, maybe I could win her over. Forgiveness wasn't one of my strong points, for Samantha I'd make the effort. All I needed was a name — the real author of the book.

He had done well with his early works, Samantha controlled the money and his emotional state. She wasn't too badly set herself. Her fashion career, lucrative with her face on every magazine in the country, set her up for life. Mariz just added to the wealth. In my mind, this was the real reason she stayed. No one could love a dote like him; not for long. I pulled myself away from her radiance, thanked her for the information and kissed her on the cheek. I wanted more, now wasn't the time. I left her to make muffins from a packet. There were people to call; my confidence wasn't high.

The ghost sat on my bed, those dead, vacant eyes watching me in the doorway. Sarina had called back and said I should follow him the next time he appears. I didn't want to; she said it was vital if we were to find out what Orlando wanted. Mariz, dressed in a black T, leather jacket, brown slacks and runners looked as real as anything else in the room. Always the same clothes, always the same look, and always the same strange blue aura.

A cold draft touched my skin. A window rattled.

"Am I to follow you?" I asked. I readied to run should he attack or throw something.

"He needs to see you."

"Who?"

"Follow."

"Is it Orlando?"

"Follow."

It was raining out, a turn in the weather. I didn't feel like walking in the rain. I'd have to change from my nightdress and put shoes on. He stood and walked towards me. I backed away, into the hall, knocking into the side table. A statue of a dolphin rattled against the wall. The smell of roses pushed into me, thick and cloying. I didn't have roses in my garden. The cold increased. I shivered. I couldn't move. He walked up close, barely two feet away. I was trapped. I reached for the statue, ready to smash it in his face.

"Follow. You won't be harmed. Follow." He turned and walked through the front door, out into the darkness and rain. I ran after him, statue in hand, opened the door; he was gone. I slammed the door and looked back down the hall. He was outside. I dropped the dolphin, and it thudded on the floor. I grabbed the mobile and called Sarina. Heart pounding, panic vibrating through my arms, my hands.

"He was just here. He was here."

"What did he say?" Sarina didn't sound concerned.

"He wanted me to follow him. Said I wouldn't be harmed." My voice shook, it was difficult to breathe. "He hasn't said that before."

"Did you follow?"

"No. I'm shit scared, Sarina. What does he want?"

"It's the only way we can find out what he wants. Let me think about this some more; there must be a solution. He did say you wouldn't be harmed, a Prelŭstitel is not known for lying, so we can almost be sure there is less danger than I originally thought," she said. "Now, did he say anything else? It is important to tell me exactly what he said."

"He said he wants to see me."

"Orlando."

"How should I know?" How could she sound so calm?

"Come by tomorrow, and we can discuss it while you work on the book." She hung up.

The book? Fuck the book. I needed answers.

Chapter 8

The Prelŭstitel

I needed darkness, the substance that helps me do what I must. I fed from a woman, took all that she was and discarded her on the roadside, her shopping littering the street. Slipping back into the colourless world of night the following of Sarina and the new woman continued.

The woman's dark energy strengthened me, deepened me and allowed me to walk in the lights of the streets for a time. During the day it would help maintain my presence beneath the sun. By the rising of the moon, I would again need to feed, to take the darkness from a living being. A dog or cat could suffice; humans were needed in order to accomplish what He had put before me — many, many more humans.

I had to watch and had to be seen watching. To see me would keep her vigilant, she would always be aware. Other reasons existed, their full meaning dissolved through time. I needed to know what the other woman meant to her. There existed link between her and what I had to find. A link I hoped wasn't true. It would complicate matters, test my resolve and perhaps even bring my final death. He had others who could challenge me; I was not irreplaceable.

I'd found out where Sarina's human lived. I didn't tell him I knew. Not yet. I stepped through darkness to her house in the suburbs. Easy when your vehicle is the night. Lights glowed through curtains, small portals in the storm that had settled over the houses.

The rain fell hard. I watched the woman's house from across the street, the single street lamp creating deeper shadows for me to hide. Would she come out in the inclement weather?

The lights in the house blinked out, a crashing sound, muffled by the rain, came from within. My ghost stepped through the front door and into the garden. He watched the door for a moment before fading, like colour washed away by the falling water. The woman opened the door; she held something. The front light blinked on. She looked frightened, stared into the darkness for a time then returned inside.

She was who my puppet haunted. Would this make getting the book and the icon simpler? I doubted she would tell me where the book was, maybe if I took her, devoured her darkness this would lead me to it? Could I risk losing another by acting too soon?

I reached into the realm, touched the skeins, felt the slight vibrations of the night. Aza'zel was moving through the fabric, searching, watching and manipulating. There were questions trickling down the threads like black blood through dead veins. He shifted. Had he seen me? I broke contact, looked to the house. Had this woman read the book? That could be the reason the puppet had found her.

I stepped to the door, ready to pass through. A force stopped me. Something protected her, and it wasn't Uttuku.

"My way." I heard His whisper through the trees.

He stopped me. Why? There was something else; it was faint, strange. Did he know? I stared at the front door, so close. Why had he stopped me? What purpose did it serve?

Chapter 9

Cassandra

Tomorrow was a long way off and a night with Mariz didn't feel all that appealing. I knew my mood bordered on the suicide line, been there before. The anti-depressants couldn't keep up with all the extra crap going on around me. I had to get out, do something, anything better than staring at the walls and listening to more of his requests. He'd be back. He always came back. Not for the first time, I wonder about the state of my mind. My doctor questioned it, and I took pills to help control it. Still, this didn't help with the questions. Could I see a ghost? Bipolar depression could create visions as real as I could imagine. Could I be lost in a world of my making and all reality be locked up in some psych ward jabbering to myself and hugging a worn old teddy bear? My neighbour across the street had gone that way. He saw and spoke to Martians, took ice with them. Police and two men in suits wrested him into a strait jacket in the middle of the street four years ago. I can remember his last words before being pushed into the back of the police car.

"Let me go; I won't tell them. Let me go. I won't hurt you. I'm going to fucking kill you!"

With shaking hands, I poured a drink, first into the glass and then down my throat. It helped. Being crazy like that didn't fit with my kind of crazy. I called Sarina to make sure she was real. She said it was okay and I wasn't going mad; easy for her to say.

Crap. That's what my life looked like tonight, absolute crap. I dressed in what I could find clean on the floor; baggy, dark clothes, a black dress and black leggings, black T over a white shirt, black, head-kicker boots laced to the knees. Dress how you feel I'd read in an old Vanity Fair. Pulling a black, silver studded bag from the wardrobe, I thought about Sarina's love of black. Could she also be a closet psycho needing a big dose of Lithium so she could see the light? Maybe I needed the drug?

Hitting the town might not be the best course of action. The keys were already in my hand and the front door open. No point wasting all this activity. The weather wasn't good and matched my mood perfectly. The pills weren't working, and the booze started its drive to oblivion, and I wanted to be on board.

Standing on the front porch, I watched the rain falling across the streetlight, listened to its fall on the wide driveway, the slap against the leaves of the trees. The car sat protected slightly by a covered carport, getting in wasn't a problem. I hated getting wet, even if feeling like a wet dog matched my decaying emotional state. How long had it been raining inside my brain, in the heart, drowning my soul?

Driving through intrepid weather to the west end of the strip only increased the misery. The wipers dragged across the windscreen, like a dirty hand wipes away tears, quick and ineffective. The sound a constant reminder of a never-ending struggle, it was a lonely sound. I hit the CD button on the stereo. Siouxsie and the Banshees smashed all other sound from the depressing thoughts. Kaleidoscope brought the hype and emotions down; the slow, melodic darkness strummed its way into my being. Crashed out my mind; I needed to be alone, needed to be seen being alone.

I knew a place, my place, my hole in the ground that allowed me to crawl in when the crap got too much. The dark river of the road, white lines glistening and slippery, led me into a world of coloured lights, secrets and hidden mayhem. Sunset Strip, W Sunset Boulevard, welcomed the disenfranchised with open arms. Not a happy welcome, more a watch your ass or die kind of thing. There had been plenty of disappearances in this street's life, more sick crimes per capita than New York it was once reported. The gangs could take some blame, but not all, still, it was an area I didn't comment openly on; I had no beef with them, and they didn't have any with me. This was the home of The Sunset Strip Killers Carol Bundy, and Douglas Clark. When coming to the strip, those were names to research; the knowledge might save your life one dark and stormy night. A cliché that could make you dead.

For the last three months, I'd been delving deeper and deeper into the Goth scene. I avoided the drug networks and backhand deals made in shadows. I had my preferred poison, and they respected that. I knew LA could be a violent place, a real bad place to be at night; in all my years I suppose I've been protected, shielded from such things. To me, everything always looked okay, dark, but okay. Maybe it was God watching over me, someone certainly was, and I didn't mind; one thing less to worry about.

Parking in front of the club - there was always a space for me - the great American author and number one patron of 'Goth Club' prepared to drop into a black, welcoming dungeon. Two huge men, not Goths, and with Security written across their over tight Ts, recognised the car. One pulled an umbrella from within the club's doorway, stepped to the driver's side and made sure I didn't get wet.

"Ms Whitehall," he said. Polite and protective.

"Andre." He led me to the door, nodding to the other guard. I paid no entry fee.

Down the stairs, black walls either side, close, I slowly immersed myself in the throb of music fighting its way to the street. The Kinks, Celluloid Heroes pulled me in, sucked at the weariness. The Club wasn't a fully dedicated Goth hangout, though many of the key figures in the culture did find their way here when the weather was bad, and the night took on the appearance better found in horror films.

Music pressed and pulsed vibrated my skin; shook the bones. Black and chrome welcomed and promised. The bar, running the full length of one wall, glittered with silver skulls and bats on its face. Flickering shimmers against the flat black of the panels. The bar-top lit from beneath and above looked like a wall of blue light sandwiched between solid banks of night.

One of the barmen saw me. A George T. sat in the pool of light before I could open my bag.

"On the house," he yelled, sliding the drink forward. I raised the glass in salute, down it went in one gulp. He poured another and again refused payment. Being a celebrity that stays close to the heart of the locals did have its advantages. Free drinks weren't one of the perks I'd been granted here. I didn't argue, let someone else flip the bill for my woes; don't expect a thank you.

Tall, black on chrome standing tables filled most of the front section of the club; above each, a tight beam of light crashed into the table top creating the effect of blue prison bars throughout the club. A cool look. We were all prisoners of something. The real Goths would be towards the back, by the dance floor, sitting on worn black sofas and chairs, smoking and existing in a moment of their choosing.

People stood about, soaked through with sound, damp with the pounding from a life they only looked at and rarely ventured into. These were the watchers, those who made sojourns into the culture to see, and gawk at others who they'd never be able to understand. Fingers pointed, heads turned, eyes fell across me like x-rays. Recognition kept the club bringing in new custom, and I didn't mind. I left the bar with my third drink, pushing beneath the haze of grey cigarette smoke, towards the reality I sought.

White faces, black eyes, black lips, tattoos, piercings and the layering of clothing usually seen on strange homeless types occupied the small section of world I needed right now. Voltaire's Vampire Club drew me towards the gutter of my heart. Two women, wearing black leather and white lace, we'd had sex a few times over the years, approached, kissed my cheek, hugged and whispered welcomes I didn't hear. Faces smiled, hands waved. I didn't know their names, didn't have to, they knew me, and that was all I needed and all they required.

Being allowed to sit in one of the chairs, an offer I never refused helped create the impression of being home and somewhere wanted. I hadn't gone the full Goth look myself, and somehow, I think they understood. Like an audience we watched the crowd drift in and out, looking to us like children watching animals in a zoo. We studied and learned more from them than they did from us. Most of us had come from the glitter life, the white side of life and already knew the social structure which drove escape. What the lookers saw were strange beings with unfathomable and unreadable faces. In the fading light of the club, their eyes wouldn't be seen, lost in the black rings of mascara and shadow. Those who came to see the Goths at play didn't get it, didn't see what we were doing, what we represented to the world. It is easy to see a Goth, quite another to understand what it means. When with this group we rarely spoke, interact as if on autopilot, and took some joy from just being. Being who they were, and not caring what people thought they were. As a writer, I couldn't afford the full mental state, the total contempt for my fellow human. I could take a moment though, step away from the me everyone knew and be the person I sometimes wished I could be. In the spiral down this was the place to be.

I couldn't talk to anyone, the music, obscure but loud, made it impossible. Drinks kept coming, and I kept right on drinking them. Mariz became more and more a blur as the sun approached dawn; its rays finding their way down the entrance stairwell. Did Sarina ever come here? Would she enjoy the spectacle? Rubbing the numbness deeper into my face I thought not. Where did something like her go to unwind? Some of the people gathered about I knew slept in coffins, had sex in coffins and lived a life close to dark legends and folklore. No matter how plastered I got, how out of my mind with the culture's meaning and influences, I could never sleep in a coffin. Then, how many of them had a real live ghost in their house? How many knew a five-hundred-year-old woman?

Bodies moved about and through the small dance floor. No one danced here. They swayed, pushed around by the strumming of electric guitars and the rattling percussion of bass and drums, or the deep melodic tones of black sound, voodoo sound. Movement dictated by sound and sound dictated by slowly decaying society. The decline into night was what I'd said of my work in an interview. Sipping, letting eyes fold in on themselves; I let the slow decline wind me down into a pit of darkness created by my hand. Somewhere I knew my problems would still be waiting; only right now I chose to ignore them.

"Time to leave." Distant voice, distant touch, dreams, murky, clouded in fog. "Help me get her outside."

Moving, shifting, sleeping. In and out. In and out with the flicker of the sun. The flicker of the sun, the flicker of the sun.

Turning in bed, I didn't remember much of the night. Fuzziness, seediness and aches held me down, pressed into the firmness of the bed. I knew where I was, the smells, the touch of the sheets against my skin; cool cotton, smooth, comfortable. The day's smell, trees and grass, the birds and the rumble of car going past my house welcomed me into the day: my world, my life.

I rolled, felt the bed. Alone. Always alone. Last night, the loneliness created by the abundance of sound kept me cocooned, separated from those around me. The crowd around the star wanting to be seen, to touch, too, for a brief time, be a part of something they weren't. I still had my underwear on; disappointment. My rescuer had left me untouched again. It wouldn't have surprised me to have had sex without knowing, not the first time, doubted it would be the last.

The bedroom blinds were part drawn, a breeze, afternoon, brushed over the bed, touched exposed skin, tickled life back into alcohol death. Someone rescued me again, delivered me to safety. Who didn't come into it? Care settled and comforted. Someone actually cared.

A clatter at the back of the house drew me closer to the day, further away from the depression I knew crept through the brain, pumped from a heart too many times strangled.

The kitchen!

I sat up. Head screaming.

Mariz!

"I hit the town last night," I told Sarina over the phone. "Tied on a big one."

"You'd better not come today. I was up late, only been home a short while myself."

"I want to see you."

"Not today. Tomorrow, okay?"

"We could maybe talk about the book?" I needed to see her, and the excuse was at least plausible. Was she disappointed in me?

"I need some sleep. Tomorrow, Cassandra." Sarina hung up. I sat on the end of my bed in my undies and bra. The shower had helped, and the glass of whiskey after a bowl of cereal did ease some of the wooziness. I had a book of my own to complete, well the last rewrite for the publisher. With anything up to four books on the go at the same time, I rarely missed a deadline or didn't have something to sell. I'd spend the rest of the day and part of the night writing. Maybe some good will come from getting words out and ordered. God knows I needed some order.

My office, as usual, waited cramped and littered with books, drafts of novels and clothes I hadn't bothered to put away. I always looked good when out, but at home, blatant slobbery took root. In the disaster area of the room, there was order of a sort. The laptop, crammed on the desk between piles of novels I'd never get around to reading, became a grey and black oasis waiting for a visit. The printer, a massive laser designed for hard work, sat under the desk, scuff marks from shoes scarred its once pristine, white surface. On a shelf above the desk, bowing in the middle from the weight, and years past staining, sat awards, texts on ancient history and two large dictionaries, which I never really used. Looks were everything I suppose.

The old carpet, once a brilliant blue and plush had been ground down to a lifeless matting, threadbare and uninviting. Today I felt like the carpet; my mouth tasted likes its underlay. I've tasted underlay; you don't drink as much as I do without being face down on the mat a few times.

In the chair, the old wooden swivel and tilt type, the computer powered up and the screen came alive with a background covered in documents I couldn't find the time to file. Cluttered room, cluttered computer and more than likely a cluttered mind awaited. I had Sarina's document, simply titled 'Bela'. This one I made a file for, not sure why, but it felt better not having the document so easily seen. I encrypted it. I hated encryption like I hated most rules and regulations. It felt like putting bars on windows to keep the nasties out. What about the prisoner within? Locking freedom outside like it presented itself as a criminal just waiting to pounce. Not my thing and he walked through doors, so bars weren't going to do me any good anyway.

Research first. I needed to find out about Bela Lugosi, his past, his family, anything that would put Sarina into the same picture. Google is a wonderful place, find anything, even information you didn't want to find. Porn is everywhere, and I swear most of it is made in LA.

The Lugosi family ran its web site, which answered a lot of background movie details; no mention of Sarina directly or indirectly. She became a fiction against the backdrop of Lugosi's life. In a way, I expected this. Sarina had said he didn't know she existed.

Straight data, Bela was the youngest son of Paula de Vojnich and the banker, Istvan Blasko and raised a Roman Catholic. He made films in Austria – Hungary between 1917 and 1918, twelve in fact. Funny, the man was famous before becoming famous. The fame dwindled because he helped create the actors' union. He wasn't allowed to act in his own country. In exile in Germany, he made a few well-received films, including a few adaptations of Stephen May novels. I noted this down. I looked May up on Wikipedia. Nothing came from it, and in a way, I was glad, this story already had all the elements of a twisted horror film as it was.

Bela left Germany October 1920 and arrived at Ellis Island in the US in March 1921. This matched Sarina's suggested time frame. I wondered where she fit in. She wasn't even a part of real history. There were a lot of references to films. The Black Cat, The Raven and Son of Frankenstein, were the most notable. I'd at least seen those, and these had him paired with Boris Karloff; more research, maybe. I knew the name, not much else. Lugosi played Ygor in Son of Frankenstein. I'd find the film and have another look; if she was about, she might have been an extra – a long shot, she did say she did extras work. There was a lot of history here, more information than I knew what to do with. Most of it wouldn't go in the book, I was sure of it, just knowing what to leave out dictated what the structure would be.

The distraction did me good. I'd finished one bottle of wine and a full pack of potato chips; a better diet than yesterday. With the sites bookmarked bookmarked I shut the computer down. The desk clock said eleven thirty, the view from the office window, dark, my garden hidden by night. It is easy to forget time while doing research, even easier to forget when writing a book. Sarina's suggestion didn't seem as weird as I thought. At least it might help keep me sane.

I watched TV with a whiskey or two before going to bed. There was an appointment to keep in the morning, which never filled me with joy. If I wanted to stay out of hospital, then turning up was a must.

I couldn't go to Sarina's, which was preferable, I had to see my shrink, get more meds and pass his questions. It became a game played every couple of weeks, like a period, it just didn't stop because you wanted it to. I'd told Sarina about it on the phone. If sharing personal stuff with her worked, she might also share back, help with the real problem.

"Can I come by after the appointment?" It was either that or face Mariz.

"Not today, I've got something to organise. You be sure to tell him everything."

"What makes you think my doctor is a he?" My slightly off again, on again feminist defence mode kicked in.

"All the good ones are, aren't they?"

"Not always." I hated being defensive; it taxed my nerves. "Okay, he's a he, and I only tell him what he wants to hear, mostly."

"Maybe call me later."

"I'll think about it." I hung up and immediately felt guilty.

I sat in the high backed, winged, leather chair, a cushion behind me for support. The room, dull illumination, looked more like a nice, private library. Dr Sholan's desk, rich mahogany inlaid with green leather was as neat and tidy as he presented. At five ten I wouldn't have called myself tall, he only came up to my shoulder. About fifty, thin and balding, in his simple grey suit and round-rimmed glasses he cut a perfect figure of an old European psychiatrist. I felt comfortable, at ease, throw in a couple of cigars and the scene would have been perfect. Throw in his questions and the whole scene fractured into defensive arguments and finger-pointing.

"How are you today?" he asked, the obvious Austrian accent pleasant.

"Pretty crap. How are you?" Best to be honest with him, he'd work it out anyway.

"Thoughts of suicide?" Raised eyebrows.

"Not this week."

"Before this week?"

Shit, I'd gone the wrong way in the conversation again, last time we went this route I ended up in a private mental home making pottery fists.

"An idle thought. Got better things to do with my life than that." He relaxed, wrote a note in the file. I wondered what he'd make of demons, or Uttuku as Sarina has said? Did psychiatrists do demons or was that up to the Catholic Church?

"Our last talk stopped when we got to your mother and father."

"Like I said, we aren't going there."

"What about them concerns you, angers you so much?"

"Next question." He always wanted the family bit; the juxtaposition between depression and growing up in a dysfunctional household. Dr Sholan wrote a few notes. I couldn't read his fine print.

"Do you think your father is responsible for your life choices?"

"You won't let it drop, will you?"

"It angers you, so I am concerned."

"I'm a lesbian; he hates lesbians. I tried to be what he wanted but I like women. Always have since a little girl. Never thought about boys, never kissed one or even had sex with one. Got it?" He nodded, didn't write. This wasn't for the file. "I tried to tell my parents, didn't work out well. Didn't change how I thought or felt, so I followed the path life dished out and the one that felt right. Simple." Again thoughtful.

"We'll come back to this one day, and I wasn't talking about sexual choices by the way," he said, his tone lower, gentler. "Have you been having visions? Hearing voices?" The checklist.

"No." Do Prelŭstitels count?

"Do you think you have behaved in a manner that might be reckless? Taking unusual risks?"

I laughed. If only I could tell him. "Only the ghost of Mariz." I also had sex with a demon who fed on light energy and who was being hunted by the evilest power known to mankind. Risks! Hah!

"Has this manifestation caused harm or caused you to harm yourself?" He steepled his hands on the desk in front of him.

"No, just the usual wandering about the place." I'd let him believe his grief angle, why complicate matters?

"I had hoped our talks would have stopped these visitations." He looked at me over his glasses. A funny look, I couldn't help but laugh.

"You find that funny, why?"

"I'm a writer. I find unusual things funny, sometimes." I kept a very forced smile going. "Look, about the only risk I take these days is going to the store to buy milk, and around my neighbourhood that can be dangerous." Now he smiled.

He sat back, placing his hands flat on the desk with exacting motion. I liked this little man, his thoughtfulness and no fuss manner helped me open, well, as much as I was prepared to at this point. If I told him everything, I'd be walking out of his office in a straight jacket.

"Do you feel high or down today?"

"Well, crap is better, but I guess down."

"Anything happen lately that might have triggered this feeling?" Again, raised eyebrows. "Anything other than your ghost perhaps? Anything strange happen since we last spoke?"

"No!" I felt sick. Did he suspect something? "Mariz's ghost is enough, and it freaks me out," I answered too fast, felt the edge of panic. The room became oppressive, warm. Could he see I was lying?

"It is common, in grief to see the departed. I think we might be able to work through what you believe you did to him. You are progressing, and that is important."

I relaxed a little. I needed a drink. Anxiety was one of the reason drugs were needed. He was a shrink; of course, he'd see my heightened state. The panic returned. I should have cancelled the appointment. I looked to the door. Maybe I should have just left, said nothing more and went home, or to a bar, anyplace that had alcohol would do.

"Any pressures on you?"

It was hard to concentrate, but I had to, or he would get suspicious, call the nurse and have me admitted for observation. Forming the right answer was imperative.

"Pressure of a few deadlines, late nights working, being by myself most of the time. I guess it's got to me a bit. Worn me down." It wasn't quite the truth. Being down in the darkness had become normal lately.

He looked at my file, flipping pages, reading.

"I might increase the Effexor by seventy-five milligrams a day and increase the valproate to stabilize your mood."

"Side effects?"

"Have you had any from so far?"

"Not that I've noticed."

"Then this should be fine but read the insert in the box to understand side effects that you could experience." He wrote a prescription. "If they are severe comeback and see me immediately, no need for an appointment, just come in. It will take a couple of weeks for the new dosage to take full effect."

"Thanks."

"I do need to ask you about alcohol." This time he looked grave, a little look down the nose. "Your last blood test showed abnormalities in your liver function test. Caused by too much alcohol."

"I do like a few drinks now and again." The frown deepened. "It helps me sleep. Makes me feel less depressed."

"You know drinking isn't a good way to deal with bipolar?" I nodded. "And drinking on medication isn't advised." He sounded like a concerned parent; the eyes softened then lips shifted to sad lines.

"I know."

"If you want to feel better, Cassandra, really feel better, we'll have to look at your alcohol consumption."

"Today?"

"No, not today." He laughed, a light sound, friendly. The parent look disappeared. "But eventually."

I leaned forward, and he handed me the prescription. Time remained to talk, though he always let me leave when I felt I had to and stay longer if it helped.

"I'd like to see you in a couple of weeks, get some more blood tests done to check your levels, thyroid function, more liver function, maybe get an ECG to check your heart."

"Should I know what that all means?"

"Do you want to?"

"Not really. I'm sure you'd tell me if there was anything serious to deal with."

"Bipolar depression is serious."

"I know." I shook his hand as I opened the office door. "Thank you. I'll make an appointment with the receptionist."

"Please do, Cassandra," he said. "It is always a pleasure talking to a fellow writer."

Dr Sholan was indeed a writer; he wrote books on the psychoanalysis of famous people in history. When I didn't feel miserable, I'd get one of his books.

The bill paid and a new appointment made, I headed into the sunshine. The happy day most people enjoyed looked bland and empty. I had nothing to be happy about. Even my old yellow Volvo looked depressed sitting by the sidewalk. Out of the corner of my eye, I saw a black limo moving down the street, the place had lots of limo these days, a kind of status symbol of success. I could have bought a new car, a Chrysler perhaps, they looked good; but why? I'd still feel miserable, and I liked the unassuming look of my car; the 'don't bother me I've got nothing' look. Right now, I wanted sex and Sarina was my choice.

Chapter 10

The Prelŭstitel

"Why did you write the book?" Aza'zel asked.

We walked together through a forest, the shadows of trees pushing in around us. Above, the stars flashed between the small openings in the canopy, and a sliver of moon gave the only real light. Just how he liked it.

"A memory. I didn't want to forget the life I once had."

"What you have isn't enough?" His blackness passed through the trees like light through glass.

"It happened a long time ago."

"Where did you keep it?" A fair question. He didn't express anger.

"Uri always guarded it." He waited for more; I didn't want to say anything else.

"Very well."

We stopped by the mirror of a lake. Black glass in the night. I remembered such things when alive, their beauty, at the time, enough to remind me of times best forgotten. I wouldn't, couldn't change the way I lived now. He stood beside me, partly in me. His touch, cold, empty and black, empowered me to achieve my goal. Being empowered still wasn't enough.

"I understand you." Aza'zel was in my mind. "I have no such desire."

"You understand what I must do?"

"No," he said, his coldness leaving me. "I know. Knowing will not help you."

"Very well. Why are you protecting the woman?"

"For you."

"Does she know where the book is?"

"You must find out." His darkness spread.

"I do not understand you."

"You heard my words?"

"Yes."

"Then you must find another way."

"And Sarina?" I still had to get back the icon — the one I'd allowed her to steal.

"Things are merging, Prelŭstitel. Opportunity will come, you must act. In time your completeness will serve me better."

"Then tell me what I need to know!"

Aza'zel shifted into the starry sky, for a moment the stars winked out, swallowed by his size. He said nothing more. Why did he protect the woman? He wanted the book found and destroyed as much as me. Was this a test?

I watched the lake, lights glittering on its surface, a night sky reflection. The woman, Cassandra Whitehall, she was the important element in the riddle, the subterfuge Aza'zel wove about me. If I could not use her, then who? The ghost of Mariz Sanchez?

Chapter 11

Cassandra

No matter how much I needed to lose myself in Sarina's body, she wouldn't let me go to her place after the visit to the doctor. She said my mind wasn't right and I felt so morose I agreed my company would have been worse than pointless. I grabbed 'Leaves of Blood' from my bedside table, a small press collection from a group. I'd been sent a copy to look over and comment on. It was okay for small press, but my mood didn't warm me to the task of reading. I'd met the group of writers when I was in Michigan on a book tour; an odd group who all mostly lived in Brighton. From memory, they knew a lot of weird stuff and had hooks into the not so pleasant side of the business. I called Mike Brown; we'd met while I was investigating Mariz's book.

"Mike. Cassandra Whitehall."

"Hi Di wondered if I'd hear from you again."

"Got a question."

"Shoot."

"Doing some research for a new book and was wondering if you came across Uttuku in your horror work?" If anyone knew something, he would.

"No, can't think of anything. What are they?"

"Just something I came across." I heard some tapping in the background; he was on the net. I didn't even know if I said it right and didn't know how it was spelt.

"Got something," he said. "It's a demon, or collection of desert demons. The link here says associated with the Babylonian goddess Lamashtu." More typing sounds. "Got a reference to Lilith in Wikipedia, this is old stuff, almost pre-legend even. At a guess, it has some connection to vampires. I haven't come across this reference before. Does that help? I could email you the websites if you like."

"So how do you say it and what's the spelling?"

"Well, I'd say oo-to-koo." He then gave me the spelling. I'd look it up later myself.

"Yeah, thanks." Even if I did find this stuff out myself, it sounded more real coming from someone I knew. Like a confirmation to remove lingering doubts. Of those I still had plenty.

"Since you called, I got a new book in the works, could I interest you? Maybe a short story on this Uttuku angle?"

"Thanks for the invite, let me think about it." I poured a drink. "I have to go now, say hi to the guys."

"You bet." He hung up.

I dropped the phone on the couch. At least there was some historical information, though I doubted it would be anything like the reality I was learning about. I should have asked Mike about Prelŭstitels. His collections did deal with things a bit like this; it might have drawn him into my mess. No. This was my problem and something that needed dealing with without endangering others if I could avoid it. I checked the computer; Mike had sent through the websites for me to read, the idea was there that Uttuku took life light. Okay, it wasn't much, but it did help with creating a reality around me. Mood deepening and frustration catching up, I drank myself to the edge of sleep.

My eyeballs ached and my temples throbbed, sleep was restless, and the painkillers weren't living up to the TV claims. Mariz wouldn't let me alone: he had sat, luminescent like a projected hologram, on the Hepplewhite chair at the foot of my bed. When having decided enough was enough, I'd risen and kicked the chair out from under him; he still sat there, suspended in space, with that reproachful look in his dark eyes. A double whiskey or five and two sleeping tablets had me face down on the bed. He'd gone and I had broken one leg of a three-thousand-dollar antique chair. He said no more than; just knowing he was watching kept me anxious. He wanted me to follow and again I couldn't, even with the promise of no harm. Real fear, fear I hadn't ever experienced since I was ten held me tight. Like the time my mother, drunk beyond sense, held a carving knife to my throat because I'd forgotten to make gravy for dinner. My muscles ached when I did stop struggling with the pillow. Morning offered feeble hope, and I took it.

I took my medication, showered and dressed, then headed out for the day. Today I had someone I did want to see.

My knock was answered by the clicking of locks and rasping of bolts. Sarina wore a similar black tracksuit I'd worn on the morning she told me she was an Uttuku. Her feet were bare, toenails black, and her hair tied back from her face. Despite my shell-shocked nerves, she looked beautiful. I took my place at the kitchen table; I'd brought my laptop and would write straight into the book file. My handwriting was shoddy and getting worse, so taking notes for later wouldn't work. Shaking hands would create a few typos, but at least I'd be able to know what the words were meant to be.

"Why do you want me to follow him?" I asked as she joined me. It took a moment for the computer to come alive.

"The book first, then we talk about him, Orlando and what he wants." She sounded definite.

I sat back in the chair; I wasn't sure I could concentrate enough to write down emotional experiences. I had plenty of doubts and paranoia to frazzle any woman. Rubbing at my face I realized I hadn't put any makeup on; my skin felt dry.

Sarina watched for a few minutes, searching my face, looking concerned. "Come to bed; it will relax you, and settle your mind, then we can work." She stood and helped me up. "You need to trust me, Cassandra."

I wasn't going to argue, it was what I wanted after all, and I needed to feel that euphoria, the depression barked at me louder today and if I had to give away some of this light to find peace, then be done with it.

"Do you trust me?"

Right now, I didn't trust anything. I was drinking heavily, eating little and sleeping even less. Sarina's hand on my face radiated a comforting warmth. Just for a moment, everything would be okay, the pain would slip away, and I would be held by someone who knew what I was going through. I didn't know if I could trust though, it was a big word, a big commitment. I shook my head and averted my eyes from hers.

"Trust me."

She took my hand and led me into the bedroom. I let her remove my jeans, jacket and heavy shirt. Standing before her in my underwear I just felt tired and very unsexy. She removed her tracksuit; she wore no underwear. She kissed me. I resisted a little at first, my strong need getting mixed up with even stronger fear. The touch was so soft, fresh; I gave into it eventually. My tension seemed to flow from my body and into her. She kissed my shoulder.

"Please." My floral undies looked wrong against the black. I felt wrong; she had to make it right. Had to.

She touched my cheek, fingertips cool. I lay on the bed, letting the smoothness of the cotton sheet welcome me. Sarina lay next to me. Pressed into me. It wasn't sex I wanted only I didn't know how to say what it was I desired.

"Not sex." I rolled onto my side, back towards her. "I want you to do that light thing, please. Please, Sarina, I feel so lost in the darkness."

She wrapped her right arm around me, squeezed. I stared at the wall; the picture of Bela Lugosi looked back.

"Just try and relax," Sarina said into my hair. Her breath was warm on my neck.

I closed my eyes and snuggled back into her, the press of her skin welcoming. Her hand caressed my brow, pushed down my frown and eased hair away from my face. Tension stiffened muscles, back and neck, the expectation unbearable.

"It doesn't hurt, and I only need a little every few days, a bit of life light to keep me away from the darkness." She stroked my shoulder, the soft scent of sandalwood in the air. "That's all."

Euphoria came. I gasped and fell, fell into softness, light and warmth. The darkness fell away like the dropping of a robe. I gasped again as the light lifted me away from the pit of despair.

I woke in her arms, unsure of how long I had been asleep. There was a slight ache behind my eyes, but I felt better, not happier just better about myself and the woman cradling my body.

"Why do you need the light," I asked softly. She opened her eyes and smiled.

"An Uttuku need the light of life to live. I need it." She stroked my cheek; I leant into the touch.

"Tell me why." I had to know more. "But keep holding me. I like it." She gripped me tighter, my face buried between her breast now. The subtleness of her skin, the sweet, pleasant scent brought a deep sense of peace.

"I take a piece of people's life light to sustain me. Cassandra, I no longer have a strong life light of my own. I take from others in order to get what I don't have." It wasn't a great explanation; it was enough. "I don't know how to explain this more."

"I won't turn into what you are?" Sarina didn't laugh. She kissed my shoulder again.

"No, you will not be changed."

I slid up the bed, so our faces were close together, my lips brushing her chin, her cheek, breathing into her dark hair. I didn't care. The world was already screwed up. What was one more strange event in the mess of the last two weeks? Sarina shifted position, gently rolling onto her back; her svelte form making me feel old. She was tired and old. Gently I pressed my lips against hers, tasted her air, felt to wetness of her tongue. The kiss was deep, long and hungry.

"Now it's time for sex." I kissed her again.

This time when I woke Sarina was gone from the bed, and I was so comfortable I didn't want to move. A black tracksuit lay on the end of the bed. I felt refreshed, the anxiety and tension gone. Dressing, I thought about having to go home to face Mariz. The thought didn't hold long, this moment was what I wanted, and it felt good.

I found Sarina in the kitchen typing on my computer. A glass of dark liquid on the table to her right. Was it blood? Did blood look black?

"It's Pepsi," she said, answering my frown.

"How long was I out?"

"Five or so hours. How do you feel?"

"Better, much better thanks." I pulled out a chair and sat. "What are you doing?"

"Adding some notes for the book. You weren't up to it." She turned the computer so I could read.

Reading seemed easier; the words clear on the screen. The notes were a bit fractured, but I did understand most of what she had entered. Bela had moved to the US in 1920, that much added up, he became a US citizen in 1931 and she a citizen in 1922, though her citizenship came through other means, suggested, yet undisclosed. Sarina had launched into gushing pages of prose on Bela's wife, Lullian Arch. She obviously liked this woman. I scanned the rest of the names. The others received light touches, nothing noteworthy.

"How many times did you say Bela was married?" I looked at the file and made a new text document for my notes. I knew from the Internet; she had to tell me. Sarina wanted to work on this book, and for what she had just done for me I owed her some time, and if this was what she wanted, I could manage the task.

"Five, though Lullian was the nicest," she said. "She was the only one to stick by him. She had his only child, a son, Bela George Lugosi junior. I liked the name." Sarina had that brightness in her eyes again. These were good memories. "I think she was also the only one who knew what a great actor Bela had been. How Hollywood had destroyed him."

"You met his wives?"

"Not directly, but I did have a brief conversation with the second, Ilona once. She made Bela laugh, and I liked to see him laugh." Sarina folded her hands on the table before her, trying to stay composed. "Lullian made him happy. Happier than I think a life with me would have been."

"You wanted him to love you, though?" I paused with my fingers over keys. "If he had, his life would have surely been different, better even."

Sarina shook her head. "No, his life wouldn't have worked with me, and I couldn't have changed it even if I wanted to."

I moved away from the wives; this was her story, not theirs. I read a few more pages, skimming the text; all emotional and personal, little about the man.

"You don't mention much about his acting career." I thought some of this needed to be in the book. "You've given me plenty about your desire to meet him, but if I'm going to do this properly, I need a bit more." The rest had given me the energy to write. Had Sarina known this? I didn't let her know I already had a research file. She had to tell me in her own words. I had to believe who she said she was.

"Bela was already famous in Hungary and Germany, he was a wonderful actor, making films almost every month. He also did Shakespeare, you know. His classical training made him a star." It became obvious the memories weren't just a recount of events. "I was getting noticed more. I had to leave Germany, come to the US," she said, her smile infectious. "He had problems of his own so emigrated to the US as well. I'd told myself it was so he could be with me. At the time anything he did I would have twisted, so he looked like he was doing it for me, it just helped me deal with the situation. I was in love, what could I do?"

"Why didn't you talk to him?"

"I'm an Uttuku; he was human. Can you see my problem?"

"I'm human, and you're talking to me."

"Things have changed. Time move forward, and I need to..." She looked away. Was she crying?

I pushed on I couldn't have her bursting into tears, call me selfish but I wanted to remain good for as long as possible. With both of us sitting in black tracksuits in the equally dark room we looked like disembodied heads bobbing about the table.

"He didn't act when he first arrived in America?" Questioning might stop her feeling sad.

"He did after a few years; he started on stage again doing Bram Stoker's Dracula." She tugged absently at her sleeve. "Before then he suffered, and I couldn't do a thing to help. I had some friends in the business, others like myself, some famous or were famous, but I couldn't bring myself to speak with him."

"I find it surprising. You being an Uttuku and afraid to talk to a man, it doesn't quite gel in my head."

"I know, but there you have it."

"What did he do to make ends meet?" I knew the movies didn't start until 1931; he'd moved to America in the 1920s. The story needed more facts, her facts. I could do the emotional stuff easily enough. I also needed to know more about her, and this seemed to be a good way to go about it without being pushy.

"He worked as a labourer for a time." Sadness in her voice. "I could see he hated the work and I hated seeing him like that. Then something happened, he returned to the stage." She looked down on the table for a moment. "He loved the stage. I think he loved working with a live audience. He began theatre work with the Hungarian-American community." She looked pleased. "The Bela I knew back in Germany was back, happier than ever. You know, he played Dracula on Broadway for three years. I was at every performance, always backstage, and away from the lights; sometimes I even worked as a stagehand to see him perform."

"I thought he only did Dracula in film." I'd only ever known the movies.

"Oh no, he only got into Hollywood movies later." She took on a more serious tone. "Rumour says he only got the part because Lon Chaney died." I made a note of the name; I'd look it up later if need be. "Lon couldn't do it even if he wanted to; his contracts wouldn't let him. Bela got it in his own right. I'm proud of that, even if others have doubts."

"That was what, around 1931?"

"Yes, two years before he married Lullian." Sarina was becoming animated, hands moving in small circles before her. "He worked hard." She gushed. The hard face always vanished when she spoke about him.

I found I liked the happiness in Sarina's voice; her whole manner changed when talking about Bela Lugosi. In a small way, I felt jealous that someone could affect her so much. I had never had anyone in my life that I could

69

remember so affectionately, even Samantha didn't come close to Sarina's pain. Sarina seemed to drift away for a moment and her eyes dulled, the smile faded. A shadow fell across her features and the joy of minutes before was replaced by the cool, measured woman I usually saw. My heart sank. I wanted to hold her, give her the same comfort she'd given me. I didn't know what she was thinking or how I could help. I had been found wanting.

I recalled some of my research, shift the subject away from Bela and perhaps to his films, his work; it felt like safer ground.

"Did you ever meet Boris Karloff?" He'd worked with Bela.

"Who? That fucking cock sucker!" I was startled. My surprise must have shown, she laughed. "Sorry, it was something someone told me Bela had said in an interview. It has stuck with me ever since. And no, I didn't meet Boris. I'd seen him on set while doing some crowd scenes in his movies; he didn't seem like someone I wanted to talk to. As I said, he wasn't the actor Bela was."

"What films were you in?" I'd look them up, see if I could find her.

"A few of Bela's, the opening crowd shots in The Black Cat and near the swing in the opening scene of Murders in the Rue Morgue, a few of Boris' and other bits and pieces. Most of the time no one knew I'd snuck onto the set. I just costumed up and drifted in with the extras. I had to do some work that kept me close to Bela; I couldn't do the party scene; no top placed friends, besides Uttuku need to remain inconspicuous."

I'd get a few titles later, for now, I needed personal information about Bela. "So, he didn't like Karloff?"

"I think they were friends once, but I had the suspicion Bela hated gays. Maybe when he found out Boris' leanings, things changed between them."

"But you are gay."

"I'm not gay. Uttuku have an ambivalence to sexuality."

That was probably why my gaydar failed.

"I need a break." I just wanted a drink. "This should be plenty to make a start on." I shut down the computer.

"Are you doing anything tonight?"

"Only another encounter with Mariz."

"Let's go to a party." Sarina's calmness was catchy.

"Where? I haven't anything to change into. I haven't any makeup." I didn't want to go home and didn't feel prepared for a party either.

"I have everything you need, you go shower, and I'll get the clothes." The changes in her mood were startling, and I thought I could mood swing, I had nothing on Sarina. The Karloff line in the book seemed pointless, stay with Bela and her as much as possible. Things were already weird enough. Whatever demon Sarina might have been she was one capable of expressing great love, and the knowledge of this helped settle some of those niggle doubts and fears. She began to look a little less crazy.

"What type of party?" I called from the bathroom.

Sarina laughed. "Goth, of course, what other kind is there?"

Did she go to the Goth Club as well? What would the club think when I turned up with this stunning woman in tow? Or was this a private party? Nervousness churned in my gut.

I stepped into the heat of the shower, some apprehension washing away. The guilt of pushing the man to kill himself had lifted, though the rejection from my peers still held tight. While washing my hair, the feeling of scratching at my scalp distracted my thoughts. The flow of hair through my fingers, liquid and smooth, reminded me of touching silk for the first time when I was a little girl; one of the few happy memories. The black tiles, the black fittings, even the black soap did nothing to keep my spirits high. How did she cope with blackness all the time? Once the conditioner, Schwarzkopf, which did make me smile, was rinsed out, I turned off the shower and stepped out onto the mat. The over-large towel made short work of drying. A blow dryer wouldn't go astray, even if there were a risk of frizzy ends.

"You'll find a new toothbrush in the cabinet," Sarina called through the door.

I looked at myself in the mirror, dark glass — slight rings around my eyes and the early signs of crow's feet. Without makeup, I looked excessively pale, dull and lifeless. I needed to do my brows; I also needed to shave my pubic hair. I looked like the wild bear down there. I thought about it. There was only one razor, and it seemed a bit off sharing a razor for such private areas. I grabbed a black toothbrush from the cabinet.

Sarina adjusted my jacket and stepped back to admire me. She'd lent me a long black dress with full-length sleeves and lace gloves at the ends. We were pretty much the same size, though she was taller by a couple of inches, so there was no problem in wearing the offered black, knee high, lace up boots. The jacket was all lace. It looked handmade and very old.

"I'll do your makeup as soon as I'm dressed." Sarina gave me the once over, pleased with herself.

With all this black I didn't think I needed too much makeup. Sarina dressed in a similar fashion, clearly indicating we were a couple and insisted on doing my eyes and applying black lipstick. Looking the part only deepened my depression. I was now mimicking the darkness of my thoughts. Had I become my fears? I offered the usual light exterior while inside the curtains were being closed against the light.

We travelled to Broadway Street down by the Oakwood Recreation Center; not the area I would have expected to go to a Goth party. I hadn't ventured into those parts since I was 10, a long time ago now. Sarina had booked us a black chauffeur-driven limo which fit with the image we projected. The interior was also black, leather and trims. The driver was Sudanese.

"I had the hire car company build this car for me." Sarina patted my knee. "It was cheaper than trying to look after a car myself."

"This black fetish, it's a bit much, don't you think?" I didn't want to upset her. It was getting to me.

"It's not a fetish; it's just who I am. You will never look at another black thing and not think of me." She had a point.

The car stopped on Broadway St out front of a house that looked deserted. Goth's did party at unused establishments, so no real surprise. The recreation centre was a little way up the road. For a party, everything seemed quiet.

She whispered something to the driver, and we got out into the cool evening. Again, strange mist fell close to the ground; the air was damp. The faint glow of street lights created ever-shifting shapes between the houses. I thought I saw someone standing at up the street. A dark figure. Straining my eyes all I saw was a light post. Did Sarina see it? Paranoia? I'd have to talk to the shrink about that. Paranoia was the last thing this girl needed on top of everything else.

"I've got a key," Sarina said as we walked up the front step. She opened the door into darkness and silence.

"No one's here." I was glad to be out of the open. At the end of a long hallway, both sides showing two doors, a backlight, dull, low watt yellow became our destination.

"You'll have fun." Sarina took my hand, which I liked, and she led me towards the light. I had never heard of a quiet Goth party and not one in such quiet location.

The light showed another shorter hallway, at the end of which were five steps leading down to a black door. What is it with the black, I thought, surely some colour is allowed? Down the steps, Sarina inserted her key and opened the door into a wall of noise, loud noise. She quickly dragged me inside and slammed the door behind us — a basement Goth party. Now the basement was a real surprise; I didn't think too many places had them in these parts. The place looked exactly like the Goth Club across town, except there were no tall standing tables, just couches and chairs. The difference here; no viewers, nobody who wasn't a Goth stared at the proceedings. I felt immediately at home, less exposed to what I endured at the club.

"I'll get some wine," Sarina yelled over screams of Marilyn Manson, a mainstay of the movement in Santa Monica over the last couple of years.

I stood by the door, feeling a little awkward. Though my look fitted perfectly, I was sober, and I didn't know how to act. The half-light cast the room full of pale faces into macabre shadows, black lips and what looked like empty eye sockets. A bar stood in one corner of the room, a replica of the one at Goth Club, the small crowd around it parted for Sarina. I noticed a large woman; it was Beth. I knew her from parties I'd been to over the years, I'd confided in her about Mariz's book. She looked my way but didn't show any recognition. She stood there, serving, bedecked in silver jewellery. She poured two glasses of dark wine. No money changed hands. As Sarina made her way back, I watched the bar; the other patrons didn't pay either. There would have been around fifty people in the room; it didn't feel crowded, just comfortably occupied. A few girls jump danced in a corner, thrash dancing I called it. Sarina handed me the wine and, taking my hand again, a definite show of 'she's with me' led me to a crowded sofa against the wall. The occupants vacated the three-seater for us immediately. Sarina must have substantial pull in the scene to get such a response from these people.

The blue haze of cigarette smoke, and its pervading stink dripped from the ceiling and clouded the subdued lighting. The music roared like a train in a tunnel, it invaded my thoughts, pressed against my mind. The screech, thump of base and then the deep rhythms rattled against my chest.

I clinked glasses with Sarina, she said something I didn't hear, then sipped the wine. A large plasma screen flashed to life on the wall opposite. An old black and white film flickered into motion. A Bela Lugosi film. 'Dracula'. Sarina sat close to me as we watched the action without sound. The wailing of Manson fit with the film, captured the darker and more sinister emotions of the character. I touched her hand; she turned her hand over and clutched mine, fingers entwined. We watched the film, sipping wine and holding hands. When I looked at her, she was smiling; a happy face. During the film more people came through the door, only none left. The room didn't fill; the space remained comfortably occupied. How did they do that? They must have all had a key to the place and knowing the culture; you would have to break their arms to get them to tell you where their secret club was. Sarina must have known this. Otherwise she wouldn't risk her safety in bringing me here.

"I own a place like this in the city," Sarina yelled into my ear.

I only knew one place. Goth Club?

"Well, one of my companies does." She bit my ear, a fun gesture. Now I understood how she kept herself. Rich as well as being bloody old. I went to ask what the name of her club was.

Then I saw him.

"Mariz." I yelled, pointing my glass towards the figure standing by the door. Sarina gripped my hand tighter. He stared at me, his blue glow out of place amongst the shadows and black.

"Follow," his voice said in my head, the sound drowning out the music.

I turned to Sarina. She nodded as if she'd heard and I should follow him. No one else noticed him; no eyes turned to the glow of the ghost. He stared but made no move towards me. Sarina gave my hand a shake. I looked into her face, and she nodded again. She could hear him.

"Follow him where?" I yelled.

"The park follow me to the park, by the trees. He waits. He will not harm you," he said as he turned to the door. He passed through and out of the room.

73

"Park?"

"I think he means the recreation centre grounds."

"I'm not going there by myself." I pleaded with Sarina, hoping she heard me. She waved over a man, more a boy who looked to be about twenty at a stretch. She stood, helped me up and all three of us headed for the door. He had already vanished.

Standing on the other side of the door, the sound of the party shut out, Sarina explained to Zeek that he had to accompany me to the trees in the recreation park. He was always to stay with me. Look out for me.

"He won't hurt you," Sarina said, hugging me. "I know Orlando, and if he has said no harm will come, I believe him." I wanted to believe her. I had a bad feeling in my gut, a feeling her embrace didn't drive away. "Find out what he wants. He will bring you back here." She pushed hair out of my face and cupped my cheeks in her hands. "Things are going to be okay. I have a feeling they need you, and I doubt harm is their motive."

"I hope not." Sarina gave my hand one last squeeze before returning to the party.

Zeek led me out of the house. His heavy boots clumped on the sidewalk as we walked down to Broadway Street. Traffic was moderate for this time of night, and some of the locals watched out through their front windows. We looked out of place. Me looking like a woman from an old horror flick, and him in his Manson T-shirt, ripped black jeans and multiple facial piercings, almost pure punk. His hair hung down his back, died black, blonde roots showing down the centre of his scalp.

"You know Sar long?" he asked as we approached 7th Ave. I could see the dark expanse of grass and trees on the corner.

"Couple of weeks."

"She must think something special of you." His high, girly voice didn't fit his dark exterior.

"What do you mean?"

"She's a loner that one. I've never seen her with anyone before." They crossed 7th and headed across the grass to a solitary stand of trees; looming giant shadow to our left. I wished it was Sarina with me rather than the boy. If Orlando were what Sarina had told her, the lad wouldn't stand a chance if he wanted to attack me; neither would I come to think of it. We approached the trees; I felt more than a little scared. I could see nothing in the darkness.

"Who you meeting?" We neared the trees. My feet were damp with dew.

"Someone you don't want to know." I kept anxiety out of my voice. "Just let me talk to the man, and you make sure he doesn't do any funny stuff."

"A wacko, is he?"

Nothing unusual for times and probably not too out of place around the park; I didn't like this one bit, even with a bodyguard. I could smell the soil as we stopped before the trees; a picnic area and low fence stared back at me.

Steve stepped from within a tree. He blue hallo form weird in the street lights that crept into the park.

"Fuck, man." Zeek yelled. "Don't go creeping up like that." He could see Mariz?

"It's okay, I know him." I touched his arm.

"Come," Mariz said.

Zeek looked at me. I sighed, this was it. Mariz walked between the trees I lost sight of him; the sound of traffic on Broadway clearly visible and audible. I took several deep breaths, clenched and unclenched my fists, willing my feet to take those final steps. Zeek set off immediately, and not wanting to be left alone I caught up. It was dark, very dark. Someone had knocked some of the lights out; shadows danced as car headlights move by. Mariz was gone. I made out the shape of someone standing close, by one of the picnic tables.

The figure stepped forward, out of the shadows. He jumped in front of me, being protective of a pretty girl. The man stopped within arm's reach of the boy. I could see the young man had taken a defensive stance, fists clenched. Then I froze. I couldn't move. It felt as if every muscle in my body had seized. The man reached forward with both hands, like knives they passed through his eyes, speared his head. The boy convulsed, stilled and convulsed again. The man's eyes shone like blue lights. I wanted to run. Something held me. I tried to scream and couldn't. The man released him. He stepped around the boy and with both hands threw him over the wire fence and out onto Broadway; a screech of ties and then the thumb of a body being struck by a car. I was next. I thought of Sarina. I thought about Mariz and Samantha. The blue eyes stared.

"How much do you know about the book?"

Whatever held me in place released its grip and I stumbled forward. "You killed him!"

"The book. How much do you know?"

"What book?" I took a few paces back. If I made a break for the street would I make it?

"The book. Give me the book." I couldn't escape the eyes.

"I don't know what you're talking about. What fucking book?" He couldn't mean Mariz, could he? That was fiction written from...

"You've seen it?"

"I...I... I..." Would I die if I said yes?

He moved closer, face hidden in the blackness, eyes beaming like two LCDs on a sound system. He was going to kill me, take my life light like he'd taken Zeek's. In the distance, I heard a siren. I turned, broke contact with the eyes. A police car was coming up the street. I felt cold. I ran towards them, towards the spot where he had been thrown. Orlando didn't stop me.

"Help. Help me!" My voice a wail in the night. I ran onto the street. An SUV was stopped, a body lay on the ground nearby. The driver looked my way, but was in shock, they just stared.

Two police car stopped beside the SUV. In the distance, I heard another siren, perhaps an ambulance. Two officers got out of the car.

"My friend," I turned to the trees. Orlando was gone. "My friend's been..."

They ran over to the body, both shining torches over the scene, one kneeling to check for life. I knew it was too late. He was dead before the car had hit him.

"What happened here?" one officer asked coming up to me. The other officer went to the driver of the SUV.

"He... he ran out on the road... and..." I pointed as I shook my head. What did happen?

"It's okay ma'am, just settle down and tell me what happened." I felt sick. Vomiting came next, then dizziness.

Chapter 12

The Prelŭstitel

The woman left the house with a young man. I followed, the meeting set, my problem half solved. I watched them walk to the end of the street. Tonight, the moon hung full, the sky clear. I'd sat beneath such moons in another time, as another being. Something would come, and it would bring me closer, I could feel it. Aza'zel would be easier to deal with, once the book was back in my possession. The woman I knew, the boy posed a problem. I considered approaching them before they entered the park. It would give me away. I didn't like to reveal myself unless necessary. It would take but a moment to shift through space, to be somewhere else. I shifted.

He would be pleased, of that I was sure; I was not. He took the boy, questioned the woman. He stepped between me and what I wanted. Why?

She lied. He knew. What could be gained by this? People gathered around the body on the road. I left. I would wait for Sarina, follow her home. Wait and watch.

I shifted back into the shadows, away from street lights. The cool of the night allowed me to create a soft, damp mist through the trees, a sprinkling of cover for those humans who prowled in the darkness. In the end, I'd take them as well, take their darkness and make it my own. Humans could enact darkness, become one with it, and when absorbed by their desires of sexual need, I show them the truth of the dark. Introduce them to the pit. His pit, the *Abad*. Then they are no more.

I waited as I have always done.

I didn't see Sarina leave. No one left as sirens rang through the night. Did they know what had happened? Sarina would have thought the woman was meeting me as I had arranged through the ghost. Her actions were now unpredictable. He had brought this on, moved on the woman. She would tell Sarina we searched for the book. Did he intend for a closer involvement between the two be created? I saw no reason why it mattered.

A police car pulled up out front of the house. The woman inside. The house stood empty. Sarina had fled. I shifted.

No lights shone from the window — a black rectangle in the wall. Sarina wasn't there. What had Aza'zel done? And just what was I to do now?

Chapter 13

Cassandra

I must have fainted. I opened my eyes to find myself laying on an ambulance gurney with an oxygen mask over my face. I tried to sit.

"She's coming around," a woman called. It was an ambulance officer, her uniform bright under lights. Searchlights. The whole area looked like it was bathed in sunlight.

The face of one of the police officers came into view. I pulled off the mask, forcing myself to sit. He waited until my legs were over the side of the bed before speaking.

"Can you tell me what happened here, Miss." His tone flat, officious.

"Is he okay?" I had to ask.

"What is your relationship with the man?" He sounded suspicious.

"We'd just met at a party; we were taking a walk." They wouldn't believe what happened. I couldn't believe it.

"Where was this party?" He wrote something in his small notebook. He had that no-nonsense look all cops got when they talked down to you. Couldn't he see I was in shock? Where was Sarina? Surely, she should would have heard the sirens, there are always sirens when something like this happens. "Please, Miss, where was the party?"

I couldn't tell them the address, so I directed them from the back seat of a police car. The house was quiet, as I expected it to be. I told them about the basement party; only I couldn't tell them I'd arrived with Sarina. Bringing her in didn't seem like the right thing to do. I waited in the car while two officers walked around the house flashing their torches through the windows. One of them made a call on his radio. Ten minutes later a car pulled up and a woman, looking bedraggled and carrying a bunch of keys opened up the house. I hoped the Goths wouldn't get into trouble, after all, it was one of their own who'd just been killed. The officers exited the house, and the woman locked the door. Something was said that made the woman laugh. The officers climbed into the car only to inform me there was no one there and that the house had been empty for about three months. They asked again where the party had been, and of course, I insisted this was the place. I then spent the next six hours in an interview room at the Venice Police station. After three hours they told me that Zeek had been killed instantly when he ran in front of the SUV, and his family had been notified. An officer recognised me from a book jacket and cleared me to go home. There were some perks to being famous. A police car dropped me at my front door at 7 am, with the notice they would be talking with me further.

As I unlocked the front door, I realised I was both witness and prime suspect in Zeek's death. I couldn't explain what had happened to the party, and I couldn't adequately explain why I was out walking in the recreation centre's grounds with a boy almost half my age. I dropped on the sofa in the front room, rubbed the ache from my temples before calling Sarina.

"Get out of the house," she said as soon as she picked up. "Cassandra, you must get out of the house."

"He's dead." Emotion was shot, the admission came out all flat and lifeless. "Orlando killed him." I fell to one side, weariness taking its toll. I closed my eyes, let the spots dance and weave beneath the lids. I pulled a cushion to my chest, something to hold.

"You will be next if you don't get out of the house and get out now." Sarina was persistent, urgent. "Take a cab and get off at the corner of 2nd and Colorado. I'll meet you on the there."

"I need sleep." I'd had enough for one night. "I'm going nowhere."

"Don't let anyone in. I'm coming to get you..." I flipped my phone closed and dropped it beside my head. I felt so tired, just so tired.

"I've got something to tell you." It was Mariz.

"Go away; I've had a rough night." I held the cushion tighter and rolled to face the back of the sofa.

"Cassandra, I'm free of him, and I have to tell you something."

I squeezed my eyes closed, willing him to go away, to leave me alone. I didn't care what he had to say. This was my time, my little piece of reality. I breathed in the smell of leather, let it distract me, lure me towards sleep.

"I have to tell you why I'm here."

"No!" The scream echoed off the walls, rang in my ears. "I don't care why you're here; I don't want to know why you did what you did. Do you understand that?" I didn't want to face him. I just wanted to be left alone. I'd witnessed a murder, a crime I couldn't explain to anyone who some fucking twisted weirdo wasn't.

He stopped bothering me, my stomach twisted with expectation. Was he still there, still watching me, waiting for me to turn over? My mobile rang and vibrated near my head, the standard Nokia ring tone. Morse code for SMS; funny how useless information like that comes to you when you are wasted. Why remember something so trivial? Why? Then it rang with a voice call. I ignored that as well. Please leave me alone, I begged, forcing the cushion into my face. Please. I lay there tense, anxious and screwed up. Even though tired, exhausted by a night of questions and bad coffee, sleep wouldn't come; even this small blessing had fled. In the silence of my front room, I heard the laugh of one of the neighbours in the distance, the twitter of a bird in the garden. All sounds that usually brought me relief from the world at large now became just noise, an interruption to the one thing I desired. The outside world continued without me, flowed ever forward as if I didn't exist, or mean anything. I knew I was crying; the tears failed to relieve me of the fear that gripped so coldly around my shoulders. "Why me?"

The doorbell rang. I ignored it, tried to pull the cushion over my ears. Go away, I thought, fucking leave me alone. It rang again and again and again — frantic ringing.

"Cassandra." I heard Sarina's yell. "It's me, open the door." Again, the ringing.

Struggling against weariness, I made my way to the door. My heels tapping on the floorboards. I was too tired even to unstrap the boots. No sooner had I unlatched the lock, Sarina was inside, shouting, shaking me.

"We have to go." She pushed a mess of hair out of my face. She smelt good. Better than coffee.

"Too tired." I didn't want to argue. I had difficulty focusing on her face. She dragged me outside and into the drive. The sun blinded me.

"Get in the taxi." She pushed and steered me towards a silver car — the red writing hurting my eyes.

"My stuff." I still needed my pills, my clothes, my pillow.

"I'll get it, now get in and put your seat belt on. It'll only take me a few minutes to grab the essentials." She opened the door.

"She okay?" the driver asked.

"She's fine." Sarina put her hand on my head and pushed me into the car.

"You don't know what I need." I fell into the seat, the smell of polish and garlic thick.

"I'm a woman; I know what you need." Sarina slammed the door, while I fumbled with the seatbelt. The driver had turned and stared at me. He looked Chinese; white, white teeth smiled in a dark, oval face.

I didn't know how long Sarina had been gone; it only felt like a few minutes until she climbed into the back with me. She pushed an overnight bag between us — my stuff. The driver reversed back onto the street and headed towards the highway and undoubtedly to Sarina's place. I couldn't keep my eyes open, the car felt warm, the sun soothing as it reached through the windows. I felt Sarina ease my head back and stroke my brow.

"You're safe now," she whispered.

Finding the true author of Mariz's book was proving more difficult than I expected. His contacts wouldn't speak to me or would have little or nothing of value to say. My yearning for Samantha increased the more I probed into his life. I kept seeing them together whenever I ventured down to Venice Beach to have coffee. Him in his baggy clothes and unkempt hair, Samantha in short skirts and revealing tops. How could she love such a man; how could she have shared my bed and not thought anything of it? To find what I wanted, I attended every writers' workshop I could find. I felt driven, determined, and in my quieter times, felt obsessed.

Completing and meeting my latest novel deadline, which was a task considering the time I was spending away from the computer, I had more money in the bank and more resources at hand to continue my search for the truth. Someone had written that book or at least the original draft it had come from. I knew it, and I suspected others had thought of the idea but were just too self-interested to care.

He and Samantha had been swanning around like the greatest couple since Brad and Ange. I knew jealousy drove me as much as anything else, and that all the tension was messing with my body. Late periods, stomach cramps and constipation, but if I was proven right, it was worth it. And if I also got the girl, that was even better.

I grabbed my coat off the back of my chair, and the keys from the hall stand. I had a writers' meeting to attend tonight, a new one. Perhaps this one would turn up that much-needed evidence.

"He was going to kill me!" I'd started yelling again. I'd been yelling at Sarina for the last hour. She'd brought me back to the apartment, took some light energy so I could sleep. Eight hours later I was alive enough to let her have it right in the face. "You sent me out to die, you selfish bitch."

Sarina said nothing. She'd said nothing ever since I let my emotions spew all over her. She must have known what Orlando was planning; she must have known the danger, otherwise, why send Zeek as a bodyguard? I stormed about her front room, clenching and releasing my fists, waiting between barrages to get my wind back, to find greater strength in my voice. My face was wet with tears, my white (yes white, fuck the black shit) singlet soaked with perspiration. I'd been pushed too far. Because of her I'd been forced out of my home, made a suspect in a suspicious death and had my life put in danger. I'm a writer; I write stuff like this, I don't live it. I'm not Amalia, the super Goth-girl. I'm Cassandra, the positive and slightly forward lesbian.

"Are you ready to talk?" Sarina asked. Her first words since my ranting began.

"Talk! Talk!" I stood directly in front of her. "What's there to talk about?" I couldn't control the screaming. "You fucking took from me again as well. You've got a hell of a lot of explaining to do, girl, and you're damn lucky I don't just kill you myself." My energy was waning. Breathing became harder, deeper.

"I didn't know he wanted to kill you," she said, placid, unemotional.

"What did you know?" It was a half yell the pacing continued, being still was an aggravation.

"I just wanted to know why he'd been following you. After all these years of being followed, I needed to know why the sudden urgency in you. You're human. Prelŭstitel kill humans they don't stalk them."

I stormed into her bedroom, grabbed a jacket from the wardrobe, my purse and went out. Talking was going nowhere, and my anger only increased at the sight of her. How could she, how could she do this after all she'd promised?

The waves, black at night with white crests created a low murmur over the beach. A relaxing sound often compared to the sound of the womb. I ate pizza and had brought a six-pack of beer, Heineken. I rarely drank beer, right now the bitterness matched my mood. Lights bobbed on the water a long way from shore. Fishermen. The pier, alive with couples out for an evening walk, despite the winter freeze, cast its light over the beach. The sand, usually bright white in the day, took on the colour of parchment. My father used to bring me to the beach when I was a kid, especially after Mum had drunk herself into a frenzy. Those had been happy times. I was still Daddy's little girl then. I hadn't seen my dad in five years, not since Mum's funeral. Liver cancer, an expected outcome; seeing as she was an alcoholic. Dad had been polite but refused to talk to me beyond hello. I wasn't the daughter he wanted, so as far as he was concerned, she'd died the day he found out his little girl was gay. Today everyone is gay; it isn't a big deal.

The night air, cold, the breeze even colder off the sea, caused me to shiver. The chilled beer numbed the nerves, and the pepperoni settled the knots in my stomach. I'd searched the dark place beneath the pier; no one watched me; the beach was deserted. Cool sand, fine and soft, squeezed up between my toes as I wriggled my feet down until they were covered. Anger still bubbled inside, clawed for a way out. The sound of water crashing on the shore and the smell of seaweed had leached much of its rawness away. The taste of beer filled my mouth. Three empties lay beside me, the pizza box was held down by their weight. What do I do? Eventually, I'd have to go back to Sarina's, sleep on the couch and keep my distance. Tomorrow I'd have to go home and decide what needed to be done. Orlando was after me, or more to the point, the book I'd briefly seen. I didn't have the manuscript, even though I had read part of it. I didn't know what it meant; I didn't even know why the old man who'd given it to me had sought me out. Evil was after me, all because of Mariz and his desire to be famous.

Do I tell Sarina I know what Orlando wants? It was a difficult question; the woman couldn't be trusted. I had grown to like her and the strange mannerisms. Black also had its moments, getting used to it would have taken some effort; I was prepared to make the effort. Now? Confusion and disappointment. There were just too many mixed feelings, too many problems to deal with, too much to consider. Last night I thought there had been a connection between us, a developing understanding. My gut said good things, was it wrong this time?

I felt a presence beside me. I turned to see Sarina sit down in the sand a little back and away to the right. She hugged her legs to her chest, put her chin on her knees. She didn't speak. I looked out to sea and the bobbing lights. The last of my current bottle slipped down my throat, and I dropped it into the pile. Even though the sky was clear, the lights from the pier dulled the stars and only a few in the distance could be seen.

"I'm sorry," her voice soft beneath the crash of waves.

"So, you should be." It came out curt, nasty.

"If I'd known he wanted to kill you I wouldn't have let you go." I listened, afraid my next answer would be too cruel. "I don't want anything to happen to you, Cassandra."

"You should have thought about that last night." I looked her way; she was looking out at the water. "Zeek's dead because of this."

"I know." She sounded dejected. The mostly even-tempered Sarina sounded hurt.

"I have to find a place to live." I opened another bottle.

"Every night I come down here and look at the stars. Take in the enormity of the universe. Everyone needs to put their lives into perspective sometimes. Even an Uttuku." The words came from somewhere deep in her. They touched me. Her voice a caress I wasn't expecting. I didn't want to look at her, didn't want to break the spell she'd just woven. I had to see. The heart that beat blood to my mind, temper and frustration needed to see the speaker of these words. In peripheral vision I watched.

Sarina stood, face pointed to the sky. Without another word she turned and walked away. The sound of the sea cushioned my thoughts, the beer drowned and killed the pain. It was my turn to look to the stars.

We were all outside the church before Mariz's funeral service. Only Samantha looked my way at first, and the look was reproachful, soon others joined in the staring. I squared myself, holding a small wreath tightly in my hand. I had a right to be there. On seeing me, reporters rushed forward; microphones pressed into my space, men and women yelling over each other. Question after question fired like bullets into my chest.

"How do you feel?"

"Did you see this coming?"

"Do you feel any guilt for what you've done?"

I pushed through them. It wasn't that I didn't have the answers, it was I couldn't believe the answers I'd given myself — the justifications. He had killed himself because I told his publisher he plagiarised his latest book. I should have spoken more to him about it first, should have met with him and Samantha about what might have been done to avoid the scandal, but no. I chose to bring him down. I thought of only myself and what I wanted. I thought of Uri. Mariz had put the poor old man in danger, and he was dead as well. Did Samantha know about him? I had wanted to tell the reporters about this; only I would have also been exposed to even deeper questioning. Why didn't I tell the police? How did the book I'd seen get back into his hands? I'd denied, at first, contacting his publisher, but Maxine didn't waste a lot of time dropping my name. What a mess all this had become. Mariz, his actions had been explained away by claiming depression and being a troubled but brilliant soul. I had become the murderer, the one who'd turned against one of their own. Though I didn't want to admit it openly, I had become a victim of my own doing.

Samantha's look, venomous as it was, didn't seem directly aimed at me. She almost looked pleased with herself. Beside her was his mother, a large woman in a blue silk suit. She wore white stockings; the kind diabetics wear to help with circulation. A dragon of a woman. She hated him. She enjoyed the trappings he brought to her through Samantha's relationship and took every opportunity to bring her son down. There was one woman who would be happy with his death. Standing before the old Church, its dirty grey-white walls competing with the straight sides of office buildings, I thought I was better than the others. My motives might have been skewed, but what I'd done had also been right.

Julian Westwood, a big man in a grey suit, one of his friends, blocked my path up the steps. I tried to walk around him. He just moved in front of me. His face, bearded and pocked on the cheeks, stared at me in suppressed anger. His body odour, strong in the heat, assaulted the senses.

"You're not welcome here, Ms Whitehall."

"I can either come in, or I can talk to them." I indicated the reporters. He looked over my shoulder, then up the stairs to where Samantha was standing. Deep down I wanted to hold her and say how sorry I was, and to offer my shoulder and support. That path was closed to me now. Samantha nodded, and he let me pass. I felt satisfaction, elation, all the wrong feelings to have at a funeral.

Chapter 14

The Prelŭstitel

I watched her on the beach.

I knew who she was, knew where she lived. Cassandra Whitehall had been in contact with the book. Aza'zel blocked me, stopped me from moving on her. His way, he'd said. His way what? The skeins of darkness were no help, offered nothing more to what I already understood. I watched Cassandra, sitting alone, drinking beer. I shifted to her side, went to take her. Aza'zel's force got in the way. I could no more touch her than reach up and touch a star. I thought of the ghost and his connection, the lure, did Aza'zel know more about him than me? He was pushing the two women together, had to be. My role might simply be to create the fear they needed to come closer — a human response. Aza'zel harboured no feelings that equated anything humans could muster. He was using me in a way I couldn't fathom. I sat beside Cassandra on the sand, she wiped tears from her face, ate pizza and stared out to sea. If I could only dip my finger through her skull, probe thoughts and seek out what she knew. If he didn't want her dead, I wouldn't take her darkness. Her smell was sweet; anger hung about her like a black haze. Sarina would know this and could move to protect her.

Cassandra knew of the book; how much wasn't clear. Would she tell, or had she already told Sarina? It didn't matter, she already knew about Aza'zel, what would it reveal about me and the secret I kept?

Sarina approached through the lights of the square, arms folded across her chest and face creased. Concern? She walked down and onto the beach. I shifted to the pier and faded into shadow. She looked beautiful in the yellow light, hair down, face perfect. I couldn't let him absorb her, even if she was an Uttuku. A part of me still needed her, why I needed her wasn't clear; it was a past I think I was supposed to remember.

I watched and listened. My thoughts had been correct. Was this part of his plan?

Chapter 15

Cassandra

I found my laptop open on the kitchen table — the bright colour of the screen incongruous in the black of the room. The screen saver, an open field against the backdrop of a lightly clouded sky commanded attention. My neck ached from a night on the sofa. The memory of the funeral was as fresh as the day I attended. I needed a coffee. Finding the kettle and what I needed was easy enough, only I had to drink the coffee without milk. Sarina's door had been shut when I went to the toilet. I was relieved she still slept, then wondered did she sleep? I'd never actually seen her do so. I shivered at the thought. *Don't go there.* I touched the mouse pad on the computer; the screen saver was replaced by a text document. The page counter at the bottom of the document read thirty pages. I sipped the coffee, the taste stale. I didn't know how old the coffee was; I should have checked the expiry date.

Sarina had written about Bela. My first reaction was to delete it. With no morning paper or anything in the apartment resembling a book, I read just for the sake of reading. Sarina wasn't a writer; the obvious common flaws were everywhere. She wrote with a mix of old and new language, sometimes poetical and at others flat and lifeless. It would be a challenging read. I had to edit out the flowery prose about love and beauty to string together some kind of history. Perhaps knowing more about her would help. Perhaps not. Fathoming why this story was important. A five-hundred-year-old woman would have greater historical stories to tell than unrequited love with a B grade actor.

Away from her secret love for Bela, a real story emerged. Not as detailed, but it had been captured in threads.

Reluctantly, Sarina moved away from Bela after a call from another Uttuku in Berlin, Eva, a friend from the early 1700s. Aza'zel, as Sarina wrote, was coming for her. It was out of love that she moved away from Bela. She feared this being would take him from her. The year was 1936.

I thought of Aza'zel mentioned in Mariz's book; the employer referred to by Uri. Were they the same? Aza'zel in Sarina's musings had no form, though she had said he took life light as well as darkness. Mariz's book didn't venture into the role of this Dark One; it had sat within the text as an unknown, an ever-present feeling. Orlando was after the book.

The coffee's bite helped shake out the questions. There were just too many, and the answers felt more like speculation than anything based on reality. Sarina had no connection with Mariz, hadn't even read his work. I felt torn between wanting to know more and fleeing. He had become the bonding agent for everything and I, as a catalyst, should know what was happening. How much did Sarina know?

I read more; an answer had to be here somewhere.

Soon after arriving in Germany, Sarina was invited to a rally by a young and handsome German officer. No name given. During the rally, she was introduced to Adolf Hitler. This tied in with the photo. Sarina's comments on the man weren't flattering, and she disliked the way he spoke. A reporter had taken the photograph, something Sarina didn't appreciate. She lured him outside with the promise of sex, took from him and then took the camera. He wouldn't remember her, no one remembered her after a taking. That was something I didn't know. I remembered? Why? Something else to ask her if speaking to her was something ever worth doing again.

Sarina felt something wasn't right in Germany and told Eva. She suggested they leave together for England or France. Eva wouldn't go. She insisted she had a plan to get close to Adolph, change him and avert what was to become World War II. The only thing written after this entry: 'The bastard killed her'.

After some romantic encounters set up for maintaining her life light, Sarina arrived in London. Getting travel papers was easy in those days if you knew how and who to contact. In London, Sarina took to only getting around at night. Before seeing Bela in Austria during World War I, she'd been in London. To be out in the open would have brought recognition and questions about how young she still looked.

I had trouble with that myself.

She'd thought of Bela every day, watched some of his movies in secret cinemas. There had been a ban on Hollywood films at the time. It ached in her heart that she couldn't be with him. In a way I understood. I ached a little, the feeling I had for Sarina had been squashed by Zeek's death.

During the grey London days, Sarina would stay in her hotel room with thoughts of going back to him. He had changed, she wrote. The 'return' she'd called it, wouldn't help him now. She didn't write with much detail, which I found annoying. I wanted to know what London looked like, what it smelt like, she wasn't an artistic writer, she'd just written what happened. If I weren't so depressed and lost, I would have given up. Still, there was nothing here for me to us in understanding the woman any more. Sarina had known famous people as well as ordinary people. Nowhere except for Bela Lugosi did she show anything other than disdain for humans, there had to be more than love to this story.

Winston Churchill came as the next surprise. She'd met and befriended him at a dinner party. They were never lovers. Their encounters centred around shared cigars and drinking, whenever he could steal time away from the parliament, which wasn't often. She took from him once a week, the action always lightened his mood for a few days. The photo I'd seen showed them sitting on what looked like a Chesterfield couch, holding cigars in one hand and a glass of liquid in the other.

'When he was down, we would smoke and get drunk,' Sarina wrote. *'He didn't like Hitler either and often felt dejected that others thought he was overreacting to the German Chancellor. I believed in him, and to Winston, that made a difference.'*

The photo of them together had been taken by his secretary. Winston signed it and gave it to her just before the war. Sarina noted after taking light from Winston; she would feel miserable for a day and found she couldn't get out of bed. I understood this as well. Not a great deal was known about depression back then. Black Dog indeed.

I looked up from the screen, my coffee had gone cold, and hunger entered my thoughts. The only things in the place were bad instant coffee and a tin of Prince of Wales tea. I'd have to go down to one of the cafes for breakfast. I needed cash. A Wall-Bank not far from the apartment would fix that. I'd read enough, for now. With all the other stuff crashing about inside, I had to get out. See the sun.

Sarina stood in the doorway, she leaned against the frame, hair glossy and brushed, robe hanging on her like a fashion queen. How long had she been watching me?

"Any good?"

I wanted to ignore her, push her aside and head out for breakfast. The calm vision of her just standing there weakened last night's resolve, reminded me of the last thing she'd said. I had to tell her about the book. If everything was how she said, then there was no way in hell I was going to survive alone. My pride might have been hurt, my trust damaged, but she was all I had.

Sarina listened to my story about how I brought him down, the visit from Uri, the book; no interruptions, no questions, no judgement. She'd raised an eyebrow when I mentioned Uri and nodded when I told her about putting the book in his house. It felt like the time I'd told Beth, only I knew Beth wasn't interested.

"We have to get that book." Her first comment.

"How?" I doubted it would still be at Mariz's.

"Right now, I don't know." Sarina toyed with the neckline of the robe. "Did you read what I'd written last night?" The question was gentle. "From what you've told me there might be something in it we can use."

"Hitler, Churchill, doesn't appear too much there to draw on."

"There is something; we just aren't seeing it."

"You know nothing about his book, and his version doesn't mention any historical figures, I don't even know how much of the real book is in his novel." I rubbed at my eyes. I'd read *Me and Him;* it was pure dark fantasy set in a possible place on a possible world.

88

"How much of the original did you read?" Her brow creased, she too struggled to find a connection.

"Not much, the opening page or two, it was in stilted English, something he hadn't totally removed from the book."

"We need to go further."

I stared at the screen, the words all running together, becoming a blur. "Sarina, I can't. Just don't have the drive to do this."

"I don't mean finish writing the book."

"Then what?"

"Maybe something in my life holds the key."

Well, nothing in mine made much sense. "Why didn't you go back to stalking... I mean watching Bela after the war?" I had to start somewhere.

"I couldn't," she said, pulling out a chair. "I was still twenty-five, and easily recognized in Hollywood. I didn't go unnoticed here, I'd been in a heap of films and explaining away my age with makeup got harder and harder." She pointed at the chair. "May I?"

"It's your apartment." I might have wanted to know a bit more about her, but I wasn't forgetting or forgiving anything.

"I did see him in the early 1950s; I can't be sure of the year, it was a tough time emotionally. I shouldn't have gone back." This was making Sarina uncomfortable. She deserved discomfort.

"When did Orlando start following you?" Did Orlando follow her to Bela Lugosi's house and cause the heart attack that killed him?

"I arrived in New York in late 1950, with all the displacement after the war, getting a passport wasn't a problem." She offered a short grunt of a laugh. "A pretty young woman can get most anything she wants if she puts her mind to it." Sarina rubbed her temples. "I started seeing Orlando, I think, around then or a bit later. At my age, you don't have flights of imagination, so those shadows at the end of a hallway and the feeling of someone watching or following were real."

"Did he follow you to LA and maybe kill Bela?" I didn't want to die like Zeek or anyone for that matter.

Sarina rested her arms on the table, she looked troubled. "For a time, I thought he had; only I didn't think..." Her voice wispy, airy. "...I had seen Bela around a few times and later wondered if Orlando had followed me there. I'd sometimes park out the front of his little house and wait for him to come out. He'd grown so old. It was then I understood."

"Understood what?"

"Just understood why he couldn't have followed me to Bela's." I didn't press it; this was obviously a no-go area.

"Did you approach Bela? Talk to him?" This wasn't in the story she'd written. "Maybe he mentioned a book?"

"No, I didn't talk to him. Couldn't find the right moment. Why?"

"Just trying to make sense of things."

"There could have been a book, but I hadn't seen him in a long time, and I only wanted to say my last goodbyes," she said, sounding ashamed. "You know I was hiding in Bela's house when Ed Wood offered him the role in Glen and Glenda. He'd left the back door open, I thought I'd approach him, confess, but I heard voices in the front room. For just a moment I thought I might be wrong about him."

"That he wasn't an addict?" She nodded once — a slight, firm action. I knew addiction well. I still had some fine scars inside my elbows as reminders.

"I thought the film offer was wonderful. The Bela I had known had been wasted away by morphine, and this small break could have helped him." She brightened, though it was short lived. "The movie was awful, and so too was the next one with Ed, Bride of the Monster. I cried all night after seeing it. My Bela was a laughing stock."

I waited while Sarina became lost in the memories, this was new. No love is perfect, I thought, there is always a downside, always something that clouds the rosy view. She regained some control. Was I doing it again? Manipulating her like a character in a book? Could I influence the life of a five-hundred-year-old woman? A concept that brought a shudder.

"You left again?" I tried to sound more sensitive.

"Not before considering taking away his pain and make him young again."

"How?" Interested, I sat forward, almost knocking the half-filled coffee cup over with my elbow.

"I ... all Uttuku have the ability to pass on a part of themselves." She looked past me, or through me, I couldn't tell. "I could have offered to make him an Uttuku. Make him young again, and we could have been together." A tear broke free, sliding like a single rain drop down a window.

"Why didn't you?"

"Love has to be by both parties, he didn't even know me." She wiped her face on the back of her hand. "I should have introduced myself when I first saw him. I should have danced with that young soldier." The tears multiplied. "I saw him on his porch for the last time that night. I moved to Washington and went on a feeding frenzy for a month. Two hundred souls later I'd flushed a good part of him out of my life. Something I should have done in 1917."

"That isn't a great memory to part on."

"In 1994 I managed to add a symbolic farewell to him that did paint him in a better light." She looked sombre, voice soft. "I had another extras role in Ed Wood with Johnny Depp."

"You for real?" I'd seen the film a few times, I was quite a Depp fan, and didn't recall seeing her. Then, an extra could mean anything.

"Nothing standout, a couple of quick screenshots." She dismissed it quickly. "Martin Landau did a wonderful job of my Bela. Johnny made Ed better than he was, but it was good to be involved in that small way."

"Sarina, I know this is going to sound weird, but I think there is more to this book than we realise and somehow, despite how we met."

She wiped tiredness from her face, long fingers pressing ever so slightly into her skin. "I know, I know. Right now, we don't know, do we? If you'd only read more of that book…"

Despite my anger and my concerns, I did feel for her. I had never lost anyone I truly loved. The odd relationship breakup did cause pain and anguish, but nothing like this. I told her to get dressed, and I'd take her out for breakfast. Silently she agreed, and to ease some of the trouble between us; I changed out of my white singlet and into black T-shirt, windcheater and slacks. Orlando was still the issue though, and there was no way to forget the threat.

Chapter 16

The Prelŭstitel

Standing under dimmed light of the hospital's morgue suited my mood. I'd told him the taking of the young man's darkness was a mistake. He shrugged and that was the end of the conversation. We stood either side of the body of the young man.

"It will take some care," I said, which he accepted. "Both prizes are stronger when the women are together; we can use this."

He nodded, dragging his ephemeral fingers through the boy's chest. He plunged his hand in deep, the body twitched once then returned to its dead state.

"Now there is nothing." He dragged his hand free.

"I will..."

"Does Sarina know of this book?"

"Only if Cassandra has told her."

"No other way?"

"No."

"Are you sure? You must be sure." He broke apart like a graphite cloud, reforming standing beside the autopsy table.

"Yes." There had been no reason for her to know.

"Have you discovered how she got her hands on the icon?"

"No. It could have been luck." If he probed me now, I would have difficulty in hiding the truth.

"Once we have it back, I will ensure it is never out of my influence again; it would be useful to know how she acquired it, then that avenue could be removed."

"I will find this as well, though it is not my primary task." He could never know how Sarina obtained the icon. It was my final gift to her.

"You won't fail me, Prelŭstitel." He drifted away from me, and through the wall, for a moment a black stain spread across the white tiles, slowly fading.

I needed fear, real fear to help create what I felt he needed me to do. I made a dream from history and shadow. Formed it in a way only the right person would see. With a wipe of my hand across brow, the flutter of eyes I sent it into the void, into the web of darkness. Who was it meant for I didn't know? The dream would find itself a place to unfold. All it needed was darkness, the ever-present night. A gentle push to bring them together, strengthen their reliance on each other. This dream would remind the women of what I could do and just how near I was. With the focus now on the book and Cassandra, the recovery of the icon could easily be... be delayed.

Things had turned in my favour, and maybe I wouldn't need to trick Sarina after all.

Chapter 17

Cassandra

The Observer ran the headline, 'Goth Writer Causes Suicide'. Talk had started I would be charged with contributing to Mariz's death. I hadn't spoken with the police since the day after his body had been discovered, so the news came as a surprise. Little had been said about his fraud. I immediately hired a lawyer, and in less than a week she had confirmed no charges were to be laid. He had committed suicide.

But I had been found guilty by my peers, and the headlines which appeared around the country made for several terse calls from my publisher. Over the next month, my book sales increased tenfold, and the publisher went from angry and wanting to cancel my contract to glowing with new offers. Goth girl might have been cast aside by the literary clique, but the readers were sticking by me and increasing their support.

Who could know what he would do once his fraud had been revealed? It was well known he was a troubled man, suffered severe depression, like most writers, including me, and was prone to alcohol abuse and fits of anger. No one expected he'd take one extra step over the line and kill himself.

In my gut, I knew he'd probably take the step, and in a way, it was my intention the line would be crossed, or I'd convinced myself I had deliberately created things to come out that way. I started to believe the feelings of the reporters around the country. I did drive the man to suicide. The woman I loved and hoped to win over, slipped away and the death drove the rumour mill as it strove to bring me down. The one I desired became my enemy. I'd only told the truth. But just how much truth can anyone take? In my interviews with the police, I didn't mention Uri and simply stated the front page of the book had been mailed to me. Uri's death had frightened me, I had to admit it, and whoever was responsible might come after me looking for the book. The media helped create the distance I needed from the discovery, by protecting me they also convicted me.

I drove out to Venice Beach for a walk along the shore. The day was warm, the sky clear and the air the usual Californian dry. My light green shirt and baggy white shorts wouldn't look out of place walking amongst the swimmers and screaming children. I used to like going to the beach and wading into the water; no more, another time had stolen that from me. I parked a few streets from pier. The wind, light and blustery, blew my hair about and into my face. I tied it back with an elastic band and tucked what I could under a straw sun hat.

The crashing of waves became a solid background noise; it wasn't until getting closer did I hear the light laughter of children. I walked down to the water feeling sand, blown by the wind, sting my bare calves. Coloured beach hats and umbrellas were everywhere. I slipped off my sandals and let the early morning coolness of the sand engulf my feet. Soon, small waves broke and washed up on the shore. Wave boards rushed in on the tide, their riders running back into the water ready to catch the next wave.

For a time, I just stood looking out to the flat horizon, water rushing over my feet and then just as fast rushing back. My feet sunk in the wet sand. A tanker, coming up the coast sat like a black smudge against the sky where it met the sea. They were going somewhere. I wished I was going somewhere.

I waited for the group to arrive at the small house about the Pacific Highway; another chance to find the true author of the book, another straw to grab to hopefully bring that bastard, Mariz, down.

I'd heard rumours about this group, how it was hard and fast, the participants dedicated to getting work published. All or most of the writers here were accomplished, well published but outside of the literary circle. Some in the business believed this group even had a special, secret meeting place, a stony room in the basement of a rundown inner city building. This was where they created the *Leaves of Blood* collections each year.

The house was a typical modern building with lightly painted rooms and big windows. By attending, I wondered if I'd get an invite to contribute. I had bought a couple of copies of this secretly published text, and on the most part, the stories were indeed mysteriously dark. The editor, Mike Brown, was a member of the group. Mariz's book had been dark, if anyone could recognise the book's style, it would be them.

Maybe, just maybe one of these writers was who I searched for. I arrived early, trying to work out how I would approach the subject with them. The car light was dim, but I could read the poem in his book enough.

Overcame the fair one
Terrible incantations
Helped by the herb
She trampled the picture
Evil triumphs
Over innocence

KVT, the letters tiny, were directly underneath. Were these the initials of the poem's true author? Perhaps the author of the original book? Did anyone in the group have these initials?

I walked in at five past seven. Six people sat around two-fold-away white tables.

"Please, come in," a rotund man said. He looked like he'd just walked in off the street. Hair a mess, face unshaven in the 'couldn't be bothered' look, and he wore a denim and wool coat. I pulled out a green plastic chair and sat opposite. There was a definite funk in the air, a combination of body odour and smelly running shoes. The room was cool, and the atmosphere relaxed in a jovial manner. The only female member, an English girl, slender with short hair in her forties I smiled. I couldn't imagine what it would be like in a group of all male writers. How would any of them understand the female point of view? Once my pad and pen were on the table, the rotund man, Gary, introduced the other members. All welcomed me and commented on how much they enjoyed my books. I thought the night would digress into writer worship, but these writers weren't easily influenced by fame. They continued in the normal fashion as if I were just another member. It was a good feeling.

I listened and took notes and offered comments where I felt they were appropriate. All their styles were vastly different, only none matched what I was looking for, and none of the personalities in the room hinted at them being willing to allow someone else to use their work. Mike Brown seemed to have a good handle on individual styles, and he was the most likely to recognize what I had. After the readings, I asked if they knew an author with the initials KVT. They all did, he had been a member of the group. Kurt von Trojan had been a client of an LA literary agency who sponsored the group up until his death a few years back.

"How did he die?" I asked

"Cancer," Gary said, it was clear he was still upset about it. "A great writer, just unknown most of his life."

"Is this his work?" I showed the group the poem in Mariz's book.

"Certainly is," another member, Kain Massin, an Australian who was visiting for a few months, and winner of the ABC book award said, reading the page. "He had a unique way about him."

"I thought it was a nice touch by him," Gary said, also reading the page. "Kurt mentored him when he was younger."

A connection.

"Does the rest of the book sound like Kurt?" The group looked at each other as if I were a little nuts.

Kain took the book and opened it to the first page. "None of this except the poem remotely sounds like Kurt, so I don't think he showed too much of his influence here, but..." He read a few lines from the first few pages. He stopped, closed the book and handed it back to me. "I hadn't noticed that before. The opening page sounds just like how my father speaks English. So, I am guessing he has some Hungarian influences."

"I didn't pick that up," the English girl said. "I just thought it was a crap book." Good, not everyone was a fan of his work.

It wasn't much, but I had something to go on. Sadly, I couldn't talk to Kurt to find out why one of his poems was in the book. I thanked and prepared to leave. I asked Mike if he could place the style. We stood on the steps of the house, puffing on a cigarette, Gary was trying to roll one in the breezy conditions. Mike agreed with Kain; only he added that the overall style was very old, and he thought a bad attempt was made to spruce it up for the modern market. I thanked the pair for their insights.

It was like I'd known these writers for many years, especially Gary. He had immediately commented on just how beautiful I was soon after I'd sat down. At first, I thought him to be a typical male sexist pig, though during the night I discovered he just wasn't afraid to speak his mind, and he didn't care much for what people thought about him maybe if Mariz were more like him, I'd have some respect for his work.

I'd exhausted the writing groups in Santa Monica, and it became clear the book didn't come from within the local industry. The only person I could realistically approach for the truth was Mariz Sanchez, and he wasn't about to tell me what he'd done. If Samantha knew, I might be able to ease the information out; only when it came down to evidence, she wouldn't do anything to harm her lover. I knew her well enough. I sat in my car, engine running, the smell of gas and fumes coming through the open driver's side window. I should have just gone home, be done with my search for the night. I felt frustrated, annoyed and more than just a little tense. O'Daniels Irish Pub would still be open, and I could do with a few stiff whiskies to settle the mess of thoughts. The original author might have been Hungarian and knew Kurt, after weeks of dead ends this gave me some hope.

More than a few drinks later, and a swerving drive home, I collapsed in front of the TV. An old horror movie was playing on late night; my vision, too bleary, created a grey haze in front of my eyes. The images moved and shuffled, sprayed shadows over the darkened room. Whatever it was, it sent me to sleep.

Chapter 18

The Prelŭstitel

Cassandra drank at a bar; four part filled glasses of alcohol. I could see the despair and fear about her like an aura; it was growing with each drink, someone like her would give me the strength to stand in the light for days. The city teemed with people steeped in such darkness and finding a supply to keep me in the human realm required little effort.

Today she'd taken to wearing all black, much like Sarina. They were growing closer. The dream I'd sent would soon do its work, and this bond would get ever stronger. I needed it to get the book and be seen to be going for the icon, though with this closeness would come a problem, one I didn't know how to address.

She left the bar, walked across the street to the park. She sat on a bench and stared at the grass. She looked to be lost in thought. What thoughts? I approached and sat beside her; his wall didn't prevent me. How close could I get, I wondered? She had a faraway look in her eyes.

Carefully I dipped my index finger into her mind. He didn't stop me. Her eyes fluttered a little — just a touch, a slight caress to see what she could see. I withdrew my finger; she caught her breath, hand to her chest. What I'd seen confirmed what I knew. I wanted more; the second touch stopped by his barrier. Once more, she fell into his protection.

"Enough," he said.

"I need more."

"No."

A brief look he allowed, a deeper look, no. I sat back and watched her, studied the soft lines of her face, the small nose, the strong, yet feminine set of her shoulders. Being attractive could have been the reason Sarina was drawn to her. It made sense, though it rarely happened that she would make a human friend; bring a human so close into her life.

Cassandra's thoughts were a mess of emotion and vision, a crazy collection of strengths and doubts that played off each other like two bad comedians. I made sense of some thoughts, gathered what I needed to understand her faraway look, but not enough to put anything together in a solid form. He wanted her for a purpose, one that involved Sarina and me.

She stood, thoughts collected, and began walking along the path. Following her led nowhere for the moment, his purpose would be revealed when he saw fit. My purpose? Push the women closer together and then use it to get the book and use Cassandra to get the icon. She'd seen it, but she didn't know what it was. If I could do this, then Sarina would be safe.

Chapter 19

Cassandra

I sat drinking George T Stagg in the Ocean and Vine lounge at the Beach Hotel; I'd given up looking for the original author of the book for the day. In a way, I was hoping he did write the book, though there were still too many inconsistencies in style that plagued me. The relationship with the dead author Kurt von Trojan, though tenuous, did give me some cause for concern. For now, I needed a few drinks, a quiet place and a place where I could safely observe people going about their everyday, boring lives. These observations helped me to develop characters and fictional lives. The hotel felt comfortable and far removed from the turmoil I'd let consume me for the last few months. I'd dressed for clubbing later in the evening, not kids clubbing, but the get-togethers where Ozzy Osborne was King and Marilyn Manson his daughter. I hadn't applied the dark eye makeup yet; it would have drawn attention to me in such a pricey hotel. Polished brass and comfortable lounges helped settle my mind, the whiskey eased the emotional turmoil and drove thoughts of Samantha in Mariz's arms away. He was doing a US-wide book signing tour, and he was the darling of the literary press. Whenever I turned on the TV, he was there, on a talk show, a news program, even selling breakfast cereal to children. The man made me sick.

"Cassandra Whitehall?"

I looked away from the ocean view to see an old man standing before me. He looked ninety if a day. "Good evening," I said. Usually, only the young fans recognised me.

"May I sit?"

Polite too. I offered the tub chair on the other side of the small drinks table.

He looked nervous as if he shouldn't be seen with me. He placed a briefcase on the table and wiped sweat from his age-spotted, bald head with a handkerchief. His suit was straight out of the fifties, dark, wide pinstripe, wide lapels.

"How can I help you?" I put my note pad down and placed my hands in my lap.

"Sanchez stole something from me," he said. The man had my full attention.

"Who are you?"

"Paslenov, Uri Paslenov." He didn't sound Russian. "I hired Mr Sanchez to edit a book that had been poorly translated. The Austrian-English reminded my employer of bad times, so I sought out Mr Sanchez to rectify this affront." He wiped his brow again. "He stole the story and wrote a book based on its contents," Uri said Mariz's name with obvious distaste. "Now I am in trouble with the... with my employer."

"You have evidence to prove this?" I sat forward; the pad slid to the floor.

The man placed his left hand on the case. "Here is the book, the one he copied."

"Why haven't you reported this?" If he knew, then why not tell the publisher? The Police? "Why have you brought it to me?"

"My time is short. I heard whispers about you. I'm sorry Ms Whitehall I can't say any more, other than to not read the book. He will come for it."

It was hard to hear his small voice. "Who will come for the book?"

"I have to leave." His eyes, wet and red-rimmed, showed age and absolute fear. "I broke into Mr Sanchez's house two hours ago and stole the book back, but it is too late. I am being followed." He looked to the main doors, searching.

"What's too late, Uri? And who's following you?" I tried to sound friendly, contain my excitement.

He watched the door, a man full of fear and expectation. "Someone will..." His face reddened, eyes afire with new fear. "I have to go." He stood, muscles not as quick as they once were. He hurried away, an old man shuffle.

He left by the side entrance; I looked towards the main doors, someone was leaving in a hurry, too fast for me to make any kind of identification. I should have grabbed the bag and followed him, but this was what I'd been looking for, and it had found me. Why me? I didn't know, and I didn't care. I spun the case around; the tumbler security locks were locked. I felt a moment of panic, then tried what I'd seen in a movie, I turned all the tumblers to zero. The locks released and I opened the bag. What looked like six hundred handwritten notes stared up at me — old script, written by a skilled hand. By the look of the style, it had all the ornate curvature of European skills. No one wrote like that anymore. I pulled out the top page; it felt stiff, equally as old as the script. It had been written with a fountain pen, the dobs of ink at the ends of the letters, the fine starts until the nib began to pump properly. I'd tried calligraphy for a time; I didn't have the patience.

The whole first page was pretty much straight out of Mariz's book. Word for word. The title of the book, simply *Me and Him*, was authored by DBD. I snapped the case closed, left my pad on the floor and my drink untouched. I had work to do, an email to write. It was Thursday night; I could have an email and a scan of the page to his publisher by morning. Now that lying bastard would get what he deserved.

I spent the night reading more of the manuscript. I didn't understand the story, and it was clear the translator's poor English didn't help. It was obvious he had made some major changes and added his story line to create a mystery, it was the areas dealing with someone simply known as him, and the dark that sounded too real to be fiction; the sign of a good storyteller. DBD could tell a good story, but the translation was appalling in places. I'd already sent my venomous letter to Maxine Rickson with the attached page. I also put the original first page in an envelope and addressed it to her, with a note saying I had six hundred other pages to the original book. Vengeance was mine. I opened a new bottle of George T. to celebrate, feeling good for the first time in months. I masturbated while thinking of Samantha, glass in one hand and touching myself with the other. I knew I had won. Samantha had no choice but to leave him now.

I'd slept well, and for some reason, I didn't feel quite so depressed. The phone rang. It was Maxine; she was cautious, worried. She tried to buy my silence at first. Fifty thousand to forget about it. I got more than that for the release of my first children's book last year. I refused, she abused, and I refused some more. I told her if she didn't release the information, I would, and I would do it through the gossip columns, who were notorious for brutalising people. Maxine agreed after a barrage of abuse, saying a press release would be out by noon. She called me a fucking dyke, then hung up. Dyke's a compliment, again hetero ignorance.

I felt vindicated, elated after the call. I sat on the sofa reading the morning's paper. The usual crime stories crowded the front page; basketball great retires; it wasn't until the fifth page that anything of the news outside of the state emerged. The big stories, surrounded in advertising were boring, so I read the little outtakes and brief items that ran the columns alongside large photographs and ads. Guinea pig falls to death off house roof in China, that one made me smile. Old man found dead alongside highway. A lot of homeless people die along the Pacific. I read a little further. Mr Uri Paslenov was found dead last night by a passing motorist, cause of death unknown. The story went on to examine the dangers to old people wandering by busy roads at night like the homeless could afford a paper to read the warning in the first place.

Feeling unnerved I had a shower, using the water to try and help me think of what to do. I had the book from a man who just turned up dead, a man who had told me his employer was unhappy with him and was being followed. Damn it, a book Mariz had stolen in the first place. I had wanted Samantha; the old man's death wasn't what I wanted. Should I contact the police? No, there wasn't anything to tell them, besides it would distract the media away from Mariz. He would pay for causing the death of the old man. If he hadn't have stolen the book, Uri would still be alive. I dried and dressed, trying to think of what to do with the manuscript. Did the old man say who he'd given it to? Was I now in danger? What was he going to tell me before he abruptly left me with the case? Someone would come for the book. Now it was out in the open I wanted nothing to do with it.

I threw the case on the back seat of my car and drove down where Sam and he lived in a townhouse. They wouldn't be home, I knew where the spare key was kept, a typical fake rock in the garden, a professional house thief's dream. I let myself in. I placed the briefcase in the middle of their dining table, no note. The investigation into his fraud would find the book in his possession, I was sure of it. I wiped my prints from the case and left. My part had already been done; I didn't need the book anymore. The media would hound him, and I could sit back and watch the show. I'd parked a few streets away so that no one would notice my car, so the walk back helped calm me some. All the time while in the house my heart felt like it was going to explode. Someone was sure to see me, call the cops and I'd be caught inside, and then it could be claimed I was planting evidence against him. Even with the case gone, my mind had difficulties with what I was doing. There was a lot more than just a stolen manuscript here, did I want to know? I needed a drink. I need a lot of drinks.

Beth lived across the road from Reed Park. I parked in her drive and sat in the car for ten minutes struggling to come to terms with events. Had I done the right thing? Had Uri died because he was old, and I was seeing too much into it? Sickness churned in my gut; guilt pressed on the elation of earlier. Getting too involved might bring consequences direr than just uncovering a literary fraud. I could tell Beth what was going on. She was a good woman, a hard-core Goth with money, and a good friend, sometimes. My hands had stopped shaking enough for me to get out of the car, though my knees buckled a little. The house had been painted bright white with black borders around everything. The place had once been the New Age Bible and Philosophy Center, or so Beth had claimed. The worst part about visiting Beth was the doorbell. I steadied myself with my left hand against the door before pressing the red button.

Even knowing it was coming, the female scream still made me jump.

I'd known Beth for about three years; we'd met at a blood party and hit it off straight away. She was a big girl, wide-faced and wide-hipped. Her husband had cheated on her, and she got the house and the bank account, "He got a young, unemployed hooker with bad hair," as Beth put it.

The door opened. Her white made-up face, dark eyes and black lips stared at me. She tilted her head to the right slightly, like a dog unsure of what it is seeing.

"It's me, Cassandra," I said. Beth could phase out sometimes.

"Oh, you." She unlocked the security door, turned about and walked down the hallway to the back of the house. I followed, closing and locking the front door behind me. Beth often didn't say much. "Coffee?" she asked, as we entered the large, back kitchen. Dishes cluttered the sink and the place smelled of incense.

"Anything stronger?"

"Vodka?"

"A big one."

"You can have the whole bottle; I hate the shit." She grabbed a bottle from a grime-stained, supposedly blue, overhead cupboard. It was filled with bottles. I recognised a label.

"Can I have a George T.?"

"Whatever." She grabbed the bottle, eighteen-year-old, slammed the cupboard closed and put the bottle down hard on the table. She was in one of her better moods. I found a glass that wasn't too dirty on the sink and poured myself three full shots.

Beth studied me while I drank, then sat at the cluttered table, pushing junk onto the floor so her pudgy arms could rest. Beth could be slow to engage in conversation; she was a minimalist in pretty much everything she said. The whiskey burned my throat, but it worked.

"You look like shit," she said, doing the head tilt again.

I told her about what I'd done. Beth stared, and stared some more, saying nothing. Her placid, brown eyes framed with badly died hair looked on like a sad clown face. I didn't know if she heard anything I said or understood the implications of my actions but talking about it was helping. What I did was right, it had to come out that Mariz hadn't completely written the book himself. He didn't deserve the SPA. I downed another glass, the bite gone; my nerves calmed or numbed.

"Party tonight, do you want to come?" Beth said, as though I'd just walked into the room. "Special gathering."

I poured another large one and drank it in one gulp. My neck tensed as I forced it to stay down. "Why not?" It took a few moments. I preferred the smoothness of aged whiskey. Right now, I dare say I would have even had a beer.

"It's at ten. I'll have to take you." Beth's voice was pure monotone, her stare empty, large eyes lost in the black eye shadow. "Be ready by nine-thirty. You still live in the same place?"

"I have to tell you something first," the whiskey freeing my tension. "What I've done might have caused the death of a man." Beth, still vacuous, didn't blink.

"Good," she eventually said. "Less men the better."

I laughed, not because it was funny because I was suitably drunk.

The party, loud, dark and moody was all death looks and vampire parodies. I'd done my best to fit in. I didn't dress to the full theme, I found it depressing, and I had issues enough. I had a black T and jacket, black, long beaded earrings, blue jeans and red shoes. Red lipstick made me stand out considerably in the crowd. Beth had supplied all the drinks, she could afford it, and a private donation supplied the location, the equipment and furniture. These people might have looked disconnected from the so-called normal world, but they weren't without substantial resources. Someone had got the latest Magnum

Carnage release by the sounds coming from the back of the house. I knew the band, and some of the music; this sounded new. Beth left me in the front room with a group of women, well girls, drinking Vodka from long-stemmed wine glasses. A large LCD screen on the wall played an old and very scratchy black and white horror film. Vampire, of course. I found it distracting, the grey light flickering across the smoky, muted candlelight of the established mood.

"You that writer chick?" a tall woman asked, handing me a glass. The music didn't drown out conversation in this room.

"Yes, I am." I took the offered drink and sipped the Vodka; it burnt my throat. "Have you read my books?" She shook her head. I didn't know what else to say; she just looked at me as if I were an oddity in a museum. She left me standing, feeling dumb and joined a group of men sitting on a long, leather sofa. The smell of cigarettes and patchouli oil drove me toward the back of the house and the loudness of the music. Fifty or more people crowded the hall, the rooms and the spacious modern kitchen. A band was moving away from their instruments in what could have been a games room. If things weren't screwed enough, it was Magnum Carnage; someone had pull as well as money. Black curtains blocked off the window; the ceiling ballooned with black lace curtain, a reddish standard lamp offered the only light. The recorded music started up and was loud enough for me, being in the same room as a full band would swallow conversation, crash me so far into oblivions I doubt I'd get back out. I was starting to think the party idea wasn't the best in my state of mind.

I found Beth out in the back garden; she was smoking a joint with an equally overweight man, her laughter seemed out of character. She wore a long black Indian dress with tassels around the hem, a thick black coat and a deep plunging black blouse. She'd covered her impressive breasts with what looked like hundreds of silver chains with charms. In the dark, where the only light was low garden halogens and the moon, the pair looked a little frightening.

"Cassandra," Beth called. She sounded happy. "Come here and meet The Ax." The big man turned and offered a crooked tooth smile. His eye makeup accentuated the wideness of his eyes.

"I have to leave," I said, joining them. "I don't feel well."

"But you haven't met our special guest." Her smile looked out of place. I rarely saw anything approaching joy in Beth.

"I'm sorry." I kissed her on the cheek, the smell of dope strong, laced with the ivory perfume she liked to wear. "But I have to go. Thank you for listening to me and bringing me here."

"I'll get Ax to drop you home; he doesn't drink." Beth even sounded more coherent than usual. Perhaps she could be a case for when marijuana is helpful?

I kissed her again, and the large body of the man cut a path through the darkness down the side of the house. He drove me home in his silver BMW. He didn't say a word, just grunted when I gave him directions. I stood in my driveway watching the moon for about an hour after he'd left. I was drunk, very drunk; it still wasn't enough to drive away the death of Uri. Was it a coincidence he died after giving me the book? I hoped so, I seriously hoped so.

Chapter 20

The Prelŭstitel

There were other Uttuku in the city; would Sarina draw on their support? If so, could I manipulate Cassandra through them? I could sense the Uttuku, but they were not part of the web of night, so making any links between them was impossible. Cassandra Whitehall had to be the way, and He had already managed to steer her closer to Sarina. I needed them so close that when a decision was made it would be the one to benefit Aza'zel and me.

Aza'zel had led me to a house, a strange house. I could find no light about it or within, even though it looked lived in, occupied — an Uttuku's house, perhaps. The walls were white, black-bordered, clearly the house of a Gothic, could this be a friend of Cassandra's? Standing across the street near the building siding tennis courts, I watched and listened. Night would soon fall, and the waiting would be less demanding.

The front door opened, a woman stepped out into the sun, walked up the drive and gathered her mail. I didn't know her, hadn't seen her with Sarina. If an Uttuku, she didn't look like someone Sarina would know; too open, too exposed. A trusted human, perhaps? Cassandra. This could be an access point to her, a close friend? A confidante? If I could not take Cassandra then maybe I could take this woman, find out about her through an alternative method. I crossed the street to the driveway, I needed only dip into her mind, and I would know. I could go no. Further, I felt weak. Something here repulsed me, it wasn't him, and it didn't feel Uttuku – something else, something else entirely.

Another Prelŭstitel? No, we do not live in the human fashion, though the fashion shown by this woman was human in appearance and action.

"What is she?" I asked, reaching into the darkness.

"I don't know; she exists outside of the realm."

"With whom is she connected?" Aza'zel formed beside me.

"Again, I do not know. I felt her presence. It is old, very old."

"Can we use her?"

"That is what you are to discover. She has an influence that has crossed Cassandra's path, find out what it means."

"What else can there be beside us, what we know?" I knew of little else with such influence on the forces of darkness.

"I must think," he said, dissolving. "She may be..." He said no more.

May be what?

Something new had been added and with it a very real concern. Something Aza'zel didn't know. What could this woman possibly be? Nothing was as dark as Aza'zel, and nothing as full of light as the Uttuku. I drifted back across the street, into the shadows of trees. I could not watch Sarina and this woman; I already had difficulties with following Cassandra. What could this mean for my plans?

Chapter 21

Cassandra

We sat sipping coffee inside the Carousel Cafe. Sarina, subdued, had said nothing for the last thirty minutes, I, on the other hand, had vented a little more. I didn't yell, just spoke using harsh words and tones. I told her we should tell the police about how Zeek died, and how we were being stalked by the man responsible. Sarina just looked at the table top, her black coffee half drunk in front of her. The cafe was quiet with only a few breakfast diners. I had Bacon and eggs, the usual speciality first thing in the morning, if I ever was awake first thing, not only filled the air but enticed me into considering having a second serve. Sarina ordered toast with blueberry jam. It was the first time I'd seen her eat a whole meal of something.

"I don't want you to leave," she said, looking up from some spot on the table.

"I can't see any reason to stay, Sarina." A waitress took our plates. I also couldn't see the need to go and put myself in greater danger either. I wasn't giving in, not just yet.

"I can protect you." She went to reach across the table for my hand, hesitated, pulled back to rest her hand on the table before her. "Together we will be able to work this out."

"Then we have to be honest with each other." I wasn't even sure I could deal with the whole truth and nothing but.

Sarina bit her bottom lip, a trait I hadn't seen before. Was this the Sarina beneath the Goth, the person I'd come to know?

"I know the name of the author of the book," I said.

"Will I know him?"

"Name is simply DBD." I watched her face for signs of recognition. Nothing.

"That's all you have. Do the initials mean something to you?"

"No, I haven't been able to find who the initials belong to." This was getting difficult. "I was hoping you'd know him."

"If we are to stop Orlando, we need that book, Cassandra!" Though calm, her words were deliberate. "You have to get it back. I will think on the initials, but I can't guarantee I'll know any more than you."

"He's following you. Why?" She clenched her hands together. "He's following me for the book, but why is he following you?"

"If I tell you, he will take your life. I need time."

"Maybe if I'd told you about the book sooner, he might still be alive."

"You could have died." Sarina looked up. "If I'd known..." This time she did take my hand.

"Tell me what Aza'zel is." I could see pain in her eyes. It was as if the Sarina of yesterday had slipped away to reveal the real woman.

"Not here. Back at my place."

Maybe now my life would start making sense.

Once safely inside the dark well of Sarina's world, she told me more about Aza'zel, the one whose name mean death in entirety. He, as he has always been represented in the form of a male, has been in and part of the world since the dawn of time itself. Where there is light, there is always darkness. He was born of the primal fear of the night and the base fear of the unknown. He is a feeder on fear, on humans' dark desires. He feeds because he can, not because he must, or needs to. He needs to do little to remain present in the world, for he will always be with the world right up to its very end. Only he will remain, always remain. This wasn't the devil story I'd known as a kid. Satan, the dark one from the Bible was merely a poor representation of what he meant to the world. Knowing what he was created a sense of hopelessness around me. If he was so powerful what could be done to stop him?

Sarina sat beside me on the sofa as she spoke. It felt this wasn't something she spoke about often. She chose her words carefully, let them free softly, a sense of defeat in her every utterance and the intention, though not meant to frighten me, did. Occasionally holding my hand and squeezing to make a point, she said Aza'zel did not require power like the living, he did not survive for vengeance, lust or desire. He took what he could whenever he liked and nothing more. The fear of the darkness fed him, the primal instinct against night a satisfaction. But Aza'zel did need completeness, and its hunger for this was immense. His Prelŭstitel's purpose was to hunt Uttuku and to take the light of those whose darkness was ready for his feasting. The Hunters took the darkness of humans, and they took it easily, Aza'zel took the darkness that remained. One he had taken what was left the soul would be cast into the *Abad*, the well of eternal nothing.

"Eventually the victims of a Prelŭstitel's feeding die," Sarina said. She stood and walked to the floor to ceiling window, the afternoon sun shielded by the heavy tinting. She touched the horse statue lightly. "Once the darkness is gone the victims can't feed themselves, they can't do anything. Human light needs darkness to shine, once taken away the light simply fades and without light, you die."

"Like being in a coma," I offered, not understanding what she meant.

"A coma is still a kind of life." Sarina put her hands on the glass, leaning her head forward. "This is no life. Everything is gone. All that is left inside the victim is nothing. Even Aza'zel is something."

"But aren't you also like him?"

Sarina laughed, a sad sound. "Uttuku only take a piece of the light, the energy that makes you alive. Never enough to cause any harm, just what we need to exist. Maybe we are like him in a way. We feed on life energy, even if it is only a small amount, and we can live forever if we choose."

"You are immortal." I could feel her growing sadness. This was something hard for her to speak about. I wondered why she was telling me if difficulties existed. She didn't have to tell me.

"You have to understand, Cassandra. We preserve life, Aza'zel decays it. It goes beyond what is known as death to humans." She turned and faced me. She went to say more but remained silent.

"We know why it wants me." I stood, she needed someone. "But why is he after you?" I had to know. "Sarina. I might be able to help."

She took both my hands, holding them down in front of her. We didn't make eye contact. I felt if we did the conversation would end. Too much honesty can be a strain on the heart, a real test on your emotional makeup. I thought I was holding together well, but it was only because I was with her. I wondered what would happen if I were alone and had to think about all this.

"It is an enemy and a threat to life in general. He cannot take the life energy of an Uttuku easily and can be driven away by them." She sighed. "There is much you need to know in order to understand why I am wanted by Orlando and Aza'zel."

"Please tell me, Sarina. I've learnt a little about you through the writing of Bela's story, but it isn't enough, nowhere near enough." I looked passed her and out at the ocean, the gentle waves rolling across the distant shore, the few people dotting the white sands. Without binoculars, I couldn't see if Orlando stood beneath the pier watching, though the knot in my stomach said he was. Turning back to Sarina's downcast face I rested my brow against the top of her head, smelt the peachiness of her shampoo.

"The first of us was Lilith in Mesopotamia," she whispered, "the birthplace of our kind. Some believe she was the biblical wife of Adam."

"So, there is a religious thread?"

"No, that is just an old story. Lilith's story is very different from what you might find written. She is a gentler woman with..."

"So where do you come in?" She seemed to be relaxing, her disclosure helped.

"My line came out of Assyrian," Sarina said. Her hands felt cool, moist. "It is said that in Egypt Aza'zel took a Queen for a rare pleasure, using nightmares to hide his form. He thought she had died in the desert under the eye of the moon, but she didn't." I squeezed her fingers. I wanted her to continue. "On the outskirts of her town, T'aru, Tiyi became the first Uttuku of Egypt, part darkness, part light. It was rumoured that her husband, Amenhotep III, loved her so much he didn't notice that she never aged. Before she was killed. Her son, derelict in his duties, beheaded her and cast her into a fire pit. This isn't known of that time." Sarina's story helped deepen my understanding of her great age. "But before she died, she converted some of her servants, which were later set free. From there we have spread."

"That means there would me millions of you by now?"

"After the first Age, Lilith decreed that only conversion for love be allowed; she made a blood pact with the night." She now lifted her head to stare into my face. "A world of immortals. Think about that, Cassandra. We would have starved, become weak. The development of the human desire and discovery would have been snuffed out. Someone like Alexander may not have existed."

"Who was Alexander?"

"A great Uttuku, who, because of love, died."

"I don't understand," which wasn't true. I stood before a beautiful woman who could live forever; there existed a vital question. "How does an immortal die?"

"Are you thirsty?" she asked. "All this talking has given me a dry throat."

"All this history has given me a sore head. I'll go a double." She left me to get drinks. I returned to the chair and sat. Sarina was opening in a way. Still, the personal area was developing, I felt comfortable learning about what she was, and felt relieved that Uttuku didn't kill their meals. I wondered where in real history Sarina came in and what deeper meaning hit beneath the Lugosi story.

She returned with two drinks. A George T. for me and a tall glass of Pepsi for her. She sat on the sofa, drawing her legs up under herself. I could smell the faint scent of roses, and I knew Sarina wasn't wearing it.

"I want to read a copy of Mariz's book." Sipped the black liquid.

"I've got one at home, but I'm not going back to get it."

"That's okay," she shifted forward, putting her feet on the floor, elbows on knees. "There's a store not far from here; we'll go look there." I didn't like her chances. This was off the subject. Sarina wanted to distract me. Why?

"Well," I started, after a good drink, "how does an immortal die?"

"We aren't truly immortal." She turned the glass around between her fingers. "Provided we don't sustain too serious an injury, we can live for as long as we like."

"Like beheading?" I shuddered at the thought.

"We can heal very fast; my saliva can even heal small human wounds." I shuddered. "If I am injured, it only takes a few minutes for my body to repair. Beheading isn't, usually, a repairable injury."

"Usually?"

"Under the right conditions survival is possible."

It was difficult imagining someone surviving their head being lopped off. Maybe a few more stiff drinks were needed before the day was out and if the mood swung sex and one of Sarina's light tricks could help re-establish some order in my life. Talking and drinking lessened the anxiety of the night but didn't truly push away how I felt about what had happened. Fortunately, Sarina had packed my medications so depression, though not absent, wasn't cramming for attention. What would the doctor make of all this? I couldn't tell him; he'd have an obligation to tell the police about the death and an obligation to put me in an institution for my safety, maybe even rehab for my drinking — another shudder. Rehab now there would be a nightmare. In the silence I thought about what Sarina had written, she had a friend in Germany, one she said Adolph Hitler had killed. With my meagre grasp of history, I knew Eva Braun hadn't been beheaded.

"But Eva, she hadn't lost her head."

"You did read it, good." She smiled. "The poison Adolph gave her must have immobilised her, but it would have been metabolised in twenty minutes. So that bastard burnt her, she couldn't recover from that."

"You know this sounds like a mix of every horror movie I've seen." I sipped my drink. "Have you seen the Highlander films?"

"Legends have their roots in truth somewhere along the line."

Cassandra raised her glass in a toast. "To Legends."

"To finding the book."

"To you telling me why Orlando is after you." She winked.

We browsed one of the shelves of an out of the way bookstore. Sarina wanted to read Mariz Sanchez's book, to try and work out what was so important about its contents. The book was several years old, and because of the media scandal, it had been pulled by the publisher. I'd known a few booksellers in my time, and they were reluctant to give a book back if it stood a chance of earning some extra money through notoriety. The book wasn't on the shelves, I expected this, and there was no point in asking the girl behind the counter. I doubted the lanky eighteen-year-old would even know of him.

"Wait here," I said, approaching the counter. The girl's eyes brightened.

"You're Cassandra Whitehall?"

"Hi." I should have known escaping my fame would be difficult in a bookstore. "Is the manager in?"

"Sorry, no." She looked excited. "But I can help you." Her enthusiasm was charming.

"Do you have a copy of *Me and Him* by Mariz Sanchez?" She wouldn't know.

"That the guy you..." she paused. She did know. "No, Ms Whitehall, we don't have any. A man came in the other day and bought the last copy the manager kept out back. He was a local you know?"

"Thank you."

It was worth a try. Maybe a second-hand bookstore would be better. I found Sarina in the Science Fiction section. She was talking to a man with glasses. I recognised him.

"Li," I said, interrupting their conversation. He turned, like Sarina he wore all black, his head shaved to leave a fine stubble on his scalp, and his small round glasses gave him a serene modern look. Not very authorish.

"Cassandra. I haven't seen you in an age." Li handed Sarina a book. "How have you been?" He kissed my cheek. About the only man, I allowed this close.

"Do you know each other?" I asked.

"Just met," Li said. "But Sarina did say she was a good friend of yours."

I thought I saw Sarina blush. She held one of Li Peng' books. The Last War of Earth. I had the series at home; he'd given them to me at a convention in Finland. I hadn't read them yet.

"Li's picked out a book for me to read," Sarina said, sounding more like a dumb blonde than the person who'd sucked blood from my wrist. "He's offered to sign it." Why was she sounding all girly?

"What brings you to California, I thought you'd be in New York for the launch." He had a new book out.

"It gets bit crazy there, so I thought I'd spend some time over here, you know Venice Beach and all that," he said. "Can never resist a book shop." He smiled a nice smile. Li Peng might have been one of the big names in Science Fiction, but he was also one of the nicest men I'd ever met. Like me he'd shared a NY Times bestseller, I think he would win a Hugo award before me. It was quite a surprise to meet him so far away from home. It was nice, but it also troubled me, something about it wasn't right.

"Li and I were talking about agents," Sarina said, composure returning.

"Why?" I had one in LA, a real prick, but the contracts were good.

"Sarina says you are looking for one?" Li gazed up at Sarina, a touch of confusion in his face.

"In the future, you are going to need a discrete, small agent," Sarina said. She caught my eye. I didn't know the game; I decided to play. "Someone who could keep a secret, maybe."

The only secret I had was standing right in front of me, and I didn't need an agent to hide the truth on the matter. Sarina was planning something else, had manoeuvred Li into a position only she understood. I had no choice. If I needed a new agent, I needed a new agent. I'd find out why later.

"I know a guy," Li said. "He in New York."

"Well known?" Sarina had taken up my speaking parts.

"A little does boutique stuff mainly."

"What do you know about him?"

"I think he represents all the profanity and profundity of living in a modern age," he said. "Passion-on-his-sleeve kind of guy."

"Is that good?" Sarina asked.

"Let's just say; I wouldn't have him any other way." He took a pen out of his black shoulder bag and signed Sarina's book. "I have to get going," he said. "Just look up BG Literary Agency, ask for Big Gary."

"Have you used him before?" My turn to join the conversation.

"No, we've met a few times at functions, a straight shooter."

"If you say so." I didn't get it.

"Have to run, ladies. Maybe see you at the World Fantasy Con?" he said, making his way through the shelves and out of the store.

Sarina took several other of Li Peng's titles from the shelf. My gut said by the end of the day the covers would be black. Would she read them? I'd never seen her read before. I trailed her to the counter where the still beaming girl took payment for the books. On the way out I grabbed Sarina by the wrist.

"I hope you are going to explain what that was all about?"

"Later. Much later," she said.

Chapter 22

The Prelŭstitel

"Sarina is planning something," he said, sitting on top of a burnt-out car. The night, clear, created shadow about its hollow interior. "That other woman is involved. Have you discovered anything about her?"

"No, I cannot penetrate whatever it is that protects her."

"Then it is vital we get the icon back. I can feel something powerful."

"You said it had no real power." The icon was a symbol, merely a representation of the past, nothing more.

"I can feel these things; it is part of me."

"What is she planning?"

"Perhaps protections for Cassandra, perhaps this other woman is to protect her."

"If she does the icon will be lost, perhaps the book as well." I couldn't afford to lose the book.

He laughed a sad sound of dying; his sound, my sound. It was not amusement that made him laugh, something darker had crossed his thoughts.

"Prelŭstitel, you do what you must, I will uncover this new strangeness. It will not get in our way."

The smell of burnt rubber and metal hung about us, the gravel beneath my feet crunched as I moved around the car.

"I suspected Sarina would find a way to stop us," he said. "This woman must be part darkness to wield such strength. Her presence eludes me for now, but I will find her."

"Do I take Cassandra?"

"No."

"Then what?"

He spread wide on the light wind, a black cloud dispersing into the night sky.

"Push Sarina and Cassandra closer, even with this new event I will still be able to create a choice Sarina or Cassandra must make."

"And my book, am I to also take such slow measures?"

"Yes, it is vital that you do this as I have planned, Prelŭstitel, the reason you will know when it comes." With another gust, he was gone.

I would know when I got it. As if I didn't know my needs.

A car approached, its lights flashed. I let the occupants see me. It stopped, the interior light came on, two young men, I could smell alcohol.

"You alright, buddy?" the passenger asked when his window was fully down.

I plunged my hands through the car, through metal and cloth and deep into their minds. They made no sound as I dragged their darkness free. Strands of black snaked from their bodies as I fed, pulled their existence through their skins, sucked them dry like a desert sucks water from the ground. Both men fell forward, empty, gone. I stepped back, clapped my hands and the burst into flames. I had work to do.

Chapter 23

Cassandra

Zeek's death was eventually declared an accident, and the investigation closed. The police warned me to be more careful, and not to venture near the recreation centre again at night, it wasn't my place, so stay away. These days Santa Monica was growing more notorious for mysterious deaths, and just about all of them happened in quiet places by unassuming people. I blamed the lifestyle.

I walked from the parking lot to the start of the pier. I'd decided to have lunch there and meet up with Sarina mid-afternoon to discuss just how to find the missing book, and then how to get it back. She was sure Aza'zel, and Orlando, would leave us alone once they took possession again. I wasn't as confident.

The afternoon heated up and the walk warmed me enough to take off my jacket. I hadn't been home in a week, and now wore Sarina's clothes. Black wasn't my colour, and in the colder months, I found it quite bad for my mood. That and yellow. Effexor's a wonderful drug; great for keeping me even, never happy or joyous, but flat and even. I had grown used to feeling down most of the time, so much so it was pretty much a normal state for me. But after Mariz's death, those dark times got darker, and I'd been driven to finally see my shrink more regularly. The latter was helping, to a point.

I accepted the madness of the last few months. I was happy in a way if depressed happiness is a real feeling to have. I had other feelings as well, only no time to deal with them. Keeping busy and creating distractions allowed me more time to spend with Sarina. Another mental distraction, only one on which the future depended.

I didn't expect Samantha to still have the book, I called her anyway. Her number was in my phone. It rang. Women never change their numbers.

"What do you want?" Not the friendliest of welcomes. My number was still in her phone as well.

"We need to talk."

"I don't need to talk with you."

"You will if you still have the book." There, it was out.

"What book?" She didn't hang up, so she knew what I was talking about.

"The one I left on your dining room table."

"It was..." Pause. "What makes you think I want to talk to you about it?"

"Let's just say a very nasty person is looking for it, and they will do anything to get it." This time the pause was longer. "Sam?" I asked after the pause stretched for too long.

"Where are you?"

"Thought I'd treat myself to gourmet food on the Venice Beach Pier."

"The Carousel." She remembered. "I'll be there in half an hour."

I touched the end call icon and felt pleased with myself. I hadn't expected it to be so easy. Maybe Sam knew more than I thought and maybe she had the book. Things would be much easier if she had.

I'd already eaten my turkey baguette by the time Samantha arrived. The place was alive with young people stuffing their faces with burgers and fries. It felt good to be in a place that sparkled with life and colour. Samantha didn't order, she pushed her way through people and sat directly opposite me at the small table. She didn't look happy, which suited me just fine.

"Not eating?" I said, taking a mouth full of coffee.

"You're kidding me, right?" I knew she hated the pier.

"Where's the book?"

"What book?"

"The one I gave you, the one Mariz and you used to win the SPA."

Samantha toyed with her hair. I had her.

"How much?" she said, placing both hands flat on the table.

"I'm not wanting to buy it from you, Sam."

"Then I don't know what you are talking about."

I should have expected greed. I did need the book, and my royalties had all come through for the quarter. Samantha wasn't going to give it to me, and I couldn't tell her why I needed it.

"Fifty thousand," I said. It was all I had. Not much for my life, I thought.

She laughed. Face hard, determined. I wondered what I'd seen in her; love had blinded me. This wasn't the woman who'd invaded my desires and my fantasies for so long.

"You look like you're in trouble, girl," she said, sitting back. "I can see it in your face. If you need the book as bad as I think then come up with a hundred thousand and I'll gift wrap it for you." She stood, straightening her pink blouse. The conversation was over. Even if I had that much cash there would be no way in hell; I would hand it to her. "If you can't offer, then I guess I don't know what you are talking about."

"But that's ridiculous; it isn't close to being worth that much." She was nuts.

"Someone died for this already, remember," she said, "and you are responsible. The amount is fair. How much a life?" she said, walking away.

I shrugged; there wasn't much else to do. She left. I had to find another way. I hadn't expected her greed to be so unreasonable. What had I expected?

He to hand the book over with and forget what had happened? Maybe I was the one who was nuts.

"I could pay what she wants," Sarina said as she watched Orlando under the pier. "Anything to get you out of harm's way." She lowered the binoculars and stepped away from the window.

I hid my surprise at her offer, but then she would have plenty of money accumulated over the centuries.

"No." I poured myself a drink. "We'll find another way to get it, now that I know she still has the book." I sat, mind racing through what I could realistically do. "To think I loved her."

Sarina moved away from the window and put the glasses on the pedestal beside the horse. Her expression one of question.

"I slept with her," I said, emptying my glass and pouring another. Sarina said nothing. "I thought I loved her, this morning only showed I 'd fallen in love with my fantasy, not her. For someone, I knew I could never have. It wasn't real, Sarina." I sipped the whiskey. "I suppose meeting you has helped me see my love for what it was."

She understood the truth of what I'd said. Her love for Bela was equally tainted by desire over reason; she'd stalked the man. She approached and sat on the arm of one of the chairs, her favourite spot. The room felt stuffy and tense. We both shared something in common, something that stood in the way of our emotional freedom. I could have just paid Samantha and been done with it, got the book and saved my life from immanent doom, but for a reason buried deep in the misery of my life, I couldn't do it. I couldn't pay the woman; I didn't want to pay and find myself owing her for my life.

"Do you have any music?" I asked. I hadn't seen a sound system or a TV, and the furniture gave no indication of storing such devices. She pointed to a low cabinet along one wall. Above hung a black square in a black frame.

I left my drink on the coffee table and pressed the door of the cabinet. There were no handles, so it had to be a magnetic lock. The door opened to reveal a black system with black buttons but no operational icons. I touched a corner square on its face; a panel lit up in red on black screen.

"Where are the CDs?" I asked.

"Press the panel beneath the system."

The panel popped open to reveal dozens of black CD cases and a black iPad. I took one of the CDs out. The whole case was black, no writing. I opened the case to see a black CD, no writing, no indication of the artist or what might be on the disk.

"How do you know what to put on?"

"I like it all."

"And what would that be?" I liked to know what I was listening to before putting it on.

"Black Sabbath, AC/DC's Back in Black, Fade to Black by the Rolling Stones, Black Betty." She came over and knelt beside me in front of the system. "I have Black Night, Black Muddy River by the Grateful Dead and some George Benson."

"George Benson?" I frowned.

"He's black."

She put the CD I was holding into the player, closed the cabinet's door and went back to sitting on the arm of her chair. I returned to my seat and picked up the drink. With some idea of what to expect, I sat back and wondered what part of black I was about to hear. Alice Cooper's Black Widow etched its way through the walls, the volume up, but not too loud as to discourage conversation.

"Met him backstage after a concert once," Sarina said.

"Do you have anything that doesn't deal with black?"

"No, why?"

If she didn't know, then there was no point going there. I listened to the music, the black themes sometimes dark, sometimes light. It created a mix of emotions and styles, nothing fitting together. As I drank and watched Sarina, I thought the music suited her and the life she had led. How do you deal with eternity? She had her black focus, a reminder of what had created her, and something she could always rely on no matter what emotional content became attached. For me it was writing, the creation of worlds with words lives that were part me, part someone else and part imagination. No matter what my mood, no matter who I was with or where I found myself, the words always kept me settled. Perhaps that is why writing Sarina's book remained as a job to do. It was a constant, a familiar element of my being, my life. The music took its time to wash around us like a pool of ink. I listened and drank. She listened and watched me drink. I didn't mind.

The CD ended, and the soft wall of sound between us fell. I thought about putting another one on, filling the void. Sarina shook her head; we'd heard enough. Soon night would come; her time, her world. Sarina looked happy, happier than I'd seen her before. The music had brought something to her eyes. They glittered with expectancy, hope. I wanted some of that. She moved from the arm of the chair to sit in my lap. I put down my glass, feeling more than a bit tipsy. Closing my eyes, I enjoyed the feeling of her fingers through my hair, the gentle kiss upon my forehead. The madness stalled, took a step back to let a glimmer of light peek through the veil of black around us. I craved the light, not the burning rays of the sun, the light created to hold off the night. I wanted to roam the yellow and white lights that spotted the evening hours, that became fuzzy orbs in fog, that offered a strange protection from the fingers of darkness and loss.

Warm breath touched my face, my cheek. Lips pressed tight, I kissed back, letting myself fall into the sensation like I used to fall into the cooling depths of the ocean. With a sigh, we broke apart, her head dropping to my shoulder and me stroking her back. This was how things were meant to be, the real feelings that I had so foolishly craved from an impossible desire. Comfort, warm acceptance drifted through about us, raised me above the lows, the troubles and problems. Nothing seemed out of reach; everything became achievable. In the darkness, I saw a tiny light, my light, her light, our light.

By the time I opened my eyes again we were sitting in complete darkness, our forms merged as one, our breathing in unison. We'd slept. I could see the light reaching into the sky from the pier below, a halo that occupied the left-hand corner of the window. In the shadows, the horse statue became a watching sentinel, our protector. I found I liked the idea of being protected in this symbolic way. Locked doors can't create safety, bars on windows can't truly protect you from those who would invade your life. Safety came from within, and for a time there was safety within my mind.

"It's time to go," Sarina said. The sound a whisper, airy.

"Can I shower?"

"Certainly." She eased herself from my lap. "Tonight, we'll let our hair down, get away from the book and Orlando."

"Goth?"

"Strip club. Someone I want you to see and meet."

I'd never been to a strip club. I thought about women taking their clothes off for ogling men, the humility of the act; then I took a double take: naked women, Sarina and alcohol. I couldn't get a bigger distraction if I tried. I showered and dressed in a nice strapless dress and shoulder jacket. Sarina wore pants, a shimmering black sequined blouse and half jacket in silk. We applied makeup to each other, me red lipstick, hers black. We both avoided the heavy Goth eye makeup. By the time we were ready, I felt quite excited about the night at the Club. Sarina had arranged for my car to be brought down to her place, it made sense as I wasn't home much. She let me drive to out to the Imperial Highway, stating if I drank too much, she was quite capable of driving us home.

Parking in the lot not far from LAX, much to Sarina's protests, she would have happily paid for valet parking; we walked hand in hand towards the club. Two beautiful women turned heads; we didn't make the usual cliché gay couple, so we got a fair share of frowns, and head shakes as well. We arrived at the club just before midnight, paid our way in and found seats by the long central stage. Men gave us glances, and I could almost hear the cogs of their minds turning, struggling with the image. This close to the stage meant up close and personal. I wasn't sure I wanted to get that close. I followed Sarina's lead, ordering champagne cocktails and settling back for the show.

The place teemed with men. Business types, young men out for a thrill and the sleazy types that gave me the jitters just looking at them. It was a strip club after all, what did I expect? The music fired up; the intro was made, all flowery talk and spin playing up to the crowd. I looked to Sarina. She smiled. Tonight, was for me. A young woman, she looked barely out of her teens, pranced the stage, occasionally swinging on the pole at the end. She started in a small bra and even smaller panties, which I thought she looked quite good in. In a short time, everything was off, and she was showing off her vagina like it was a new Christmas present. Twice she splayed her legs before me and gave me a good look at her womanly bits. Call me old school, call me what you like, I didn't like the shaved look; it removed some of the imagination and allure. I didn't find any of the acts titillating, or remotely sexual, for me, they held more amusement than anything else. I found myself having fun in a place I would never have ventured before.

The night wore on with copious cocktails, cheering men and a bevvy of naked women of the beautiful kind. It was fun, nothing that would excite me as it seemed to excite the men. Later, as the crowd thinned, Sarina bought me a lap dance, thirty-five dollars for the full nude, which put me even more up close and personal. The woman was attractive, young and quite skilled in her moves. Again, I found I wasn't the type to find such things stimulating. By three I felt tired of the same routines and wriggling bits, and I think I'd seen enough vaginas to last me a lifetime. Under the watchful eyes of the male audience, Sarina and I called it a night. I knew what I preferred to be looking at anyway. The time had released the days mental anguish and tension, the bevvy of beauties did serve a purpose and allowed me to drift away from the real world for a few hours. Even though I didn't find the dancing exciting I did find many of the dancers very fit and beautiful, Sarina had filled my night with beauty, and for that I was thankful.

Chapter 24

The Prelŭstitel

It was easy to blend in with the walls of the club. Most of the lighting pointed to the stage, its dimness designed to hide the wrinkles some of the not-so-young women displayed. The music lifted the spirits of the patrons, its ringing volume more an annoyance than stimulation. Women danced, swung on a pole and stripped naked. If desire still existed somewhere within me, it didn't feel the need to explore this world of lights and flesh.

Sarina watched the stage, smiling and drinking as spread legs played out in front of her. This world of hers no longer registered in the darkness. What I could see was inside the men scattered about the room. Seething inkiness, black lusts and thoughts depraved to the point of Aza'zel himself. What would an Uttuku want in such a place? What did Sarina see that I could not? Was all this for Cassandra's benefit? I didn't see this when I touched her mind, although it did work in a hazardous fashion. Her desires could have been mixed, hidden inside the mess.

I shifted between the men enjoying women dancing just for them. Breasts were shoved into their faces, but they couldn't touch, dare not touch for fear of retribution from one of the sizeable protectors. I flowed with two women leading men backstage for more personal attention: subdued light, deeper shadows, quietness. The men occupied booths at opposite ends of the private arena of flesh. I had chosen well.

The woman slow danced, the man, arms stretched across the high-backed booth watched and licked his lips, eyes raping the woman with every move. His darkness ran thick. He was ready. I slid into the booth beside him. The woman, now naked, bent over and mock-played with herself. The man blinked. I thrust my hand through his chest and ripped his life of his heart free, the darkness rushed into me with his deep groan. She woman continued to dance, the man, empty of everything that had made him real, stared on. I squeezed his heart between my fist until black dust flowed between my fingers. It felt good, rich.

I stood and calmly walked from the room. The woman would finish her parade, and the man would be thrown out as if drunk. In his chest, the shell of a heart still beat. It would stop with time and then Aza'zel would take his human stain from the Earth. Merging back into the wall to the left of the stage I watched a beautiful woman dance for the women. Her face reminded me of something; her light was strong, stronger than it had a right to be. Two bodyguards escorted the empty from the club. I also took my leave. Sarina and Cassandra had left, I could catch up later. I wanted to walk into the lights of clubs and enjoy the play of colours. The man's life gave me energy I could burn, and I didn't want to waste it sitting and watching.

Into the hum of the city, I shifted, along with the throng of lives searching for something that didn't exist - love, lust, or a combination of both? The men certainly harboured these desires, the women much softer wishes. Sarina and Cassandra were close now, were they close enough? My dream cast had still not found root. When it did, I would be sure the time was right.

Chapter 25

Cassandra

The night was warmish, heavily clouded and dark. A mere smudge of the moon looked down on us as we made our way back to the car. The thump, thump, thump of the nightclub music punctuated the air. I was glad to be away from the club, and away from the gangs that lurked in its darkened corners. Sarina held my hand as we walked towards the car, isolated in the lot. I felt good, confident and at ease with her. The strip club had done it job, and I felt I could sleep better without several nightcaps.

"Someone's following us," Sarina said, gripping my hand. I went to look behind. "Don't look, just get the keys out so we can get in the car before they get to us."

"They?"

"A gang, by the sounds of it." We quickened our steps, heels clicking on the pavement.

The sound of running came from behind. I turned. A group of young men were running towards us. It looked like an Asian gang, in the poor light I couldn't tell for sure. Sarina pulled me forward; we started to run. The men were yelling, laughing, running. We got to the car. I couldn't get my keys into the door. My fingers didn't work. Hands shook. I was grabbed from behind and dragged to the rear of the car and thrown, pinned against the trunk. I could see Sarina standing at the passenger side of the car with four men surrounding her. The men had knives. I felt the blade of my attackers against my throat.

"Fucking dykes," one of the men said as he pressed the knife harder against me. I recognised him from the club. I couldn't escape. I wanted to scream. But the knife.

"We'll do the young one first," a man in Yankees baseball cap said, as three of the men near Sarina pounced.

"No!" I managed. The men holding me yanked my arms back. It hurt.

Sarina struck out. The first man was flung across the lot, his body flailing. The other three grabbed her arms, pinning her to the side of the car.

"Fucking bitch," the man stumbled back, blood streaming from his nose. "We'll cut you so bad no one will want to fuck you." He raised his knife and slashed, striking Sarina across the face. She didn't make a sound. Blood ran down her cheek. The men laughed. "Drag her here," he yelled to the two holding me. I struggled. They were too strong; I was too weak. "She can watch what we are going to do to her. Feel a real man inside you, eh!"

Sarina twitched her shoulder, a quick move. She grabbed one of the men, a flash of light and he slid across the pavement away from her. It was fast. Silent.

The bloody-nosed man lunged, driving his knife into Sarina's stomach. She kicked up, knee striking him in the balls, he lifted off the ground and flew back a few feet to lay screaming on the ground. The men holding me let go and raced at Sarina. I ran to help. I was pushed to the down. She lashed out an another, again bright light again a body sent flying. The other attackers jumped away.

"Fucking Kung Fu pussy licker," he said. Sarina turned and kicked one of my two attackers in the head. He cried out as he went down. The second threw himself at her, knocking her down. I froze. This was it. I wanted to scream for help. My voice caught. I couldn't breathe. Sarina moved swiftly. Grab, light flash, grab, light flash. It was over in a moment. Sarina was on her knees, blood everywhere, her blood. The men lay unconscious about the lot: all but the one she'd kneed in the balls.

Sarin walked slowly over to him, sent out a sudden flash of light and he fell still. She took his knife and drove it into his leg. He didn't react. "That real enough?" she said, spitting on the man.

I couldn't move, breathe, think. She yanked me to my feet. I stared at her, the blood across her cheek, on her chin.

"We have to get out of here," she said. I felt cold. She dragged me to the passenger's side of the car. She climbed in the driver's side, unlocked my door and pushed it open. "Get in." I stared at the door. "Get in!" she yelled. I climbed in and closed the door. Pain stung my face. She'd slapped me.

"Why'd you do that?" I felt hollow, voice dull, empty.

"Seatbelt." She started the car.

I buckled up as she hit reverse, driving over one of the men. Sarina dumped my handbag in my lap. Blood flowed from her stomach. Blood, so much blood. She looked down at the knife sticking out of her stomach.

"Ruined a good dress, bastard." She pulled the knife out and dumped it in the back seat. She drove us home. The cold grew worse. I was sweating and felt cold. We had to get back to the W Imperial back, to the San Diego Freeway to Venice Boulevard. Once on Abbott Kinney, I started to notice where I was and how far we had to go, Main Street would lead us back to Sarina's. She turned right just after Westminster Elementary, and for the first time, I felt I could breathe.

"I feel sick." To my ears, I sounded like a little girl again.

"Hang on; another twenty minutes, and we'll be home. Just hang on."

Sarina parked in her space under the building then pulled me along after her and into the lift and the apartment. The door securely bolted, became a protective wall. I was shivering. Shock. I turned to Sarina, her face bloody, red rivers running down her neck. The front of her dress was wet; blood dripped from the hem.

"We have to stop the bleeding," I managed to say, breaking out of my numbness.

"Don't worry about it," she said, taking my face in her hands. "How are you?" I must have been crying because she wiped my eyes with her thumbs. "You're safe now. You're safe."

"But the blood, the knife, you're hurt."

"It's okay, trust me it's okay. The important thing is you are safe."

I didn't feel safe. Sarina gave me some tablets and made me wash them down with water. She led me into the bathroom and turned on the shower.

"The water will relax you," she said, helping me undress. I could help but see the blood still dripping from her face, the stain shiny on the front of her dress. Gently she guided me in and under the warm stream. I just stood there, the water hitting my face, getting in my eyes. I felt light headed and put my hands out on the tiles above the taps. I tilted my head down until the water ran over my back. I cried. I cried hard. I could have been raped. I could have been dead. I kept seeing images of the men, seeing them attacking me, stripping me, raping me. It didn't happen that way, though it could have. My knees wobbled, it was hard to stand. I shook with deep sobs. My mind replaying the scene over and over. The blood, so much blood. Sarina was hurt, and I didn't know what to do, she needed a doctor. I went to turn off the taps. I had to help her.

The shower door opened, and Sarina stepped in. I threw my arms around her. Sobbing harder. She held me, pulled me in tight. I buried my face in her shoulder; water flooded my eyes.

"It's okay," she said, stroking my head. "It's going to be okay."

I pushed back, looking down, blood was washing from between her breasts, her belly. "We need to get you to a doctor," I said, barely managing to get the words out.

Sarina rubbed her hand over the wounds, the blood sliding from her body. There was no wound; skin intact, perfect. I looked to her bloodied face, no scar across her cheek, it was as if she hadn't been cut at all. It was too much; I couldn't deal with it. I burst into tears again, audible crying. I howled into her chest.

"I could have been raped."

"But you weren't," Sarina said, holding me, running her hands down my back. "Nothing happened to you."

"But I could have been if you hadn't been there. If I was alone..."

"You're okay, Cassandra. You're fine." Sarina turned the water off and helped me from the shower and into a black towelling robe. She led me into the front room. I collapsed onto the sofa. She pushed a full half glass of whiskey into my hands, then, wearing a robe of her own, sat on the coffee table in front of me. Her hands were on my knees. I couldn't get the images of the men to go away. I couldn't stop crying.

"Just try and relax." Sarina rubbed my knee like a mother rubs a child's skin to drive away pain. "Have a drink and relax. It's over now. We're safe."

"How can I relax!" I screamed. "We were just attacked. You were stabbed." I gulped some of my drink, spluttered and gulped again. "I've never been attacked before."

"I know how you feel..."

"You don't know how I fucking feel." It came out cruel, but I didn't intend it to.

"They stabbed me."

"But you aren't even fucking human."

That hurt. I saw it and knew I shouldn't have screamed at her; it wasn't her fault. She didn't react or counter my outburst. Instead more booze was poured and another pat on the knee. Opting for silence while I ranted seemed to calm me faster.

Sarina helped me lie down. I stared back at her perfect face, her unmarred face. She sat quietly, letting me deal with what had happened, making sure I wasn't alone when the tears started up again. I couldn't speak. The hadn't calmed, my stomach felt knotted and tight. I wanted to vomit, fought it back, let the nausea pass. We just sat there staring at each other. The black of the room closed around me, tried to swallow me as anguish at what could have happened created unwanted visions in my head. I wanted to scream, drive them out.

"Eighteen ten," Sarina said after a long silence.

"Eighteen ten what?" I managed, voice a little crackly.

"Rio de Janeiro, November 12, 1810, I was raped." Sarina didn't look at me. "Romero Sanchez gagged me, tied me to a bed and raped me."

"I'm sorry." I didn't know what else to say.

"He stabbed me twenty times before leaving me for dead. I swore never to let it happen again. I'd always been careful with whom I selected to feed from, but I was struggling, desperate for light," her voice just above a whisper. "I can fight off any attack if I see it coming, sometimes I can even kill with a single blow, but I wasn't trained to fight or to defend myself properly." She sighed. "I do know how you feel."

"Did you report the rape to the police?" I lifted myself on my elbow.

"I tracked him down and cut his throat," Sarina said blandly. "He's just another unsolved crime from that time."

"Is that why you don't like men?"

"No, for a time I hated them, thought of them as less than animals, but Bela's personage showed me true dignity, honour and the good that can come from men. That is why he of all the men I have known is of great importance." She sighed and brushed the back of her fingers over my brow. "I don't view them as I used to." Sarina's chest heaved with a heavy sigh; she looked tired. I felt tired. "Aza'zel prefers the representation of the male, and for that period I understood why. Men are responsible for the biggest atrocities throughout history; it makes sense he should find the greatest darkness within them."

"I thought it was religion that drove atrocities."

"An excuse. If religion was the cause then why didn't women also murder and rape, destroy everything in their path?" It did make some sense. "Men have used whatever excuse available to carry out their darkest desires; in this, I understand Aza'zel's manifestation."

"And watching Bela changed this for you?"

"Bela was a soldier, fought in a war that started with the death of my close friend Franz. To me, the man I saw, he came back wiser, like many men who returned. I saw the change and reconsidered my view. Wars were not fought by men they were fought by armies, an entity vastly different from that of the individual. There is good in men; I think it takes a good woman to bring it out."

Rubbing my face to push back my weariness, I couldn't see the good in those who attacked us — the pure hatred in the actions. I knew good men, Li, and even Gary at the writers' group with his up-front manner, but it still couldn't undo what had just happened.

"I felt defenceless tonight, useless; I couldn't even help you." My voice sounded mechanical. I was drained, drained and fretful.

"I can teach you how not to be. First, we have to sort some business." She stood. "It's been a tough night all around. Come on, let's go to bed." She helped me up. We cleaned our teeth and held each other on the bed. Our gowns giving me a semblance of protection against the dreams that I knew would come. I would have liked to cut those men's throats.

I couldn't sleep. I left Sarina in bed, her breathing slow and deep. I wondered what type of dreams she would have after five hundred years of life. Maybe she didn't dream. I stood at the window, lights off, looking down on the ocean and the pier. In the lights running out into the water, I could see the rain, sweeping across the view. The window, wet with sliding drops showed just how I felt. In another time the view might have been beautiful, now it looked grim and depressing. I stared into the darkened region near the pylons. Was he there, watching? Did he ever sleep? I felt old and tired, and I looked much older than the eternally beautiful Sarina. What did she see in me? Or was it just circumstance that kept us together.

Seeing Sarina shouldn't have been a shock. She'd told me about it, but seeing it, experiencing it myself put the whole idea into a new light. This woman I liked couldn't die, not easily anyway. How long would I have with her before I became too old? This evening there were no bobbing boat lights, even the hardiest of fishermen wouldn't chance such choppy conditions. The night drew me in, sucked on the negativity I felt, multiplied it and drove it deeper into my heart. I thought of my father, and what he might have done if I told him I'd been attacked, nearly raped. Would he have held me like Sarina had done? Would he have said 'everything was going to be all right' to his baby girl? For now, I convinced myself he would have. I still loved him even if he didn't love me. I had wanted to call him so many times. To visit him and sit down over a cup of coffee and catch up with life.

"Can't sleep?" Sarina said, coming up behind. She put her arms about my waist.

"Bad dreams."

"Come back to bed." She kissed the back of my head. "We have a lot to do later this morning and you need your rest."

"How did it feel getting stabbed?" I touched the back of her hand.

"It hurt. I might heal fast, but I still feel pain."

"Does your mind heal the same way?"

"Do the bad thoughts go away?" Her head pressed into the back of mine. "No."

"How do you deal with the memories, the horrors you've been through?"

"Pretty much the same way you would, I guess." She turned me around. I looked up into her face, eyes bright, smile gentle. "Sometimes the light I feed on helps me heal mentally. If it's a good light, good energy." She kissed my forehead. "Someone like you."

I rested against her, taking in her clean scented soap smell. Her arms draped about me like a comfortable blanket. I could hear the rain against the window and thought I could hear the buffeting of the wind; the buffeting my life was taking. I had to take some control back from the craziness. Last night I'd frozen in place, emotionally spent and mentally numb. Before getting involved with the Sanchez incident, before meeting Sarina I was in firm control of my life. I knew where I was going and what to do to get there. Right now, wrapped in Sarina's arms, I was struggling to hold it together.

I started to cry again, softly. I didn't know why. I knew it wasn't the attack, and wasn't about the book, or about Zeek. I felt like this before going onto anti-depressants, when life looked more desperate and everything was too much to deal with. I really wanted everything to just go away, to be better. I knew what would make me feel better, make Sarina feel better.

"It's time to give you some light."

Chapter 26

The Prelǔstitel

"They were attacked," I told him as he looked down on the bodies. The lot was in darkness. I made sure we were alone.

"Were they hurt?"

"Sarina was stabbed, Cassandra untouched." If they had got into real trouble, I would have stepped in. It would have been difficult being so close to an Uttuku, but I still had something of the old me inside.

"This could have ruined everything." He hovered over the six unconscious men.

"Their darkness is thick." I could have taken them; only I needed to give him something to show my focus remained.

He knelt beside the first man, dragged his hand through the man's head, taking absorbing his darkness and light. The body twitched for a moment then stilled, the black mist of his darkness flowed into him.

"He was the one, the instigator."

"The others?" I said as he stood.

Snaking black arms erupted from his chest, each tendril plunging into the remaining five. The men convulsed, the tendrils ripped from their bodies, they fell still. A shifting shadow growing darker with the feed. He backed away, turned to me.

"They are gone."

"I believe the book will soon be ours. Mariz's connection with Cassandra has led me to another woman." I needed to offer something for my labours.

"I know."

"Then why can't I get it? Take it back now?"

"The path has been laid; you must walk this path."

"Why?" The touch of cold through me.

"Trust me," he said. He looked to the men on the ground. "We cannot afford to have these men found empty. Mark them in human death, a bloody murder perhaps." He stepped back into the night and was gone.

I pulled the knife free of the bigger man's leg. I knew she'd stabbed him because she remembered her past. I was surprised she didn't cut his throat. This would be messy, but necessary. A gang fight, six dead, simple investigation, simpler headline. No one missed criminals. I knelt before the first man, raised the knife and began my work.

Chapter 27

Cassandra

Almost a week had passed before I managed to go outside the apartment. Sarina had taken from me daily, trying to draw away the horror of the attack. It worked, along with my medication and three bottles of George T Stagg. The black had closed around me, sheltered as well as entrapped me. This was my mood, my view of the world. I took the lift down. The reflection in the lift's glass wall showed just how dowdy I'd made myself, how unattractive I looked. Sarina was out, doing whatever she did during the day, and I had grown anxious about being trapped. I needed to see Beth, get her hard view of things, feel ignored yet accepted at the same time. Would she have seen me with Sarina at the party and would the association allow me to rant and rave, get the crap off my chest and out of my mind.

Tension was a weight on my shoulders, an aching neck and throbbing head made doing anything slow work. I tried deep breathing. And positive thinking, even running a mantra over in my mind; nothing worked. The fear sat real on my chest. I gasped, shook, felt weary and empty. I sat for several long minutes in the car before turning the ignition. It would be a reasonable drive to Beth's place. Midday traffic I could handle generally, but edgy, uptight? I didn't know if I could make it. Would I get half way and freeze up? Must call Sarina to come and get me? I had to do this. I had to.

Out on California Avenue and into the flow of traffic I felt better, more in control, driving helped steady my thoughts. It gave my mind something to do other than feel sorry for myself. I'd driven most of the way without even noticing, which would have usually bothered me, for now, I counted it as a blessing. Ten minutes of traffic holdups had me pulling into Beth's driveway a little flustered. A blue Audi sat in the drive. Beth had a visitor. I didn't want to leave. I'd made it all this way; I wasn't leaving without talking to her. I knocked on the door, the doorbell too much to handle in my fragile state.

Beth opened the door. "What?"

"Can I come in?" She turned away and walked further into the house. That was a yes.

I followed her down into the kitchen and into the mess of her life. Sitting at the table was the young woman who'd given me the lap dance at the strip club. She looked up at me, recognition in her face.

"Cassandra, isn't it?"

I looked to Beth. She shrugged and reached for the drink's cupboard. A bottle of whiskey was thumped onto the table, and a chair dragged out for me. My brand; had she been expecting me?

"Marie," Beth said, fishing a glass from the sink.

"Ah, we met last Saturday night." I sat. Marie didn't take her eyes off me.

"You at a strip club, then?" Beth poured a full measure for me. "Sarina must like you then."

"How'd you know?" This was getting weird. I downed the drink, shuddered and poured another.

"Ask Sarina," Marie said, her face pretty in the daylight, her voice soft, gentle and cultured.

"Why you here?" Beth sat, her chubby features wobbling as her rear hit the chair.

"I was attacked after the... near the strip club after the show," I blubbered. "I was nearly raped."

Marie touched my arm. Beth stared as normal. I didn't think she wanted to know, or just didn't care. I need that uncaring look of hers, the 'big deal' look that said just get on with it. Marie pulled a newspaper from the pile on the table and dropped it in front of me. The headline said it all.

GANG MEMBERS MURDERED IN STRIP CLUB LOT

This wasn't a coincidence. Sarina had blacked them out; she hadn't killed them. I read the first paragraph. The six men had been cut to pieces. The bloodied knife found at the scene.

"Fucking men." Beth looked pleased with the headline.

"You've got some pretty impressive friends," Marie said. The way she spoke sounded like she knew who had killed the gang.

Another whiskey stopped my hands from trembling. I immediately thought of Orlando; only Sarina had said he didn't kill, only took the darkness. Did he butcher the men because of what they tried to do?

I told them what had happened, Marie listening intently, Beth grunted when she felt the need. I didn't mention Sarina had been stabbed, only that she'd fought them off. Beth didn't explain how she came to know Sarina and I didn't push it. Two hours of crying and blabbering about the attack gave me a sense of release. Sarina had helped me, but she was too close, was involved, and for some reason, I just needed to tell someone who didn't care. Beth didn't care one bit, shrugged it off as if I'd just told her a traffic light had changed. I asked Marie how she knew Beth. All she would say was that they were old friends. Marie didn't do the Goth thing, was too busy dancing and stripping to attend the parties and gatherings. I found myself liking her, and it did feel a little odd at having had my face between her breasts, and vagina thrust into my private space. How do you see eye to eye with someone you have seen in positions better left in bedrooms?

"You done?" Beth said.

"Yeah, I suppose I am."

Beth looked at her watch, a bulky black studded band with an ornate face. We sat in silence as they waited for something. I poured another drink and thought about leaving. I'd said my bit, and the non-caring from Beth helped put everything into skewed perspective. The death of the gang, though shocking, felt good. I don't know how the law would view it, it was right they should get what they deserved. I drank my glass, gave Beth a thank you look and readied to leave. I heard the front door open and close, the click of heals echoed down the hallway towards us. Did Beth have a live-in lover? It would be surprising considering how much of a disorganized slob she was.

I watched the doorway. Sarina walked into the room.

"Ladies," she said. I didn't know what to say or think.

Sarina walked around Marie, bent slightly and kissed me on the cheek. I mouthed 'what's going on'. She moved to Beth and offered a sign with her fingers; Beth bowed slightly.

"It is good to have us all together for a change," she said. "I know you and Beth are familiar, but Marie you've only just met, briefly and, well, in a different light." She stood behind me, both hands on my shoulders, a calming action. I wasn't feeling all that calm.

"How do you know each other?" I managed to say, wishing my glass was filled. "Don't tell me you are all Uttuku?"

Beth grunted an animal sound.

"Marie is," Sarina said. "Beth is a Bruxsa."

"A what?" The booze softened the blow, but only just.

"A being even older than Uttuku."

Oh, I needed a drink now. Beth smiled, all razor teeth bared, her eyes turned black. I shifted away, the chair scraping over the floor. "What the fuck!"

"Now, now," Sarina said. Beth changed back into the chubby woman I knew. Sarina squeezed my shoulders tighter.

"I told you, you should have let me eat her." Beth's tone became malicious. "Wouldn't have this problem now, would you."

"Beth is Bethra, who I met in Germany in 1918, she usually travels with me and keeps her ear to the ground through the Goth and subculture networks." Sarina patted my shoulder. "She is quite lovely once you get to know her."

"Whatever." Beth shrugged.

I'd known Beth for years, this was too much to put together, too strange, and I was just way too drunk.

I looked to Marie, pretty and young. She smiled and blushed.

"Marie, of course, is of noble birth. We met in France in 1773 and became close friends."

Marie didn't look any older than twenty-five; like Sarina, her flawless skin and bright eyes were a vision of youth.

"This, Cassandra Whitehall, is Marie Antoinette."

"Let them eat cake," Marie laughed as she slapped Sarina on the backside.

"In joke," Sarina said. "Paris had no bread if the truth be known."

"Quite unfortunate. Luckily Sarina and I baked loaves in secret so the servants could deliver them to those who supported Louis." Marie cringed. "What a complete French prick he was."

They laughed; I didn't get it. Things were getting out of control. This time I drank the whiskey straight from the bottle. Who could think about what might have happened last week to what was happening? I blinked away the burning sensation in my throat and looked straight at Sarina. She knew what I was thinking.

"She was beheaded," Sarina said. Marie made a cutting motion across her throat. "I had some friends gather up her remains and get them to me quickly."

"Fortunately, the blade was sharp," Marie said. "What a mess it made of my dress."

Sarina put her hand on the young woman's shoulder. "I cut my wrist, and while holding her head where it was meant to be, I dribbled blood over the wound. Two hours I stood there, by the time she opened her eyes I was ready to drop."

"But people saw you die; they buried you?" I'd studied a little French history at school. I took another swig. I must have been plastered. Here I was talking to Marie Antoinette, who worked as a stripper. What next. What fucking next.

"I had doubles." Marie shrugged. "Once your head was off no one looked too closely." She gripped Sarina's hand. "I owe this girl my life, or is that death?"

Sarina took the last chair in the room, shoving everything off the table and onto the floor, including my bottle and glass. Beth didn't move to pick it up, and I felt a little too woozy to reach down.

"Cassandra has a problem," Sarina said.

"Obviously," Beth grunted. "Fucking drunk if you ask me. Not worth the blood in her veins."

I'd thought of Beth as a kind of friend; after what I'd seen I didn't know what to think.

"Aza'zel?" Marie said.

"Oh, him." Beth chuckled. "My mistake."

"If he's after you, then I can't see what we can do." Marie put her hands on the table, a final gesture.

"It might not be her specifically." Sarina frowned. "He wants a book, a book Cassandra once had."

"Not that thing again." Sarina looked at Beth. "She told me about it. I didn't listen. Back then I thought it a typical dumb human thing to do."

I hadn't told Sarina I'd spoken to Beth about the book's return to Mariz's place. She raised her eyebrows. It was clear luck had been on my side. I hated to think if who I told wasn't a friend of Sarina's.

"Give the book back, simple," Marie said, leaning forward, elbows on the table.

"Problem one." Sarina sounded all business. "She doesn't have it, and the person we know has it won't part with it unless we pay her a hundred grand."

"You're kidding. Who does she think she is, the Queen?" Marie said. I smiled at that. It was funny or was it because I was drunk, it didn't matter, I was sitting in a kitchen talking to Marie Antoinette, how fucked up is that.

"Tell me who she is, and I'll get it for free," Beth said. "She will tell me as I rip her heart from her chest."

"No, Beth. This isn't Portugal; the mess will create other problems we have to avoid. There is another problem. She has a Prelŭstitel after her."

"Fuck!" Marie whispered. Precisely, I thought. "Which one?"

"Who?"

Sarina sat back in her chair and looked at Beth. "Mine."

The two women nodded with knowing.

"How many of you are in Santa Monica?" I asked. The booze was talking. "You two and... and her."

Marie and Beth looked to Sarina. This wasn't something they usually spoke about. Sarina signalled something with her fingers, and the two looked back to me.

"We think about twenty or so." Sarina bit her lip. She was lying. I could feel it.

"How many you know of?" Yes, the book was important, but so too was knowing what shit I was in.

"I know seven," she said. "The others are just guesses based on typical Uttuku movements."

"They get around." Beth groaned. Her boredom worried me. "There's only me here. Let's just say our feeding is more obvious and my kind aren't all that friendly to each other." She winked. "Predators are like that."

The next hour drifted away and into wild fantasy while they discussed how to get the book back and protect me at the same time. I recovered the bottle and resumed my very quick decline into oblivion. It was the protecting me part that kept tripping them up. Marie suggested I lure Aza'zel to the person's house and let him deal with the problem. Beth agreed and added that if he killed her, it would save a lot of problems. She looked at me, and I saw in her eyes my death would also be preferable. The idea had merit. Sarina didn't agree. Aza'zel could take Samantha without ever getting the actual book; then I'd be in a harder position that I already was. How much harder could it get, I wondered. Death seemed pretty final to me.

I listened as the three planned and unplanned, ran through possible scenarios, found solutions that ended up creating extra problems. I considered raiding Beth's cabinet for something else to drink. I still couldn't believe I was sitting next to the one-time Queen of France, and I'd seen her in all her glory. I wondered if King Louis had been as close as I had? Why did the Marie work as a stripper? Surely there were other ways to make a living as an Uttuku. Sarina had a companies and nightclubs, Beth, as I learned, had a string of wealthy marriages and lucrative divorces that didn't go through the courts. She sucked the men dry in the true sense of the meaning.

The attack last week, the reason I'd come to see Beth in the first place, the emotional trauma simply got crunched under the weight of my immediate plight. Beth, a Bruxsa, I would never have believed it, given the other two were so beautiful. Apparently, Beth's size had to do with her feeding, when well fed she looked bloated. She could look beautiful when she needed to lure her prey. To me, Beth sounded every bit as dangerous as Orlando.

The three agreed on a plan, one of them would always be with me. It came with risks, not only to me but to them. I could still end up dead, as they put it. "There are worse things," Beth had offered with one of her sharp-toothed and open-mouthed hisses. "Even worse things than me."

Feeling somewhat more relaxed and far less stable on my feet than when I arrived, we left Beth and Marie to their own devices. When down, shopping usually lifts my spirits, when quite plastered shopping was about the only thing, I was capable of, and I hadn't done any since meeting Sarina. I didn't want to go back to Sarina's yet, and I was tired of wearing her black clothes. She didn't put up much of an argument, so we went shopping. I needed underwear to call my own, even if Sarina had drawers and drawers of new stuff. At the Santa Monica Place Shopping Centre, crowded and smelling of body cheap perfume we found the lingerie store. I purchased bra and pantie sets, packs of plain black panties and even a couple of sports bras. The thought of running away from danger made it a wise choice. Sarina insisted on paying for the lot, over three hundred dollars' worth. We ate lunch at a health food cafe, which I didn't like, never really got into bean shoots and coloured lettuce. At least if Aza'zel took me, I'd be wearing clean underwear.

"We need to get back," Sarina said as we left the centre. The day turned cool, the sky heavy and grey.

"I could use a bath."

"That could be nice." She took my hand.

"By myself." I wanted to lay back and soak, not be stroked.

"Maybe later."

We walked hand in hand to the car. I liked holding her hand; it felt natural, comfortable, safe. The news of the gang's death did give me satisfaction, which felt wrong for some reason. I would have to deal with it all at some stage, right now I enjoyed the distraction, closeness and wobbly head drunkenness. Nothing mattered when I was plastered, nothing.

Sarina drove me back to the apartment.

I ran a bath, dark water in the black tub, stripped and sat on the edge running my hands through the hot water. California could be desert dry in summer and water an expensive commodity. Guilt about the excess bothered me right up until I slipped into the hot embrace of the bath. Worth every drop, I thought, letting tight muscles relax.

"Thought you might like a drink," Sarina walked into the bathroom. She held a glass of whiskey and a glass of wine for herself.

"Long day." I took the offered glass.

"They'll get longer."

"I know." I sipped the drink and closed my eyes.

"Marie and Beth are good friends, Cassandra," she said. "Beth might be a Bruxsa, but she won't let anything happen to you." She stood, back against the full-length wall mirror, watching me. Looking concerned, worried.

"Marie was a surprise." I meant it. Not every day you meet dead monarchy.

"We've lived in the same places together since her conversion." Sarina shrugged. "A constant familiar face makes adjusting easier. Besides we're both Austrian, understand each other."

"But a stripper, who would guess?"

"She's alarmingly attractive, why not show off?"

"Yeah, I suppose." Not something I'd do, no matter how good the pay. "But she's a Queen."

"We've all been other things through life." She toyed with her wine glass. "I fought in Vietnam, front line soldier."

"Women..."

"The other side."

"Oh."

"I better leave you to relax, enjoy the drink and don't fall asleep." She moved towards the door. "I'll check on you in about fifteen minutes."

"How many other famous people are like you?"

She laughed. "In Hollywood, there are more than a few. It is easy to act in a period part if you were living during that period."

"Any in government?"

"Now that is a secret I will not disclose."

Not that it mattered, because from what the women discussed there wasn't a lot any of them could do for me other than help get the book back. I would pay Samantha, get the book and hope Sarina's Prelüstitel just moved along and left alone. I could easily sell my house and get the money to pay Sarina back. The warmth of the water lulled me, allowed the miasma of muddled thoughts come up with a solution that made perfect sense. There was no place for pride where your life was concerned, so what if the bitch made an easy hundred grand, at least I'd still be alive.

I felt afraid, not the fear that had gripped me for the last few days, a different fear — the real notion of actually dying. I was still young, though of late a lot more disconnected from what I'd thought of as the real world, and I had a career, a good career.

"We'll go to the Goth Club later," Sarina said. "He won't bother us there."

"Tell me, what stops him from coming here?" I wondered if I was too drunk to go out. Goth Club sounded good though, hadn't been in a little while.

"Me." She left the bathroom.

As we drove down W Sunset Boulevard, I turned to see Mariz in the back seat staring at me. I screamed.

"He's here," I cried, my eyes fixed on the blue glow in the back. "He's here."

Sarina pulled over, unbuckled and reached for me.

"Cassandra." she shook me. He stared. "Cassandra."

"He's in the back seat!"

Still holding my arms, she turned to examine the back seat. She looked back to me. "You sure?"

"He's looking right at me! I don't have it!" I screamed, trying to break Sarina's grip. "You hear me; I don't have it." Mariz vanished. I stopped struggling and started bawling. Sarina got out of the car and came around my side. She opened the door and helped me out onto the grass of the footpath. She held me. Stroked my head and whispered things I didn't quite hear. I settled. Nerves shot, mind shunting thoughts about like a madman with a Rubik's cube. I found a semblance of safety in her arms; I let her hold me. I wanted everything to stop, and for the first time in a while, I thought of suicide.

"I think we have another problem, Cassandra," she said, pushing me back slightly so she could look down into my face. I wiped tears from my eyes. "I didn't see him."

"You must have. He was right there." I pointed into the car.

"I didn't see him," she said, being firm. "Aza'zel has let him go. He is outside of the darkness now; I can't see him anymore." I leaned my head into her shoulder. I didn't know what it meant, and by the sound of her, it wasn't a good thing. I wondered if I killed myself now would I find peace?

"I want to pay Samantha, buy the book back and give it to Orlando."

Sarina patted my back. "My thoughts exactly. For the moment, let's get away from the world, it has been a tough day, and you need something I can't give you."

141

The club was loud and crowded. Onlookers were everywhere, the standing table spots looking like misty bars in the haze of cigarette smoke. I sat in a large chair, one leg over the arm, a half bottle of Jack Daniels on the low table. No George T Stagg tonight, sold out. I hadn't been down in a while. I sipped whiskey, let it drown what remained of my thoughts, pickle the mush of my brain. Hieronymus Bosch crackled through the skin, stroked and tempered the mood. I'd requested Intravenous, the deadhead on the desk turned a pasty-faced stare at me; vacant, lifeless. I gave up talking to the gravestone and settled with my bottle.

Sarina looked to be making out with a young woman in black leather and a dog collar. For a moment jealousy crammed the neurons, created distorted sparks that squeezed my heart. I would have stormed out if I could walk. She ran long fingers across the girl's brow. The girl's eyes fluttered then closed, light flashed briefly about the girl's head. Sarina left her seemingly asleep on the couch. A mouthful of whiskey and the feelings bubbled away. Sarina stepped behind me, ran her fingers through my hair. Leaned over and kissed my forehead. Suicide looked good.

We'd spent a long time talking about Mariz as she drove to the strip, the reasons why she couldn't see him, and why he was now haunting me and not just the house. The ghost was free and for some reason started seeking me out wherever it pleased. She suggested going home to find out why I said getting completely hammered and forgetting about everything was preferable. For the moment I felt like I was living inside the pages of one of my novels, seeing the strangeness of my imaginations materialize and influence my life. Uttuku, Bruxas – whatever that was - possessed ghosts, Prelŭstitel's and dead famous people all with a neat romantic thread to hold it all together. I wanted to select all and delete, start a new page, a new story.

Goth Club didn't help; now the lookers could see my decline, witness the madness I'd fallen prey to. What did they see? What did they think?

"What are you fucking looking at?" I screamed to the crowd at the bar.

"Cassandra." Sarina pressed her lips to my ear. "We'd better go."

"What are they fucking looking at?" I threw my glass into the crowd; some stepped back, others laughed. They were laughing at me.

Sarina grabbed my hand; I tried to shake her free. She touched my head. I let the anguish wash away.

Chapter 28

The Prelŭstitel

Drawing all the lines together was proving difficult. Dealing with humans, though easy when you dominated, didn't work well when you tried to lead and gently influence. I had my plan, Aza'zel had his.

I sat out the day in a park. Unseen I watched, it felt good to watch the life light people displayed as they moved past. The brightness, the blinding brightness and the undercurrent dark was something I craved, needed and took whenever I wanted. Nothing could stop me. Aza'zel didn't understand the small spark of white still alive inside, perhaps didn't understand the ways of any of his Prelŭstitels, and I didn't understand his needs. What Sarina had and desired had no power over him, had no power at all. It was a symbol of the past, an effigy of a once powerful time.

What I wanted only had power if in the wrong hands and now it wasn't, and never would be. Need stemmed from a human desire, not mine. It would come, and I hoped it came sooner rather than later. Already Aza'zel had acted before time and undone work I had put in place.

A dog ran up to me, sniffed the air around something beyond its feeble sight. I saw no owner. I touched its head, felt the fur under my palm. It dropped, collapsed beside the seat. The small light enough to keep me sheltered in the day. I would need more, human more, for now, I was content. Later I would go to a retirement village, the light would still be strong, and the slipping away of a few lives could be accepted. Unlike my master, I was careful in my presence.

"Bruxsa," he said forming before me. "That woman is a Bruxsa."

They rarely ventured far from their home in Portugal. How did one end up here?

"That is why I could not find her in the night. She has no light. She is dead."

"How?" He controlled the darkness.

"An old race, far older than legend itself." He began pacing before me, an odd thing as he never showed human mannerisms. "Her force is strong, her darkness difficult to detect. She is why Sarina has been able to protect Cassandra. A protection that has been going on longer than your search for the book."

"I don't understand. How can she protect before she knew Cassandra needed protecting?"

A tree collapsed as if struck by lightning. The sound, a crack that echoed through the park, brought a host of onlookers.

"Act. Act now."

Chapter 29

Cassandra

Dr Sholan had called. I'd missed an appointment, and he was worried. He insisted I come to his office immediately. I didn't feel up to it, and w was still boozy; he'd smell it, comment and judge. He wouldn't let me go unless I agreed to see him and be at his office in forty minutes. Sarina also suggested it would be a good idea and encouraged me to clean up and go. She called a taxi, offered to go with me, I wanted to go alone. I felt dark, darker than any other time I'd seen him. Depression grew thick about me; I didn't want to do anything, nothing but drink and hide; suicide, sitting on top of the list of things to do, a real and foreseeable option. I'd already checked out what pills I had, and I thought I had enough to do a reasonable job

All the way to the office I stared out the cab window, trying to see the world but seeing nothing. Trees were a blur, people unreal in their puppet-mastered movements. Nothing was as it should be, even the sky, painted blue and dotted with clouds looked artificial. I paid the driver and staggered into Dr Sholan's office. He met me at the door, waiting impatiently.

"Please, Cassandra, sit," he said, leading me into his room. He took his seat behind the desk while I looked at my hands in my lap.

"How do you feel?" he asked — real concern in his voice.

"Bad."

"You've been drinking."

"Einstein!" I said a little too loudly. "I smell like a bar."

"Why?" he asked. "What has changed since we last met?"

I wanted to talk about the attempted rape, the threat of violence, the horror and fear. I wanted to tell him about Sarina, the five-hundred-year-old woman I was living with.

"Aza'zel wants me."

"Really." He leaned forward in his chair, elbows on the desk. "Depression can do that. What about the darkness within, why has it affected you so badly?"

Speaking and thinking weren't meshing well. He took Aza'zel the same way he took the term Black Dog, which in my mind was fine by me. I shouldn't have mentioned the supernatural. If I were Dr Sholan, I would have me certified on the spot. To make matters worse, I became attached to a demon woman, an Uttuku. The feelings should have been good, should have been the light in my life. Instead I felt like crap. I wanted to run away, hide, escape from the crazy world around me. I wanted to fucking die.

"I love my father," I blurted. Just came out, I didn't know why.

"Yes."

"He doesn't love me." I headed away from safe ground, onto bad ground, into bad memories. As bad as I felt about my life, going back to those memories was better than venturing into now. Besides, alcohol screwed stuff up.

"Why do you think your father doesn't love you?" He made a note.

"Because I'm a lesbian. Because he threw me out of his life."

"And your mother?"

"Drank herself to death, just like Granddad." I couldn't look at him.

"Did she know you were a lesbian?" His tone had become gentle, caring.

"If she did, she never said anything." I couldn't even remember if I told her. No one told my mother anything important because it always came back at you when she was drunk. She was a nasty drunk, real mean spirited.

"Did she love you?"

"My mother," I said, delivering the comment with all the contempt it deserved. I hoped my cold stare emphasised the point "She loved only one thing."

He made notes, nodding slightly as he wrote. I knew what he was thinking; I thought the same thing myself. I wasn't her, could never be her. I felt hot, the usually comforting room gave off a sense of unease, or was it the subject? Why was I even talking about it?

"What was your father's reaction when you told him about your sexuality?" His accent made sexuality sound exotic.

"He simply said get out and never come back."

"And did you?"

"I left. Tried to visit a few times but he wouldn't let me, wouldn't speak to me. He slammed the door in my face." I could feel tears.

"And your mother, could you speak with her?"

"No." It sounded final, and I meant it. "I hadn't been able to speak to her since I was twelve. I never knew what she'd be like when I got home from school, or from being at a friend's house. No one visited us because of her. One moment she'd be all happy and smiling the next a screaming maniac, then happy again, like nothing had happened."

"I see."

"You see fuck all." He didn't take offence. "She made life a misery at home. I couldn't bring friends around; Dad wouldn't come home from work until late, just hoping she'd passed out before he'd got back. I had to deal with her. I had to cook the meals she'd throw back at me." I wiped my face.

"We can stop now if you'd like?" he said.

"Why? You want to know what made me, why I am the way I am, don't you? This is what you fucking wanted wasn't it?"

"It's making you angry, upsetting you," he said gently. "My job isn't to upset you, Cassandra, it is to listen to you, talk to you and together work out how to deal with issues."

146

"Fucking issues," I spat. "My mother's dead, never once telling me she loved me. My father considers me dead, never to love his little girl again. How do I deal with that?"

"Do you have someone close you can talk to, be with?" he asked. "I prefer you be with a friend tonight, not by yourself. Or I could arrange for you to spend the night in hospital."

Sarina was all I had. Mariz didn't listen. "Yes," I said, calming slightly. "I know someone." If I went into hospital, I'd never be allowed out.

I was already living with Sarina, though I hadn't thought of it as anything permanent. She knew as much about me as Dr Sholan, and I did feel she showed real concern for me.

"I'm going to prescribe some Neulactil to help calm you and to help you sleep better at night," he said, scribbling on a pad. My GP entered details on a computer and printed a script, Sholan was a traditionalist, I was surprised he didn't use a fountain pen to write with. "I want you to take three a night for a while. We'll see how it goes, and later we might be able to stop this treatment."

More pills. I trusted him not to give me anything I didn't need. I also grasped the importance of taking the drugs. I had writing friends with bipolar depression who kept on stopping their medication when they felt better. What a mess. They crashed and crashed big time. I didn't want to take that road, I thought myself smarter than that, drunker at least. Besides, how big would my crash be if I wasn't already on drugs?

He handed me a box of tissues so I could wipe the tears away and blow my nose. He sat and watched, not speaking, letting me calm, settle the anxiety of opening up in an area I hadn't expected to. The stress of the last few weeks must have driven the stubbornness, the self-protectiveness into a corner, broken through the hardness I displayed. I looked up at the little man, softness in his face, concern in his eyes. I did feel better, not fantastic or even happy, just better than when I'd come in.

"Have you had any thoughts of harming yourself?" The way he asked it was gentle, not his usual probing manner at all.

I wanted to say yes, but the admission wouldn't help me or the situation. Besides, he would try and stop me, and if push came to shove, I didn't want to be stopped.

"No," I said handing back the tissue box. "I'll be fine now, thank you."

He stood, walked around his desk and offered his hand, helping me from the chair. I hugged him. At first, he seemed surprised, uncomfortable; then I felt a firm pat on the back.

"You're a good woman," he said, easing himself out of my arms. "We'll address issues together and learn how to best manage your depression. If that is fine with you?"

"Thanks, Doctor." Another wipe of the eyes. I left wondering just how much help the pills would give, and why he didn't pursue my problems further, it was his job after all. He made me call him every day for a week, and not to worry about what time I called. His receptionist gave me his mobile number. I doubted I'd call, but it was reassuring to know I did have someone to fall back on.

As I waited for a cab, I let the sounds of traffic lead me into a nothing place, a no feelings whatsoever state of mind. A gentle wind blew, the smell of exhaust suffocated everything else in the air and the feel of the wooden bus stop bench, rough. Age permeated everything, the buildings, the trees, the electricity poles. Nothing felt newly developed, which was odd considering the building was less than five minutes from downtown. Sarina would have been alive before this land had even seen people before the wildland had become home for Indians and a later refuge for settlers. How could a mind so full of history cope with so much change? I had a hard time dealing with every day, how do you adjust to hundreds of years?

I needed to get settled better with Sarina, establish a more permanent arrangement with her. I required some things first, things that were me, the person I was, small reminders that might keep me together. The taxi-cab arrived, the silver Prius showing someone was thinking of the environment. There was a time when I use to care about water conservation, sea conservation and beach care; I use to write letters to congressmen petitioning environmental issues. How many years ago was that? I might have a great career but how far have I fallen, how far?

Talking about my family wasn't what I wanted to talk about. Dr Sholan wanted to hear it, use it to help rebuild me I supposed, what I needed to get off my chest was the threat of death. Fearing death didn't enter it, the inevitability existed with everyone. I feared dying to a dark force beyond his, my comprehension. Sarina had told me, explained Aza'zel and Orlando clear enough, getting a picture in my mind just didn't come. I should see my father, talk to him, make him listen, tell him the danger that threatened the daughter he once loved. Would it change anything? Maybe not.

Chapter 30

The Prelüstitel

I let Mariz go. The man had proven useless on the most part. As I expected he would be. We had Cassandra Whitehall, and his small part had been done. I would let his essence find its way home and then Aza'zel would cast him like a rag into the *Abad*.

Light passed into me, darkness seeped from the woman's body like ooze, and I ladled it into my mouth. My need for feeding met, my hunger sated, I let the woman fall to the ground — a jogger out for a night run. I had to go into the heart of Los Angeles, into the lights, and I needed this woman's darkness. She would be found by morning, an empty body. It was sad; she would not be missed. I could still feel sadness sometimes; only it was usually reserved for myself. I had to exist by the way I'd chosen. I knew I had not chosen wisely.

I left her lying on the path beside children swing. I felt solid and ready; I had to arrange a meeting with Cassandra. I must use caution because if she fled, I might not be able to get to her again. She sounded scared, apprehensive and I knew I had only one chance.

He had given me a deadline to get the book back. Finally I could act. Three days, then he would do what he had to. I couldn't let him do that. Despite everything I wanted Sarina to live, and if I was right in my understanding, it was also important Cassandra not die, not be taken.

The street lights were bright, immediately some of my strength drained. The fight to protect me within my shell of darkness, I would need to use the greatest of my powers once we were together, that drew on my darkness, and of that there was plenty. The Strip was crowded with late nighters, the stink of humans filled the air, piss and car fumes, and the sound of this world troubled me. I preferred silence accompanied by the soft whimpering of dying. I would need another feeding before the night was out, and this time I would find someone who was filled with darkness, bubbling with anger, their darkness would be blazing, the wrong kind of light to have when a Prelüstitel is hungry. I would expend a lot of energy with Cassandra, more than I had in over fifty years. I had the power to do whatever I liked, to use it was costly. Perhaps this is why power-hungry Prelüstitels rarely lived beyond a century. I had other plans — power not one of them.

As I waited for the lights to change and let me cross Sunset Boulevard, I saw a gang of ten youths harassing a young woman as they walked past the cafe. Yes, a gang. Aza'zel had commented on their anger; he wanted more of them. Easy targets, retribution blamed for their deaths. After I'd got the information, I needed I would let them drag me into the shadows, allow a robbery. Then into his pit, I will lead.

149

Chapter 31

Cassandra

I returned to my home to get a few essentials. Sarina had purchased pretty much everything I needed; I wanted more personal items, photos, trinkets, things I had collected over the years. Standing in my front room, TV on and filling the world I'd known for ten years with the sounds of the mundane, I felt as if I were saying goodbye to the place. If Mariz didn't haunt my home, I would still be living there. I didn't know how long it would take to get him to leave, if ever. He wasn't there, the cold, absent, suggested he hadn't been there for some time. I hoped it would stay this way.

Somewhere nearby Beth offered her protection. An eagle, rare for area, stood in a tree in my back garden. Was it her? Or did she have power over animals? Whatever she was, it was good to have the protection.

I wanted to only take one bag and a box, so being selective over my things became a chore. There wasn't time to relive snapshots or places I'd visited; taking only the necessities meant hard choices. The day dragged on, and I'd only managed to pick a few things out of the mess. I'd have to stay the night, finish up in the morning. I called Sarina, let her know the plan. She didn't approve but accepted I had to do this; Beth would watch through the night. I told her what the doctor had said, and it was met with approval. The stay away, though important, posed a mental risk. Her concern was placated by me agreeing to come straight back to the apartment should he show himself. Once she was satisfied, I drove downtown, picked up a bottle of wine and a Subway roll. With a lot of luck, he wouldn't come to me tonight. Sleeping in my bed a pleasure waiting to be had.

The wine and roll barely lasted twenty minutes. Hunger satisfied and mind already pushed towards its usual state, I searched in the almost empty drinks cabinet. A bottle of whiskey, a ribbon around its neck, probably a gift from someone I'd forgotten, gave me some pleasure. It would do wonders for the sense of loss I felt. I'd packed one bag, and half-filled a box with stuff; all I wanted to take.

The phone was ringing. I turned to the clock beside the bed. One am. Only friends called at that hour. I picked up, the ringing making my head throb.

"Hello." I didn't feel receptive.

"Cassandra," the woman's voice said. "It's Sissy Falloe."

I hadn't spoken to her in years, not since the last anthology she invited me to contribute to.

"Sissy, good to hear your voice. How's things?" I managed to sit. Head pounding, mouth like glue.

"Good. This just came to me, and it couldn't wait. I have a new project I'd like you to write something for," she said. Straight to business. She usually thought of me when a new anthology made it into the works. I'd had a few short stories published in her books, all under pseudonyms, so my publisher didn't get all antsy with me.

"Life's a bit, well, crazy right now, but what's the project?" Crazy wasn't the half of it.

"I was sitting in the dark, just thinking, when an idea came to me." She sounded both excited and vague at the same time. Unusual for her. "The collection will be stories set in Austria, maybe even around the time of the death of Archduke Franz Ferdinand." I gulped if she didn't have my attention before she had it now.

"Why that period?" It was hard to keep the concern from my voice.

"Not sure really, it's just a strong thought. For some reason, I've also been thinking about Bela Lugosi, the Austrian connection, Royal family, intrigue." She always had good concepts, but this one?

"I'm pretty tied up for the moment," I said, feeling sick.

"It's still early days yet, have to sell it to a publisher first, but I think I could give you a lead time of at least six months. Will that be okay?"

"Thanks, Sissy," I said. I'd have to call Sarina. This was no coincidence. "Any plans to come to the coast?" We hadn't seen each other since a science fiction convention some years ago — nice lady, a bit shorter than me, and sported beautiful, long black hair.

"Not this year, how about you coming here, stay at my place for a few days. Hit the town, maybe."

"Right now I couldn't think of anything better to do. Maybe in the New Year. I have to come to New York for a book signing tour. Catch up then?"

"You're on. I've got a few more calls to make. For some reason, I felt you needed to be the first to know about the new book."

"Thanks, Sissy. Be in touch." I hung up, raced to the toilet and vomited. Had Aza'zel got to her as well?

Aza'zel had visited Sissy. Why? To find me? I dressed, stuffed my bag and box in the trunk of the car and headed back down to Sarina's. What had just happened? How did he know about Sissy Falloe? What the fuck was going on?

It took some time to calm down enough to tell Sarina about the phone call. It wasn't Sissy or the request. I got them often; it was how she got the idea and what it involved. It couldn't have been a coincidence the setting was almost directly associated with Sarina and the mention of Bela Lugosi. The dark forces were now using things around me to get to me, people I knew. I tried calling Samantha, but she didn't pick up or didn't want to. It was getting more desperate to get the book.

Sarina allowed me to ramble, spew thoughts out like a water cannon. I knew I wasn't making a lot of sense, knew I was saying stuff that didn't apply to what might be going on. It freaked me out, screwed with me. This was a major head-fuck, and I didn't like it. I ranted about Bela, about Mariz and his fraud, the slag, Samantha. Life looked crap. The days crappier. I screamed about my drunken mother, my father who didn't love me anymore, the depression and thoughts of suicide. Everything that existed in my head dropped over her like a blanket, a bright flowery blanket full of false joy, hatred and a child's desire to be loved. Nothing but sadness came out; I didn't make sense. I cried, yelled, screamed, abused Sarina for what she was and what I'd stepped into. I blamed her, abused her like a mad woman in a bar. There was dog shit on my shoes; I couldn't scrape it off, get rid of the smell. Demons, Uttuku, Prelüstitel, death, darkness, darkness, ever-increasing fucking darkness. Where were the candles of salvation? The light so many religions spoke about in the hour of need. Nothing, everything became a nightmare just waiting to find a home, a dream to invade and screw you over. Screw me over.

"Why now?" I screamed at Sarina. "Of all the times Sissy could call, why now?"

Sarina waited until I calmed, sat and let the last of my rage sink into the comfort of the chair. I didn't even know if I wanted an answer.

"The editor in New York wouldn't have known," she said. Her even, measured tone caused me to close my eyes, to think, to listen. "Aza'zel or even the Prelüstitel would have created a dream, he is capable and sent it to find someone who would contact you with its contents. The dream wouldn't have been for anyone specific; it would search the scape until it found something close to you. She was it."

"And the references. Austria, Bela?" My hands shook so much I couldn't get the drink to my lips.

"Probably drawn from within you as much as anything else. I doubt this Sissy would have even known what the call was about until she heard your voice, started speaking. This is a reminder of how close the threat is. There isn't much time to act."

I didn't feel any better, felt worse. I'd told Sarina about my life, the crap I'd hidden away, kept secret. I looked over at her, sitting demurely in the other chair. He hair, always shiny, always brushed, framed the young face I believed I was finally trusting. She looked so white amongst the black, the copper lighting creating a bloody shroud over our small piece of the world. I'd vented on her again, called her names, I'd become the crazy bitch I'd thought she was. I bore some of the blame. Mariz was mine; the book problem was mine, these were things Sarina had known nothing about. At the end of hours of releasing all I was on to her, I ended up with one conclusion. Whether we liked it or not, I was going to die.

"I can't get a hold of Samantha, and without her, I can't get the book."

"Well, I've got the money, in cash when you do."

Sarina filled my glass and watched as my shaking hand touched the glass against my equally trembling lips. In amongst the craziness, I felt I should have felt pleasure at being asked to write something for Sissy. To be a part of one of her projects was to be held in high regard; an honour many fought to achieve — a six-month deadline. If things didn't get any worse, I could maybe do it. I looked at Sarina, the woman who at five hundred years old was the most beautiful woman I'd ever laid eyes on; she wasn't even human. Demon, cemented in my psyche, just fit her so well. Six months. I could be dead in less than a week.

"Fuck it!" I said, pouring another glass down my throat. "Fuck the lot of it."

I'd drunk myself to sleep as usual, well, I think I did. I opened my eyes and was in bed. Naked, warm and as messed up as I'd ever been. I'd slept until noon. Sarina had gone out. Though I let her take from me occasionally, she would still need to take from others to keep her strength up. The clubs served a purpose, I now knew. Goth just fit in with her penchant for black. Goth fit in with how I felt, the abject isolation, and the look. The look guaranteed privacy when out. People looked at Goths, they didn't speak to them, which suited me just fine.

Dressed in track pants and singlet, sitting at the kitchen table, drawing rings in water on its surface, I accepted a battle was looming. One I couldn't fight and possibly win. I'd never felt helpless like I felt now. I could control nothing, influence nothing. What God do you call on when this happens?

I'd tried Samantha twice already and still no answer. I would have to call on her, break in and steal the book if I had to. I might be as miserable as all hell, but I came to one realisation last night. I didn't want to die, by my hand or any one's else's.

Sarina had left a bag of croissants on the kitchen bench, and surprisingly there was a block of cheese in the refrigerator. I ate and drank wine, letting the smell of grilled cheese and the vibrancy of its colour wash through me like a spring rain. Black inside black and about black was no place for hope. Cheese offered hope.

I didn't know the vineyard or vintage of the wine; only that is was red and rich. All of her bottles in the rack had no labels — black bottles in black racks in a black room. Easily missed when heavily intoxicated; I thought I'd work through the rack top to bottom, left to right. Might take a few days, but what the hell. If I didn't know I was dead what would it matter?

My mobile vibrated across the table. It didn't recognise the number; then the number didn't make all that much sense either. It showed on the screen as all nines.

"What," I said.

"Meet me at the Griddle Cafe on Sunset Boulevard tonight," the man's voice said.

"Who is this?"

"Return the book, and you will be safe. Meet me at eight, and we can discuss how to do this without bringing harm to yourself or Sarina."

"Orlando?"

"Don't be late." He hung up.

I called Sarina, the sound of her phone ringing in the bedroom left me alone. I couldn't contact her, tell her what Orlando wanted me to do. I had four hours to kill, and I wasn't going to do it drinking, or could I? If meeting with Orlando would bring an end to this nightmare, then I'd do it, sober if I had to. I had some questions of my own that needed answers. Four hours. If I fussed a bit, it should be plenty of time to get showered and changed and down to the strip. I ordered a taxi for seven. I wanted to write a note for Sarina; only there wasn't any paper in the place. I hadn't packed any in my computer case. I grabbed her phone from the bedside table and left a message in her diary. I left the phone open in the middle of the coffee table. The black phone was only just visible. I cut open a croissant, put half in the centre of the coffee table and the phone on top of that. It looked odd, but it had the effect I desired.

I sat in the Griddle Cafe. The place, all old wooden tables and chairs was, alive with the Friday night crowd. Coffee and food smells would have usually pleased me; only this wasn't a pleasant meeting. I sat in the centre of the cafe, couples and groups ate and talked around me. I felt protected and safe to a degree. Could this man take me without anyone seeing? It was a question I asked myself all the way into the city. It was a warm night for early November, and I'd opted for jeans and a light shirt and blue suede jacket. Tonight, wasn't a night to look attractive.

I toyed with my drink, they didn't serve alcohol, and the coke I ordered wasn't cutting it.

"Good evening," a man said, looking down at me. He was all in black, hair neatly cropped and stylish. "I believe you are waiting for me."

"Oh my God!" I couldn't believe it; I'd seen his picture. He was dead.

"I am flattered that you recognise me."

"You're…"

"Please, Cassandra. May I sit?" He removed his long coat. I couldn't speak. "Thank you." He took the seat opposite. He folded and placed his coat on the seat to his right.

Sitting in his presence the cafe seemed to fade away into insignificance, the noise became muted, and the strong scent of roses pressed about my face. It took a few breaths to settle myself, to concentrate.

"I have that effect on women," he said. The accent, minor, suggested culture and wealth. "I must admit, I am surprised that you came."

"She thinks you're dead." This couldn't be happening. "I think you're dead."

"I know I look like the person she might have shown you, but he is dead and not only to the world." His tone was gentle, like a father talking to his daughter.

The man, who looked to be in his late twenties, placed both hands flat on the table, then slowly moved them apart until he was able to grip the table's edges. I studied his face, the lack of lines around the eyes and lips, the paleness of his skin and the darkness of his eyes.

"Then who are you now?

"Someone of great age."

"Sarina called you Orlando." I wasn't feeling all that brave now.

"So that is what she calls me. If it helps, I am pleased." A smile, a genuine sign of pleasure, split his face. "It is good she has a new name for me." His teeth were small, whitish yellow and even. "Forgive me," he said, extending his right hand. "Let us start with formal introductions. I rarely have such meetings, you understand?" I didn't feel like taking his hand; I didn't want to be courteous.

His hand hovered over the table, his smile stayed fixed, and his eyes commanded the appropriate greetings be made.

"Cassandra," I said, lightly shaking his hand. The touch was cold, not cold, but winter skin cold.

"For you I am Blas," he said. "Don Blas de Lezo."

"But..."

He tilted his head like a dog listening to its master. "As I said, that part of me is dead. Only the name remains, and I am quite attached to it."

I held my breath. I knew what I was seeing, but my mind floundering. Was nothing real in this world?

Don Blas de Lezo was the first person in Sarina's album. The connection might have been made, but the shock and surprise were no less weakened. Was there a union between them? The crowd pressed in around us, the noise rose, drowning out the jumble of thoughts cramming my mind. How could he be here, be alive? Blas raised his hand; the place silenced immediately, all movement ceased. People sat or stood, stopped in mid-sentence, mid-action. A man pouring soft drink from a jug at the next table froze while filling a glass, drink spilt over the edge of the glass and across the table. Blas reached across the table and pushed my chin up, closing my mouth. He looked at the drink, pouring from the table to the floor.

"Always have a problem with liquids." He reached into his coat and pulled out a silver flask. He unscrewed the cap and handed it to me. "I think you need more than coca cola."

"You're dead." I downed the some of the flask. I felt warm inside. It was brandy. This wasn't happening.

"In a way, I am."

I was shaking; the cafe felt cold, the total silence unnerving.

"Aza'zel made me an offer, and I took it." Blas turned to one of the tables nearby and took a glass of water and placed it before me. "You will need this as well."

I didn't need to be encouraged. I drank more brandy. I choked and spluttered; it sent a sensation of warmth through me. The man, well groomed, looked far too young, younger than the man in the picture. He also had both eyes and arms. I sipped the water; it cleaned away the bite of the brandy.

"But Sarina?"

"She must never know," he said, his tone softened. "I could have asked her to help me once, but I'd made my deal. Aza'zel helped me recover. I couldn't bring myself to tell her. As I am now her light is too bright."

"Then why are you following her?" The question was hard to form in my mind and harder to ask.

"It wants something she has, my part of my deal is to get it back." Blas sounded grave. "I have been following her since I secretly aided her in getting something; watched out for her and protected her; trying to find a way in which to get what he wants."

"Do you love her?" I said, feeling my own emotions for her come under assault.

"Once perhaps. Never told her though, I doubt she even knew I noticed her. I was busy with war, fighting the English, I was foolish then." He straightened his cuffs, fussing about his appearance. "I am part of Aza'zel, Cassandra. I am a Prelŭstitel. I am here to protect the interests of the darkness, to keep its secrets secret." He paused. "Sarina is one of the most powerful Uttuku in the world. I am also to destroy her if possible. Understand I have no choice in this, what is commanded must be carried out."

"And you are telling me, why?" I thought of the evil overlord plots from trashy novels.

"I might not have a choice, but that does not mean others cannot take precautions." He smiled. Light and mischievous.

"Why the interest in me?"

"I was to kill you because you saw the book. The book I wrote about things that should not have been written about."

"The name on the manuscript, DBD. Why the Hungarian voice?"

"Don Blas de Lezo, that is simple. The man who translated the work from Spanish was Austrian." He said this with a flutter of his right hand as if flicking away a bug. "Mariz Sanchez stole the story and made it his own. I took his darkness before finding the manuscript." Blas took my hand. "I still do not

157

know where the book is, I did learn that you had seen it. No one can know that the book is not a fiction. It was a mistake of Uri's to think I wanted it edited."

"You killed Uri?" Was I next? Would the cafe come to life to find me dead at the table?

"No." He was firm. "I do not know who killed him. Uri was an old man who had served me well for many decades. I would never have harmed him. But Aza'zel would have; he didn't."

"Then who did?"

Blas shrugged. A comical look.

"Zeek? The boy under the bridge?"

"Aza'zel." He showed no expression. "He also discovered you had seen the book. I couldn't stop him. The boy? Well, Aza'zel takes; no reason. I am the same in such matters."

"What about Mariz, the ghost you control? The ghost that has been haunting me for the last few months?" I was getting more questions than answers. If Blas didn't kill Uri, then who did? Was there another killer for me to worry about?

"I have occupied the vessel that was Mariz. I wasn't able to track you through him; it was only when I wanted to know the woman Sarina had spent the night with that, I discovered your involvement with the book." He spoke slowly; time had been stilled. "Has she told you that I am a Prelŭstitel?"

"You are going to kill me, aren't you?" If this man could stop time, then I would have no hope of escape.

"Not at all." Blas sounded offended. "To do so would harm someone I care about. Used to care about."

"What do you mean?"

"Sarina is in love with you."

"And how do you know that?" She'd never told me as much.

"You remember her takings, her tasting of your life light?"

"Yes, what of it?"

"You share her apartment? Dine with her?" I nodded. "She has never done this before." He smiled.

"Never?" Deep down something changed in me. Sarina trusted me. I hadn't considered this fully before.

Blas leaned forward, elbows on the table. "And I think you love her."

Confronted with the suggestion, I went to deny it; he might have been right. I didn't know if I loved her. Though, the only reason I decided to have this meeting was to protect her.

"Can you get me the book?"

"Not right away. I do know who has it." I felt at ease. I wasn't going to die. "I have been trying to call the person who has it; she hasn't answered yet."

Blas closed his eyes, pressed his fingers to his brow. He took a deep breath; everything shimmered about us. His sigh felt like the groan of the wind through an old building. I shivered. Goosebumps sprang up on my skin. Cold. Cold embraced me. What was he doing? He looked up. Eyes no longer brown but black. Two shiny black balls turned on me.

"I'm sorry," he said. "It's the lights." He moved his chair back, turned to the woman sitting at the near table. Starting at her head his right hand disappeared into her skull, he dragged his hand down, through her neck, her back. A cloudy essence moved about his wrist. She came to life for a few seconds. Her body snapped rigid, relaxed, then snapped rigid again. Blas pulled his hand free, a stream of blackness, like smoke, flowed from her to him. Another deep sigh, only this time it penetrated me, rubbed against my heart. Pain shot through me. I grabbed my chest. I couldn't breathe.

Release.

I fell forward on the table, drawing hard breaths, sucking air into my lungs. Darkness had touched me. I saw its depth; I teetered on the edge of nothing.

Soft hands touched my face. Cool hands. Blas helped me up. His eyes were once again brown. I could see the woman behind him lying face down on the table. He'd fed from her, taken her darkness right in front of me.

"I almost slipped from the light," Blas said. "Sitting close to me you would have been touched by the edges of my influence, the strength of my feeding." He must have noticed my confusion. "If I hadn't fed immediately you would have been sucked clean of life; such is my power."

"Aza'zel?"

"He is this and much more."

"Why?" I rubbed my chest, the pain gone. "Why stay in the light?"

"I needed to be in the light to find you and the book; to stay close to Sarina, to watch over her." He folded his hands on the table. "I have three days to deliver the book, after then, he will take you, and there will be nothing to stop him. Once his darkness comes, it comes forever."

I didn't like the sound of that. Three days to get the book. Samantha had to answer the phone, had to take my call.

"What about the call from Sissy Falloe?" I asked. "What did it mean?"

"Who?"

"She's an editor in New York, she called me with an offer. Mentioned Bela Lugosi as inspiration."

"Ah, the dream." He looked pleased. "I don't know who received the dream. It was cast. The person who received it would know who you were, call; the action would remind you of my power. I am pleased this Sissy thinks the subject interesting. You know Sarina quite liked Lugosi?"

"Yes, but why bring Sissy into this? I already know how much danger I'm in."

"My reasons are for me. I believe things will be in order now. We have met, you understand the fullness of the situation."

"Is anyone else in danger?" Already too many people had died over the book.

"No, only one more will die if I don't get what I want, and they are very close to you." His image and politeness unnerved me, his calm even manner, gentle movement, belied the monster I knew he was.

I shook my head.

"As you are with Sarina most of the time, I had to find a way to..." He offered his even-toothed smile again. "Let us agree that what has been done is done."

"I need money to get the book, the person who has it wants to be paid. When she accepts the offer, I will have the book, how will I get it to you?"

He laughed. A high sound, unpleasant and grating. "Humans and money."

If she doesn't answer the phone or agree to see me, I don't know what else to do.

"If that happens, I might be able to help."

Why would he help me?

"I must go," he said. "Remember. The book. It will be the only thing to appease Aza'zel." He grabbed his coat from the chair and stood.

"I'll get it."

"I know you will. I think you also need to talk to Mariz." He slid into the coat. "Now free, I believe he has something to tell you."

"You know something?"

"Let me say I also require a sense of justice; justice that can only come from the living. He may tell you something for me. I can do a great many things but talking to the dead isn't one of them."

"I have three days." He nodded — not much time.

He walked around the table, placed his hand on the back of my chair and offered his hand. "Time to go. It would be better if you aren't here when time restarts." He indicated the woman.

I took his hand and allowed him to help me out of my chair. "Why don't you act? You seem to know more about what is going on than I do?" If he knew he had the answer, then why didn't he ask him? If he knew where the book was, why didn't he get it?

"For some reason, I am not able to." He stared me hard in the face. "And I am forced to use you." He led me from the cafe and out onto the street. Everything was still and silent. Someone stood, half exiting a taxi, pedestrians, mid-stride littered the sidewalk.

"How do I contact you?"

"You don't." Blas kissed the back of my hand. "I will visit you. I can be anywhere at any time if the need arises. I do not read minds, but I can read darkness and young lady, you have a lot of darkness." He licked his lips.

"You aren't going to kill me?" He shook his head, still holding my hand. "Until later then." In that moment he was gone.

Life erupted around me, the sounds of people talking, the sounds of the cafe, the traffic closed in. What had just happened? Someone screamed.

Chapter 32

The Prelŭstitel

The child played by a bronze statue. The sun was setting, the crowds of shoppers and workers on their way home thinning. At first, I sat on a bench just watching. The child ran his hands over the statues surface, the smile on his face enchanting. The child was happy, enraptured by the size of the thing before him. Children are so accepting of things; they don't question purpose or need, they enjoy and marvel at what is before them.

I shifted. Knelt beside the child and let him see me. He didn't look surprised or concerned. He just stopped stroking the statue and looked up at me.

"I like puppies," he said.

"So do I."

He looked like a mini adult in his blue jeans, boots and dark sweatshirt. The picture of a motorcycle was stencilled in white across the front. I touched the statue as well; it's metal cooling more with the approaching night. I couldn't see his parent, the guardian of such a small soul. I stroked his hair, felt the tiny rays of darkness within, let it reach to me; tickle my fingers. I dipped a finger through the back of his head, tasted the minute memories, the visions, savoured the emotions. His darkness, filled with colour and sound, brought yearning, the need to grasp his tiny spark and rip it free.

"I want a puppy when I grow up," he said, turning his attention to a woman walking a dog. "A puppy like that."

I could have taken him then and there, fed from his small shadow and saved myself part of the feeding later; a child's darkness is too small, unsatisfying. I felt something for this child.

Aza'zel fed from children. His presence at Beslan took many small lives. He could see when someone was about to die, knew when to take and not be noticed. The school that day didn't need much effort, nothing in the way of secrecy. I couldn't see death coming and was thankful in a way. I could create death, bring it early, snuff the light from a life like wet fingers around a candle flame. Looking at the small boy, I saw something. A vision from my childhood perhaps? Whatever it was it was enough to save his life.

If I had been in Beslan, I would have taken. The terrorists, yes, but not the children.

"Where is your mommy?" I asked the child.

He turned and pointed to a small store. A young woman holding a baby was looking at dresses on a rack. This child would be an easy target to the likes

162

of me, and to those whose darkness wasn't so apparent. There were others who would delight in a child like this; others I would take in a moment. I took his hand, fighting the urge to absorb, and led him to the woman with the baby.

"Mommy, Mommy," the child squealed. "The man likes puppies too."

The woman looked down on her child. She couldn't see me. "What man?" Immediate shock touched her face. The child looked up. I had vanished from his sight.

"Don't talk to strangers," she said, taking his hand.

"But Mommy..." Holding tight she dragged the child away.

So easy, I thought, taking a child is just so easy.

I thought of Cassandra, Sarina and the others. I had to do something soon, or he would intervene. He lacked subtlety, finesse; he lacked all semblance of care. I also lacked care, though not completely, not totally.

I drifted into the movement of bodies, the lights from shops giving a different life to the night. Come nightfall I would create nightmares while I thought and planned. Aza'zel will find the screaming dreams and accept my offering. While he fed, I would be left with time to direct Cassandra along the path to my vengeance. I hoped I wouldn't have to take her as well.

Chapter 33

Cassandra

I waited in the front room of the apartment. I deleted the message from her phone and ate the dry croissant. The man I met, de Lezo was alive. I hadn't expected anything like this; it didn't seem possible. With only three of the copper down-lights on above me, the rest of the place was in darkness. Blas' face kept running over in my mind. I'd checked on Wikipedia; there was an old image of the man, his face had even been on a Spanish stamp, a real hero. Waiting was something writers were good at. I could wait month for my publisher to give me the nod on a book. Laptop open and on the coffee table to keep me company, I searched YouTube and watched the music clip for *Bela Lugosi's Dead* by Bauhaus. The clip came from a movie called The Hunger with David Bowie. I'd heard the song a few times, never seen the video. In one of the crowd shots I thought I'd seen Sarina's face, and after several replays and pauses, I still couldn't be sure.

What else lurked beneath the surface of reality, who else lived when everyone knew they were dead. Sarina was in some of Bela Lugosi's movies. Was she in The Hunger? Like Alfred Hitchcock would turn up in his movies. A shadow here, a walk by there. After this mess is cleaned up, I'd get some movies and see for myself. A dark-haired beauty around the set all the time would have been a director's dream for a walk-on, or in a background crowd shot. Replaying the song yet again, listening to the words 'Bela Lugosi's dead' it was difficult not to think about what I'd just seen and my impending death. Bela Lugosi meant something in the big picture, what was beyond me.

The horse watched me, silently and yet protectively. I could see why Sarina would keep it on display by the window. Maybe it was her version of a gargoyle, the protector from all things evil.

The locks clicked on the door. Sarina was back. I closed the laptop, taking deep breaths to calm myself. As she walked through the door, the stink of cigarette smoke wafted in with her. After a night of partying, she still looked great, makeup perfect, hair shining with its usual lustre and eyes alive with life.

"You waited up for me." She barely contained a smile; I saw the slight movement of her lips.

"I met Don Blas de Lezo, tonight."

"I wondered when he'd introduce himself. I suspected him for some time," she said lightly.

"You knew?" Another shock.

"He's not alive, you know," she said, sitting on the arm of my chair. "And yes, I've known since he died, and suspected his deal with Aza'zel."

164

"I'm sorry, Sarina, but I am getting confused here." I let the tiredness show in my voice. "He died. How can he be here now?"

"He is dead, and I am sad he is." She offered me a sad smile. "The Prelůstitel come from those who make a deal with Aza'zel. They get eternal existence if they hunt for him."

"But..."

"He's part of Aza'zel. He can never come back from there. He has been dead to me since the day he physically died after the battle with the English fleet." She stroked my hair; I let the sensation comfort.

"Then you know it's been him that's been following you?"

"I only worked that out in 1976, after Marie told me she thought someone was following me. She gave me a good description. I put a few things together." I leaned back in the chair, resting my head against her side. "I knew it wasn't the man I'd known, so I named him Orlando, after my cat in Austria. He was black."

"Why didn't you tell me?" My eyes closed. Too much shock, too little medication. "I thought you trusted me."

"In many things I do, I didn't think knowing Orlando was who he had been was something you needed to know. It does change anything."

"It's his book we have to get back."

"In a way, I figured that out as well. I couldn't be sure, and I didn't want to put you under any more stress than you already are. I'm sorry." She ran her hand down the back of my head, despite the lie I let it slide.

"He was sent to get something from you."

"I know, but I knew he couldn't." She touched my face, her fingertips gentle. "Then this book thing came up."

"It's all because of Mariz. Fucking Mariz."

"It's about a lot of things, I guess."

"I could do with a drink."

Sarina had bought me a new bottle of George T, and we drank for a couple of hours, talking about Blas, his life and unlife. The sadness in her voice, the copper light and the invasive black made for a very down mood. I couldn't quite equate the man I'd met in the cafe to the one Sarina talked about. I'd seen the power of Blas first hand, literally through his hands, and I easily accepted he was a danger to us. I wanted to believe my staying with Sarina would somehow keep me out of harm's way. His words undermined that belief, took away the surety I needed, and started to believe in.

"You know he loved you?"

Sarina looked up from her drink, eyes shadowed in the dull light. She nodded a small action. Sarina said nothing, but I noticed a tear, a slight glistening trail down her face, she made no move to wipe it away. I wondered how different things might have loved him?

I don't know what time we went to bed. I knew I'd drunk a lot, talked too much and listened too much. I let her make love to me, though I didn't feel anything. She knew. She needed the closeness of our bodies, the act, the little taking afterwards. The whiskey did its job, and my night-time pills helped everything along. Sleep wasn't too slow in coming. Tomorrow Mariz would have to be dealt with. A few stiff drinks beforehand might be called for.

I waited until eleven before driving over to my place. The traffic was lighter, and I felt more awake by then. I didn't have a drink, though I had been tempted by every bar I passed. By the time I pulled up out front I was ready for him. Sarina had said this had to be done and that Beth wouldn't be too far away should something go wrong. Set within a tidy garden of tall eucalyptus trees and small flowering bushes, my blue stucco house looked dated, old and much like how I felt. Getting out of the car I heard the twitter of the birds, the smells of car fumes. This was my place, my home. The neighbour across the way walked down the drive, happy to see me. He handed over my mail and asked if I'd be home for long. "A short visit," I said, and he offered to continue to collect my mail. Dave was a good neighbour, and he did watch out for others in the street. Hard to find people like that these days.

I walked down the path to the front door.

The house smelt musty from being shut up. I put my mail on the country style dining table. The house felt cold, despite a warmish day in the 60s. He was here, I could feel him. I wanted to call out, demand he tell me what I wanted to know, but being with Sarina had shown me that being calm and allowing things to come to you helped keep the mind steady and receptive.

I sorted the bills from the junk mail and noticed several overdue accounts. I put the bills in my bag. I would pay them through the Internet once back at Sarina's. It felt odd being in my house after so long in the blackness of the apartment: the white painted floor, the green walls and curtains, the coloured picture frames scattered about. I thought about putting some music on, or even watching the TV. Instead, I opened the curtains and stared out at the overgrown garden, which was, of course, its natural state anyway. The tall trees that bordered my piece of real estate were good for shade, though raking the leaves was a chore. Not today though. The greens and browns, the ochres and yellows stood out, drew my attention. The colours seen every day, seen in something that is truly mine created a different feeling, a new understanding of what it means to be alive.

"I've been waiting," Mariz said from the kitchen. The half-wall divider separated us.

I stared at him, surprised he said anything other than follow. Again, a change. If Aza'zel wanted to screw with my mind, then he was doing a bloody good job of it.

"Why are you here? What do you want?" I didn't want to talk to him.

166

"I'm trapped, Cassandra." He stepped through the wall and took a seat at the table. It bothered me. I sat, gripped the seat in my left hand, to help steady nerves. "The Prelŭstitel gave up on me. He knew I wouldn't be able to lead you to him a second time."

"Damn right about that." This ghost looked different, more Mariz than usual.

"I'm stuck here, trapped in your dimension."

"Like I care."

"Cassandra," he pleaded. Odd for a ghost I thought. "You have to give him what he wants."

"He wants the book back. I don't have it, yet."

"I know. Sam's got it. I told Aza'zel this. I don't know why things have gone along as they have."

"That makes you and me both."

"There's more." He looked at his hands. "What you did wasn't wrong. You told the truth about me. I would have done the same if anyone else had been caught out."

"Everyone thinks I caused you to kill yourself." I now knew better; the rest of the world didn't know. "I'm an outcast in the literary world because of you."

"I can make it right. I have to make things right. Otherwise I can't cross over." He looked miserable, in pain. "I don't want to be trapped here forever, and I don't want Aza'zel to take what is left of me."

I felt sorry for him, not enough to forgive him for stealing the book, just regular sorry. His cold filled the house, drove away the warmth of the sun through the windows. The place felt like a freezer. A lot of silence passed before he continued.

"Samantha killed Uri."

"What?"

"He stole the book back. Sam confronted him, and when her threats didn't work, she injected him with insulin." He looked up at me. "Sam and I had planned to kill him; she even stole the injection from my mother for the job."

I suspected Uri had been killed; I hadn't expected the murderer to be her. Samantha was a bitch and wanted something for the book. A murderer. Surely not. He stood and paced the room, his ghostly blue appearance like a fine shimmer of light moving above the floor. This was how he looked when alive, always nervous, twitchy. In the time since his haunting, I had never seen him so alive. I thought of Sarina. What would she do? How would she handle this turn of events? I felt empowered as I drew on the thought of her strength. Now I could bring down Samantha and remove the guilt I still harboured about him. I could change the view the literary world had of me. I had of myself.

"I don't have any proof." It was one thing to know the truth, a lot harder to prove. "Do you?"

167

"I wrote a suicide note." Mariz pacing, wringing his hands as if cold. It was cold.

"But you didn't commit suicide."

"I was going to," he snapped. "I planned it out. The vacuum cleaner hose, the duct tape, everything."

"You didn't kill yourself," I said again, this time raising my voice. "Blas killed you."

"I know, I know. But I did drive out to the hills that night to take my life. He came to me out of the trees, all surreal and like something from a bad movie. He set up the suicide for me after he'd taken everything that made me who I was. Made me this."

"What's in the note?" He was on the right page after all.

"I said how guilty I felt for the old man's death, and that Sam and I had planned to kill him once we got the book back." He stopped pacing. "The syringe is still in the case with the book. It would have her prints, Uri's blood."

"Where's the book?"

"I don't know what happened to it. Sam hid it when she found it on the table. I saw her put the syringe inside." Sam, I thought. "In the note, I apologised for stealing the book, plagiarising it, and said how Sam had helped me with the rewriting." He stopped wringing his hands, stepped towards the table and leaned against it with both hands on its surface. "Sam wouldn't agree to tell the truth, and I wasn't strong enough to go against her."

"And where is this note?" It might help get the book back.

"With my lawyer. Ben Richards." He dragged one hand through his curly hair. "I forgot to give him instructions, so I guess the letter is in my file somewhere."

I blew out a breath. Big news with even bigger consequences. It was the same when my new publishing contract came through. I blinked a few times, forcing my thoughts to order, to think, Samantha was a killer. He had suggested enough to put her away for a long time. To do so I had to get the letter, then get the letter to the police without them knowing that it was me who was handing it over. I couldn't be involved in this kind of stuff again; I didn't think I could survive a trial and cross-examination. Given the current state of affairs, it was a journey I wouldn't survive. The threat of the letter might be enough to get the book though, but I had to get on with it.

"Is the note handwritten?"

"Yes." He looked hopeful. "I want this to end, Cassandra. I want to go over. I don't want to end up in the eternal pit. I've seen it, felt its pull and damnation. Please, please, you have to help me."

"I'll try." I wasn't all that sure I could help. "Until then I suppose you're stuck here?"

"I can't go over. My business in this plane isn't finished, I have to be reconciled to go."

"I have two days to get it. Can you wait that long?"

"I have forever. I've already spent what feels like an eternity here; another few days will mean nothing."

I picked up the mail I had to deal with and left him moping about my house. If Blas made contact again, I'd ask him. I drove downtown. Ben Richards' office was on Santa Monica Boulevard, upmarket and low key at the same time. The only reasonable parking would be on top of the shopping centre with a walk down 3rd Street Promenade, maybe if I'm lucky there'd be a sale at Urban Outfitters. On the air, I could smell turkey tostada as I passed the Border Grill. It had been a while since I'd eaten there and could get something on the way back; might as well make the most of feeling good. I didn't have an appointment with Ben, and I didn't have a plan; it wouldn't hurt just to stop by and get a feel for the situation.

Ben and I spoke for over half an hour. He wouldn't release the file, and I wouldn't tell him what was in it. The file was now Samantha's property, the sole recipient in the will. Telling her about the letter would surely get it destroyed. The only way to get into his file was through Samantha. I asked about other things of his to keep attention away from the letter specifically. He'd call Samantha, tell her about the visit and what was talked about. I decided to ask about his book, pressed Ben as hard as I could. He wouldn't know about the original. By harassing him over it, I was sure he would only discuss this part of our meeting.

It wasn't a total loss, at least Ben still had the file. Breaking in and stealing it would have been a good option; knowing the filing system might have made the option viable. I needed help, and I just knew who to ask. Blas wanted the book as much as I did, he had to contact me again. He just had to. On the way back to the car I bought a yellow blouse with tiny crystals sewn into the collar. It beat black; I just hoped Sarina liked it.

Chapter 34

The Prelŭstitel

He emerged from a stone wall, an ooze that coalesced into a human shape of darkness. The walk through the graves was meant to keep him focused. We strolled together in silence, letting the spirits shift about our feet like a low mist. They called to him with reaching hands, pleading to be freed from his pit. Once inside the darkness, there was no way out. With the Devil, you had a chance, but he was not the Devil, he existed before such idols were made by the human domain. Even God would have to bow to his will.

"You won't go against Sarina?" he said, walking over graves. "I can see it in you."

"I can use Cassandra, it is easier, more efficient."

"She is protected by the Bruxsa?"

"True, but by posing no threat I was able to speak with Cassandra, the large woman didn't intervene." I didn't know much about the Bruxsa personally, but I did know I had to project more light than dark to keep from her attentions. He could not.

"The book will soon be in my hands."

"Very well. Will she also bring us the icon?"

"In time, it will take caution given her protection."

"Prelŭstitel," he said. "If you can't do it, I have another who can."

I knew who he meant. Sarina would be a match in strength and cunning, but I knew what would happen to her. I'd done enough to darken her life.

"There is no need."

"He has turned an Uttuku before," its voice stabbed through me. "He has a way you don't have access to."

"What will you benefit?" I sat on the ground, merging with the soil above a grave. I could sense the presence of an unclaimed one. Did he?

"Not me." He hovered above, blanking out the stars, the light of the moon. "He will; it would make him stronger."

"Stronger than me?" Prelŭstitels were, overall, equal. Contact with Aza'zel did increase our reach into the light.

"Darker, more equipped to deal with this Bruxsa."

I knew he would be, and he would be a threat to Sarina. History existed between them. She would remember, he wouldn't. I had to settle this business now. Otherwise all my years protecting her would be for nothing.

"I will not turn her. I will get what we need and be done with it."

"He will be waiting. Perhaps he is already here."

I had to take this as a threat. He was already here, I could feel it, and I have seen some of his doing. The author in the book store was his work; it was subtle but easy to see when you knew what to look for.

The stars returned; the moon's light shone on the headstones, revealed the names of those who had been claimed before and after death. I had never seen my own grave, read the inscription. No desire pulled me to its stone. Don Blas de Lezo, the general, the husband and father no longer inhabited the world of the living. I inhabited everything he represented in history. I was Legend, and he was dead. I thought of the new Prelŭstitel. Aza'zel never made threats and never asked permission. The attack on the women in the car park, that was also his work, it fit his profile, his manner. To search him out could bring more danger. He believed in himself too much to be convinced there were other ways to get what we wanted.

I would not turn Sarina. I had no ego to turn her for. I could not protect Cassandra. Once I had the book, she would die.

Chapter 35

Cassandra

Blas sat on a bench, reading a magazine, and looking like any other passenger waiting for the bus on Broadway. The night air felt heavy, damp. Global warming had changed the seasons, and it was hard to know what the weather would be like when heading out. My sandals clicked as I crossed the road, a black and white cruised by. I'd walked against the light. My luck was still holding.

I got his text message a little before seven. As I approached, it felt odd that creatures with so much power would use technology; a very human communication method. He looked up from the magazine, closed it and waited for me to sit beside him. The evening was still early, and a few real passengers waited for their ride home.

"Good evening. A nice night, don't you think?" He looked across the street. He could see Beth, watching. "I see you have a friend."

"It's a bit cool for me, and she's my security." My coat wasn't heavy and didn't keep out the dampness; I wished I'd worn closed shoes.

"Are you able to get the book?"

"Something's come up." I hoped he could help. "The woman who has it won't answer my calls." He frowned. "What's more, she killed Uri."

Blas touched his black tie, the whisper of a smile on his lips. "Really." With eyebrows raised, he looked like amused. Even with the comical appearance, my stomach tightened. This thing could kill without warning and as easily as I could down a whiskey.

"I need to get a letter Mariz wrote. It states what he and the woman did." I wondered if he would care for what I wanted to do. "It would clear my name." Would this make a difference? "And bring Uri's killer to justice."

"Human justice." He smiled, the idea pleased him.

Standing, Blas dropped the magazine on the seat. He offered his hand, helping me to my feet. Without speaking, he turned and walked up the street towards the Broadway Deli, its black sign blending into the night. I followed Blas, first a few steps behind, and when we reached the crossing lights, I walked beside him. Where were we going? I tried asking him, talking quickly; he remained silent. He'd called me, so he wanted something, and I guessed it wasn't only the book. We crossed the lights. Blas stopped in front of a parking garage and looked in at the cars.

"What do you see?" he asked.

"Cars."

"What is the most important thing about garages?"

Was this a trick question, a riddle I had to solve? I stated the obvious.

"You park cars."

"Precisely," he said, looking from the garage to me. "People leave one of the most expensive things they own in a place they trust. The darkness is much like this garage, Aza'zel stores his most valuable possessions there. No one can enter this place unless they have permission, or as with the garage, you have a ticket."

"And?" It was just a garage.

"Aza'zel has lost something, and it is my fault. I let someone into the darkness, the garage so to speak, and I allowed them to take something of great importance." He turned away from the garage and moved to another bench on the sidewalk. He sat, indicating I should join him.

"The book isn't the only thing I need." He sounded vague, and I found I didn't like it. My suspicion was right, and I was baffled by what else he could want from me. "Have you seen a horse in Sarina's place? A black statue of a horse with its right leg raised?"

I had, but I wasn't about to admit it. I had to tell Sarina, find out what it meant before I told him. I shook my head. He looked as if he already knew she had it.

"Is it important?" I asked.

"You might say that."

"Why do you think Sarina has it?"

He laughed, a deep chesty sound. "I know she has it I let her take the thing; I want you to get it back for me."

"Why?"

"All you need to know is I want it, and Aza'zel wants it." He wasn't going to explain. "Think of it this way, Cassandra. It might be the only thing to keep you alive."

I pressed for an exchange. I asked him about getting the book back and the letter. He agreed that Samantha should pay for her crime, though it wasn't his imperative. I gave him a card I'd taken from Ben's office; he slipped it in his pocket saying nothing. We sat watching the traffic, the people and a fog that slowly fell across Broadway. Downtown wasn't known for thick fog like this, and when I saw him smiling, I knew he or Aza'zel had something to do with it. In the fog seeing became difficult, moving around for those not wanting to be seen easier.

"I have much to do," he said, standing. "We will talk again, soon." He crossed the street, cars passing through him. I didn't like his tone, and I didn't like the change in the rules.

I met Sarina at the Goth Party house out on Broadway Street. I'd gone to my place to get changed; it was closer. Mariz wasn't there, which I appreciated.

173

I left my car in the drive and got a taxi with Beth to Oakland Recreation Centre and then walked around to the house. I had a key this time.

The house still brought bad memories. I looked at its lightless windows and thought of Zeek. Did he have to die? Did anyone have to die? Despite the bad feelings, the house seemed a safe enough place to go. The Goths were good people when you got to know them. Beth, on the other hand, was another story. Unlocking the front door, we went in and made our way to the basement party.

"If it weren't for Sarina, I would have killed you years ago," she said as we headed down to the black door.

I didn't answer, didn't want to think about her. There was already far too much to consider. She just made things murkier, more complicated. Right now, I needed a drink, and I planned to have quite a few.

Inside I found Sarina on the large sofa, a glass of wine in her hand and some young men fighting for her attention. As soon as she spotted me, they were waved away. The music, loud, pumped through me, screamed at me, the smoke haze helped hide what I knew would be showing in my face. My heart wouldn't be able to hide for too long what Blas had asked for. She'd see my worry.

I sat beside her, drawing my dress in around my legs. A very tall woman, looking like death and wearing leather shorts and a leather bra, handed me a drink. Beth moved to the bar, all bright bangles, necklaces and burgeoning breasts. She looked my way, shook her head and started serving. Why would a Bruxsa choose to be so fat? On the screen, a Bela Lugosi film played, Son of Frankenstein. Bela's makeup was impressive; I could hardly tell it was him. I wondered if this film was a favourite in the club. Sarina grabbed my hand, fingers entwining, and pulled it into her lap. She was glad to see me, and despite what I had to say, it felt good to be beside her. The movie ended, the music still pumped. Joy Division pulsed through the ambience; too many in the room, they were the creators of the Goth terminology. Others talked about The Cramps. The debate, always soft, never got heated. Fights were beneath these people.

I'd even mentioned this questionable information in one of my books, though I didn't fully grasp the whole concept of Goth music back then, and I didn't think I got it now. With the film in the background, it made more sense, became more darkly emotional. It wasn't just the music, the sound needed visuals, usually non-related images that worked closely with emotions. Old black and white horror films lent themselves nicely to the task. The film closed, the music dulled to an even white noise. It was time to tell Sarina what Blas wanted.

A disconnected scene flashed on the screen; an interruption in the visual landscape. Black and white, Bela Lugosi hovered over the exposed neck of a pale-skinned beauty. His cape spread out, his fangs ready to strike. A shadow moved across the white linen of the bed; he looked up. I didn't remember him doing this before, not in this scene. Well, I thought I knew the scene.

The shadow stepped from the screen, the film becoming a snow haze. Sarina gripped my hand tighter. I held my breath, body stiffening. The noise stopped, everything stopped. It was like the night in the restaurant. I turned to see Beth, the only other person able to move. She approached us, looking extremely unhappy.

"What do you want?" Sarina asked. I didn't feel well.

Before us stood the figure of a man, the blackest black I'd ever seen. No features, only glowing blue eyes. It had to be him, could only be him. I knew those eyes from the night Zeek was killed. I didn't want to die. I returned Sarina's grip. I didn't want to die.

"You know what I want." The voice washed over me like a thick syrup, the sound tugged down on me, dragged across my body.

"Piss off," Beth said, now standing a little to the side and in front of us. "There's nothing for you here."

"Bruxsa," the darkness said. "You align yourself with Uttuku. Why?"

"Go fuck yourself."

"Not one of my desires." A low, hard laugh followed, a strange sound lacking emotional detail – a machine laugh. "I see you have many followers, Sarina."

At least Beth didn't seem to be intimidated. I for one was.

"Why are you here?" Sarina didn't move; I could feel her tension, the tightening in her wrist and fingers.

Aza'zel expanded, increasing its size to cover the screen behind. I didn't think I could get closer to Sarina, but I tried. I tried to climb inside her skin and hide. He moved through the stilled gathering, a solid cloud flowing over, around and through the bodies.

"A lot of darkness here," he said. Again, the drag.

"Leave them alone." Beth's contempt was palpable.

"They mean nothing to you." Sarina put her wine on the nearby table. "And I will never give it back."

"You won't have to." He made an unpleasant sound. I could hear screams interlaced through his voice. He pointed straight at me. "She will get it for me. Do it or die."

"Blas asked me to take it from you," I blurted, feeling like a little girl caught out doing something wrong. "I wanted to tell you, but the music..."

"When?"

"Tonight, just before coming here." She didn't let go of my hand.

"It is about time the Prelŭstitel made a move on this." The darkness formed in front of us again, eyes piercing. "You won't be able to protect her forever, Uttuku."

"Did he tell you what it was?" I nodded.

175

"Your symbol of power will be mine." Aza'zel billowed like a curtain. "She will bring me the horse."

Beth looked confused for a moment, then searching Sarina's face, her look turned to suppressed anger. She sat on the sofa, sandwiching me. A fat hand wiped a chubby face. Slowly she turned to Sarina, looking right past me. I could see anger in her eyes, the set of her jaw.

"You took the horse?" The airiness of her voice a light brush against my face.

"I'll explain later." Sarina nodded to Beth. "I think you should leave," she said.

"The horse or the woman, your choice, Uttuku. Will you sacrifice your heart's desire? Or will you surrender the icon of Alexander?"

The darkness flowed back into the snow of the screen, the vision of Bela, the Dracula, about to feed returned, only now he lay sprawled across the woman. The woman was screaming. It was Sarina.

"I will take her, I will take her from you, and there is nothing you can do."

The image flickered. The screen returned to show the opening credits of The Raven. What was that all about?

Sarina stood, pulling me up in turn. She looked at Beth, who just sat staring off into space. I had to find out what the horse meant and just how he would make me take it from Sarina, or would she give it to me to save my life. Of that, I felt doubtful.

"You are safe," Sarina said.

"Because of you?" I didn't feel safe.

"Because of Beth. Come with me," she said, panic showing in her face for the first time. Real panic. She led me to a blank wall to the rear of the basement. She pressed her hand against the surface; a panel slid open to reveal a tunnel, a poorly lit hole in the wall. "This will take us away from here and out of Blas' contact. Everything's gone wrong."

The way, lit by candles, and stinking of wax, felt long. We jogged in a steady stream of water down the centre of the floor and seeping through the walls. The smell reminiscent of wet coats and sodden earth.

"What do you mean every thing's gone wrong?" Sarina ran ahead of me. "Sarina! What do you mean?"

"Follow me, I... I'll explain..."

We ran and splashed for an age, perhaps a mile. The stone curves of the tunnel closed about us as it twisted under the park and then under the road. The sounds of cars echoed above us. At the end of the tunnel, a flight of steep, worn stairs led up. Sarina led the way, pulling her skirt above her ankles as she climbed. She disappeared into darkness, and I followed. Nowhere else to go.

We came out beside a fireplace in a well-furnished house. The lights were off. The glow from the street lights through a bare window showed what looked like antique furniture: turned legs, winged armchairs. Sarina drew the blinds before turning on the light. She shuddered. The colours of the room must have been unnerving. All bright florals and garish flock wallpaper.

She turned on me. "What did he tell you about the horse?" The always calm Sarina looked anxious. "I need to know, Cassandra."

"Only that it belonged to Aza'zel and it was important to him."

"It's important all right." She hugged herself. "He can't get it back. He can never get his hands on it, do you understand?"

I thought of the book, maybe a selfish thing to do. I needed to, had to focus. I had two days. How did the horse affect what I had to do about the book?

"I've got to get the book," I said, not feeling all that happy myself. "I have no interest in taking the horse for dark features." I sat in one of the floral armchairs, glad to be out of the stench of cigarettes, glad not to be surrounded by black right at the moment.

Sarina paced a little, mumbling, shaking her head. She stopped in front of me, knelt and took my hands. Something was wrong, terribly wrong. The look in Sarina's face betrayed something I had never seen in her before. Fear. Cold braced my spine. Sarina was scared.

"You can't give him the horse. I know I can't stop you if you decide to take it, but I'm asking you not to do it."

"I won't. I promise." She gripped my fingers so tightly it hurt. "I promise."

"You won't be able to stop yourself. He knows who you are, Blas knows who you are and how to influence you. They will get to you, get to me through you."

"Then what can I do?" Was this a *fait accompli*?

"First we return the book, satisfy Blas' immediate needs, then we must protect you, stop him... I have to... I don't know..." She put her head in my lap. "It wasn't meant to go like this," she cried, voice high, upset. "If I'd known any of this was going on if I'd only known. Things... things..."

"What are you talking about?" I eased her head up. She was crying. "Sarina, you're scaring me."

"Our meeting, getting to know each other, it wasn't meant to be like this. It was meant to be simple." She looked worn out. "We were meant to work on my book, and the book was meant to remind me of emotions I'd buried so I could... so I could feel them for you." She shook with crying, her words flowing like a child's babble. "Through the book, you were to learn about me... I wanted you to fall in love with me... this wasn't supposed to happen, Cassandra. None of it."

"You approached me because you wanted me to fall in love with you?" I didn't know whether to laugh or cry.

"I'd already fallen in love with your writing. I could tell you were in the work, and I fell in love with the author I thought you were." She shook her head. "I didn't know about the troubles heading your way. I just wanted us to have a chance together. The chance I didn't take with Bela."

This wasn't the time for such confessions. She could have said all this well before now, picked a better moment. In another time I would have welcomed the news, right now the only thing on my mind was staying alive.

"Cassandra, I've spent every day trying to find a way to keep you safe, keep you away from danger. I was told always to show you strength, always be there for you no matter what, but never was I to admit how much I really knew."

"You've been protecting me by not telling me anything?"

"I've tried. I can't just keep hiding the truth anymore." Real anguish erupted from her. All this time I thought her strong, in control. Even this was a lie.

"No point confessing now," I said. "Whatever you planned, it's all gone to shit, and you and I have to get out of it." I struggled with my feelings, only there wasn't time to think about them, not yet, not now. I needed her to pull herself together. I needed Sarina back. She couldn't go to pieces on me now. That was my job, nut case and jabbering was what I did best.

She kept her grip tight around my fingers. "I have to tell you before anything happens to you." Her face wet, mascara running like black rivers down her cheeks. "Cassandra, Beth has been looking out for you for the last three years, just making sure you... you remained single." I knew that piece of the puzzle was there; I just hadn't wanted to put it in place yet. "I even had Dr Sholan keep an eye on you for me. I have been getting counselling from him as well."

"What?" My doctor, my shrink was a part of all this? Beth, I could, maybe, put in the picture, but him. "Is there anyone who doesn't know what's been happening in my life?" I should have been angry; there wasn't time for it.

"I helped him with his books, and he kept me informed on your health, your mental state." She looked at me. "I wanted you to be well, Cassandra, please believe me. I didn't mean any of this to get to this stage. I thought I could fix everything without you knowing."

Too much. Time to scream to the night, get locked away and pumped with drugs, block the shit out. Bring the straight jacket now; I'm fucking as ready as I'll ever be. We were both nut cases, me thirty-two and ageing, she five hundred and forever young. Now things got worse. Now of all times.

First, we had to save ourselves, well, I had to save me, and if Sarina was a party to that, then she was in. Breaking her grip, I grabbed her shoulders and gave her a firm shake. Strength, I needed her strength, false or not. I needed her to guide me, show me what to do. I couldn't deal with tears and emotions, deal with deception, not to mention privacy issues. It would have to wait. I had to go to the toilet; even that had to wait.

"Well, there won't be much chance for love if I end up dead, will there?" That worked. Sarina wiped her face and stood. "Do you know how to deal with any of this?"

"I'll call my limo, and we can go." She straightened her dress, a distraction, a self-ordering gesture.

"Sarina. Do you know what to do?"

"No," she said, regaining some of the resolve I expected.

I didn't want to hear that either.

She took her phone out of a small handbag and placed a call. We sat, saying nothing until the limo arrived. The drive to Venice Beach, in silence, took forty minutes. I couldn't get my head around Dr Sholan being involved. How could he? I trusted him above all others.

By the time we were safely in the apartment I felt extremely calm, my mind plotting and planning like it did when I got a new idea for a book. As long as I was safely within her sphere of protection, and so long as we stayed together, I would be okay. I asked about the horse as I sat in one of the armchairs. She wouldn't tell me at first, said it was dangerous to know, but if my life was going to be on the line over it, I deserved to know. Sarina joined me in several large glasses of whiskey. I'd never seen her drink anything stronger than wine. She settled on the sofa, elbows on her knees. She twirled the glass in her fingers, watching the amber fluid wash against the sides. I investigated my glass and only saw the wobbling image of myself staring back. What was on her mind?

"If I am going to die, I want to know about the horse." I couldn't believe how matter of fact I sounded. "The time for secrets, emotional protection and lies is over. I need the truth."

"The horse is very old."

"That I guessed."

"I took it about two hundred and seventy years ago." She drank again. "I had drifted close to the pit, Aza'zel's home, it is called the Abad. I'd been starving myself, denying the light." She looked to me briefly before pouring another large measure. "You have to understand that when an Uttuku can't take, their darkness increases and brings them closer to its presence. It was by the pit I saw the horse. It stood on a tall pillar of onyx, expertly hidden in shadow."

"I was falling, Cassandra, giving into the darkness. Blas had told me the horse was there, not directly, but I knew, it was him who directed me to its location. He wouldn't know I suspected him. Before he turned fully to Aza'zel, he was given some small powers. He used one to gift me the horse, tell me where it was." She drank a mouthful of whiskey, her neck tensed. "I grabbed it and used the feeble light I had left to fight my way back. I nearly didn't make it." She fell silent.

I wanted to say go on. I had to wait. Letting her remember and speak in her own time would help her settle, regain composure. If she regained her resolve, she just might be able to save my sorry ass. Besides, the talking helped me with Beth; it helped me whenever Sarina let me ramble. It was her turn.

"It was the horse that sent me back into the light." She lifted her head, looked at me with wet eyes. "It drove the darkness back. It was Marie who told me what it was when I showed her. She'd heard of it from other Uttuku." Sarina laughed with a combination of sadness and defeat. "To think I didn't know about it." She got to her feet, walked across the room and lifted the statue. "Inside this horse are the ashes, the last remains of the greatest Uttuku of all time." She stepped over to me and handed over the statue. It was heavy, warm.

"Alexander?"

She nodded. "Not all of us live for a long time, and this one was the shortest lived of all. He died from a broken heart."

"Don't you dare give me that love conquers evil shit." I might have been giving her a chance to fix things, but I wasn't about to buy into the love game, not yet.

"Not love, light." She drained her glass, her eyes looked brighter, she was steadier on her feet. "You hold an exact replica of Alexander the Great's horse, Bucephalus. Inside are Alexander's ashes."

Unbelievable. I cradled the horse, ran my fingers over its fine lines, the perfect musculature. I couldn't see any seams to suggest this was just a fancy urn. At least love didn't come into it. Light I could deal with.

"The horse was fashioned in Alexandria in his honour in 333BC," she continued, "though only he knew what it was to be used for." Sarina sat in the other chair, leaning forward and watching me. "When Hephaestion died of a fever, Alexander grieved like no other in history. He had the Uttuku gift; he could have so easily saved his friend. He hesitated, unsure of his power, reserving his love. The fever moved too fast, he became helpless."

"The story goes that he was gay." I'd seen the movie.

"He was an Uttuku, there are no sexual boundaries in our lives," she said, just a little too firmly.

"I didn't mean..."

"It's okay," Sarina relaxed. "The thing is that Alexander, faced with an eternity without his friend and blaming his physician for his death, not only crucified the poor man, he marched into Cossaeans and, for no apparent reason massacred the entire nation."

"He went mad?"

"He went from the greatest to the most despicable within a few days. Uttuku within his own army left his side, his men started to lose respect. He drank heavily." Sarina looked at me. I shrugged, took another drink. "He eventually succumbed to a fever. Twelve days of misery later he was declared dead. Some Uttuku had returned on news of his illness. They beheaded him and later cremated him. The greatest of our kind was also one of the saddest."

"And Aza'zel knows this?"

"In part, he doesn't know what it can do; you can't know what it can do, the risk is just too great."

I handled the horse with a sense of sadness myself. A broken heart, the loss of love had brought him down, when armies could not. Lost love was bringing me down, like it was bringing down Sarina.

"His body was burnt, and the ashes placed within the horse. It was the only thing that never left his side."

"And how did Aza'zel get it?"

She poured herself another drink, offering the bottle to me. I put the horse on the coffee table, took the bottle and half-filled my glass.

"Like all things through time, the statue was lost, passed on through trading, theft, seeing more markets than battles. A Prelŭstitel working for Aza'zel in Turkey found the horse in a bazaar, felt its link to us and took it to his master as a gift. Alexander's horse is a symbol of strength and tragedy to us, a reminder of the costs involved in the life we live." She sighed. "To Aza'zel it is the embodiment of death and destruction; he can draw back through history, feed on the anguish and fear through Alexander's warring ways. It was also a reminder to be used against our kind, to show the fallibilities of their lives." Sarina's strength returned with the telling of the tale. "The urn also held the last known power of the old one, the one who had converted Alexander in the first place. In an Uttuku's hands that power could be used to control the roaming of the Prelŭstitels, thwart some of Aza'zel's ways."

Sarina spoke, I drank steadily and listened. What Aza'zel would do with the horse was unknown. She thought he would use the power to find the Old One, the oldest Uttuku alive. Knowing he hadn't found her even with the horse brought Sarina and others some comfort, it would have only been a matter of time, the one thing he had ample supply of. Until he found the Old One, the Uttuku were relatively safe.

We finished the bottle and called it a night. We made slow, clumsy love, she on top with one of her toys and grinding, me simply lost in the haze of booze and soft skin. I liked the closeness, loved the way she felt and sighed with pleasure. I thought about her confession and how I felt. Inside the fugue of intimacy and drunkenness, I couldn't place my emotions. Or was it because I didn't want to? Could I love something like this? Was I indeed in love? She slid down me, energy spent and breathing hard. Her head lay between my breasts. I closed my eyes, world spinning slightly, and gently toyed with her hair.

Would I ever know if I was in love? I hoped I knew before I died, otherwise, what a waste.

Chapter 36

The Prelŭstitel

"Why did you go to them?" I asked. I had everything going as planned.

"You do not question."

"Time is nothing to you, never has been and never will be." Inside the tunnel, our voices echoed; the smell of oil cloying. He'd come through the ground above, sixty metres of it. I simply followed the track; the walk helped settle my thoughts.

"Cassandra needed influencing; she needed to see my power and the futility of her life." He shifted about me like an icy breeze. He was agitated, unable to solidify. What else was happening?

"Do you think Sarina will let her come under your control now?" I still needed Cassandra for the book, and I wanted her to stay disconnected from him until I had it. I thought of Cassandra, sent a message. If Sarina made her move, all would have to start again. I didn't know his game, the reasons behind the manipulations, but I was tired of them.

"I will get the horse back, Prelŭstitel, you will lure Sarina away. You have the means I gave you, now use them, like you should have fifty years ago."

I would not lure her, as he wanted; I could not. The protections I had afforded Sarina for so long had come to an end; if he were to take Sarina, he would need use of another hunter. I hoped I could get the icon and the book before he realised I would not go against her. I hoped she could protect Cassandra because the next time I saw the woman, I would take her darkness and rip the life from her like a page from the manuscript.

Chapter 37

Cassandra

We'd slept late. Sarina was having a shower while I worked out a plan to get the book from Samantha, she still didn't answer my call, and I was getting desperate. I needed to get the letter from the lawyer; it came later my priority list. Checking my phone, I found a message, sent last night. I hadn't heard the phone's tone. It was the 555 number and simply said:

'Meet me at the woman's house. We get the book today.'

I waited for Sarina in the kitchen. The laptop showed two files in my work in progress folder. Sarina's book, which had been a ruse to get us together, and something I didn't think needed anything else done, and 'The Seething', a book I had to complete over the next six months. I couldn't concentrate enough to look at my latest novel. Once I would have shelved my life to get it done, things being as they were, I doubted I'd even make the deadline.

Aza'zel wanted me to bring him the horse, and if I wanted to live, I would have to do it, go against Sarina. All the history and reasons behind it were like milk – black milk. My view of history had been fractured and partly reassembled into a new form, one that made sense but didn't make sense. As I combed fingers through my hair, letting the soft strands quiet my thoughts, I couldn't help but think of Hitler, Churchill, Bela, Marie and Beth. What was the connection here? I logged on to the Internet. None of this was random; it was a gut feeling. With Google, I started my search.

Hitler was Austrian, not German. An easy and straightforward link. Churchill wasn't as direct, but he did view Austria as a war tool to be used against Germany, used against Hitler. Not a great link, it made some sense. Bela Lugosi came from Austria-Hungary, but he was Hungarian, and Marie Antoinette was part of the Austrian Royal family. Beth I couldn't find, except for some site associated with Bruxas. She didn't sound all that nice, and I was immediately glad she was on my side. I was guessing there was an Austrian tie-in here as well. I didn't know what it meant and how it applied to me. As an afterthought, I searched up Kurt von Trojan, the man Mariz cited in his book.

This was a messy search and I'd almost given up when I found an obscure reference on a site with more links then all of Japan's golf courses put together. Kurt von Trojan was Austrian, a journalist who worked in Vienna and later moved to Australia, that was easy to find. His father was the last Knight of Austria. Sir Trojan. On Wikipedia, I found Kurt had died of bone and kidney cancer. The listing mentioned his last book, 'When I Close My Eyes'. I made a point of ordering this. There might be something in it that might help make sense of all this. The Austrian connection was strong, but why? Sarina mentioned she'd lived in Austria.

Sarina entered the room brushing her hair and looking radiant, fresh. I felt dull and lifeless.

"What are you doing?" she asked.

"Research." She looked stunning in a black business suit, black shirt and tie. Masculine but feminine at the same time.

She stepped behind me and looked at the screen. She sighed.

"Everything seems to point to Austria," I said. "Even someone mentioned in Mariz's book is Austrian."

"I know the name." Sarina read the Wikipedia entry. "I was there when his father received the Knighthood. I made a lot of friends in there, so of course, there would be strong associations."

"Hitler, Winston?"

"Winston wasn't Austrian."

I dropped it; she was avoiding something. I would have to work it through later; I had other things to do. I handed Sarina my phone, the message from Blas still on the screen. She sat, put the brush on the table and rubbed her brow.

"This is going to be risky," she said, handing the phone back. "I can't be with you."

"Will Blas protect me?"

She shook her head. "Beth will follow you, keep her distance. Blas won't be able to harm you."

"Can you distract Aza'zel?" I needed two hours, maybe less if Blas had a more direct plan.

"I'll try," she said, taking my hand. "Just promise me you'll tell Blas whatever he wants to hear." I frowned. "I don't want to lose you, Cassandra."

"How reassuring."

It was agreed that I meet Blas, and together we would visit Samantha. I managed to get her to pick up on my fourth call for the morning and the promise of money, and in cash, didn't make it hard. I knew Blas wouldn't pay the money. As Sarina explained it, the darkness does not need such human commodities. It takes what it wants whenever it wants. I also didn't want Samantha dead; I needed her alive to face charges of murder, to clear my name. Sarina stood in the front room looking out at the sea. She turned as if knowing I was watching her.

Unfolding her arms, she touched the sides of the horse. I heard a stony clink. Carefully she lifted the head free of the body. I'd never seen a seam, even the slightest flaw in the body. Sarina dipped a finger inside, then drew it out, covered in a light grey powder.

With her free hand, she replaced the head, and the clink locked it home.

"He will come to me as soon as I am outside, he will detect Alexander's essence," she said. "I will keep him for as long as I can."

I kissed her goodbye. A long, hunger-driven kiss. We both knew this might be the last time we'd see each other. I held her as close and as tight as I could.

"I love you," she said into my hair, then kissed the top of my head.

"I know." I wanted to say those words, found I couldn't. I didn't know how I felt. She gave me a little squeeze then released me.

I had to leave. For a time, I wanted to know why it was so important, what was in the book to cause the death of so many people, but now I just wanted it gone. I didn't care about its contents any more, let it keep its secrets.

Out in the street, I climbed into Sarina's limo for the trip. I couldn't afford to have my car recognised or seen anywhere near Samantha's place. With a black scarf covering my hair, and large Hollywood glasses covering most of my face I felt confident in my anonymity. The limo pulled up around the corner from Samantha's. The road was packed with cars. Blas, the one-time Spanish General, was standing, leaning against the side of a silver Chrysler 300. He looked like a young business executive in his trim black suit and tie. He wore thin dark glasses. I instructed to driver to expect my call soon and waited for him to drive off before approaching.

"Are you ready?" he asked.

"Not really." He placed his hand in the middle of my back and gently eased me toward Samantha's house.

If I sighed deeply once I sighed a hundred times, facing Samantha in her and Mariz's home would have been difficult under normal circumstances, but with a Prelŭstitel in tow, I didn't know what would happen. The tree-lined streets offered welcoming shade from the sun. The day would be warm, and I was already feeling uncomfortable in my black dress and rib-high jacket. As we walked, I thought we looked like The Adams family out for a stroll. By the time we arrived at the front of her house, my heart was trying to climb out of my chest, and I thought I could smell my sweaty underarms. Blas looked as cool and as comfortable as when we hooked up. We stood in her narrow driveway, the house hidden a little by trees and bushes. I felt the gentle hand in the back and the walk to her door. Tall, standard roses, white, gave off a subtle scent. Blas sighed.

"The Bruxsa is near, isn't she?" I nodded.

The doorbell didn't scream. I could hear its tone somewhere in the house. I heard Samantha's heels approaching down the entranceway's tiled floor. I drew in a deep breath as the door slowly swung inwards. Sam was all smiles and easily welcomed us inside.

She looked at Blas. "One of your Goth freaks?"

"Please," Blas said pointing to the main part of the house.

Samantha led us into the large, open planned living area. The dining table was where I remembered it, though the place had been repainted in soft

185

yellows since my secret visit. She stood by the table, her summer floral dress more akin to the weather than mine.

"The money?" she said, looking between us and not seeing a bag.

Blas looked at me. I nodded, couldn't speak. He approached Samantha; she took a step back.

"What's going on?" She hid her fear well. "I won't tell you where it is this way."

He moved quickly, right hand plunging through her forehead, his hand disappearing up to the wrist. Samantha gasped. Eyes closed. She fell forward into him.

"No!" I cried. "Blas, no!"

He released, and she dropped to her knees. I ran to her aid, kneeling beside her and holding her. She was breathing rapidly; sweat beaded her brow, the top of her lip.

A ceiling access cover above the table crashed upwards into the roof. Blas, a blur of black disappeared through the square opening. I laid Samantha on the floor, using a chair cushion as a pillow. Her eyes were still closed; breathing began to slow.

Blas dropped from the hole; he could have been a feather drifting to the ground. In his hands, he held the briefcase Uri had given me. He placed it on the table and ripped the top off as if it were made of paper.

"Have you read it?" he asked. The words sharp.

Now wasn't the time for honesty. "No. I just looked at the first few pages."

"Good."

I stroked Samantha's brow; she was hot. "Will she be okay?"

"I took what I needed. She will feel a little empty once she wakes." He turned away from the book. "I saw through her memories how she killed Uri." He looked pleased. "Though I don't need it, Uri needs justice to be done."

I left Samantha and joined Blas at the table. The handwritten pages stared up at me. The old script, the fountain pen marks. What now?

He placed his hand in the centre of the pages, fingers splayed. His hand looked as if it were soaking into the top page — black ink on blotting paper. Wind whipped up around us as he removed his hand. The pages in the case were lifted, scattered like confetti around the room. The wind, brief and fierce, stopped. The pages fluttered to the floor, onto the table, settled over everything. I picked up a page. It was blank. Every page from the case was now blank.

"Now I am meant to take your darkness," he said, flatly and plainly. He turned to me, his eyes blank and face hard. I could feel my end radiating off him. "I suggest you leave."

"The syringe, is there a syringe in the case?"

"Yes. Cassandra, I will take care of things now, so go. I will not give you another chance, take it."

I didn't have to be asked again. I was out of the house and running back to the corner as fast as I could. I'd kicked off my heels and held a shoe in each hand; my small shoulder bag slapped against my back. I had to get back to Sarina's. I'd be safe if I could just make it back. I called the limo, and in a few minutes the car was back and me inside shaking and about as scared as I could ever be. The book had been returned, and yet still I was going to die. This wasn't fair, not fair at all.

Chapter 38

The Prelŭstitel

"She held the horse before me, taunted me," he said, enlarging himself to consume a whole wall of the Egyptian room in the museum. This was part of the history of where Sarina's line had begun. A reminder of his mistake. "I could not take it from her. There is more to this symbol, much more."

"I got the book," I said, the one task he had blocked me from accomplishing had finally been completed. "It has been destroyed."

"You didn't take, Cassandra?"

"I couldn't. The Bruxsa was near."

"There is still something that must be done." He formed into human shape lying inside the sealed case holding the mummy of a woman. His black fingers traced the edges of the wrapped face.

"I found Uri's murderer." He nodded. "I owe the human a final act."

"You owe nothing. Do what you must, then get the horse. Use Cassandra; she is Sarina's weakness, use it."

I watched as he flowed through the glass to reform, standing before me. The soft lighting of the room sucked at him like an exhaust fan. The museum was closed for the night.

"I don't think Cassandra will bring us the horse. She is too close to Sarina, too involved. Her protection too strong."

"She will. There is no choice for her." His eyes became brilliant, almost blinding blue. "Lure her away so I can use her." He spoke so loudly one of the cases cracked. "She trusts you."

"That trust has gone." Sarina wouldn't let Cassandra go so easily.

"I am taking steps." Aza'zel turned his back. "I will make the ultimatum; there is a way to influence Sarina's decision and to motivate Cassandra to do what we ask of her. You have been clouded Prelŭstitel; you must know I have now made you clear."

"I don't understand."

"You will." He broke apart and scattered like sand in a strong wind — black sand.

I walked through the wall of the lawyer's office, surprising him on the phone. I leaned across his desk, took the phone and placed it in the base. I could see he was finding it hard to put words together. The shock of seeing me appear like this does it every time. The office was typically ego boosting — one wall floor to ceiling legal books; all show, no meaning. The picture window behind the desk was bad Feng Shui; it still gave a good view over the shopping district. Two buttoned leather chairs sat in front of the overly large, polished wood desk. This man wanted to show strength and power. Where was it now?

"Who...who...are you?"

"Someone you don't want to know."

His mouth worked a few times before he could find more words to use. He looked like a puppet without a master.

"What do you want?" He gathered himself. "How did you get in here?"

I slid over the desk, pushing myself between him and his power. Before he could cry out, I wrapped my hand around his brain and squeezed until he began to cry. I knew what I wanted him to do and I showed him what would happen if he didn't follow my demands. As I released his mind and dragged my fingers from his forehead, he slumped forward. Gasping, struggling to breathe, he slowly raised his head to look at me.

"You have the letter, and you know what to do?"

He nodded.

"If you see me again it will mean you are about to die. Do you understand?"

Another nod.

I left the same way I arrived. The action should drive home the point. In a strange was I felt good about what I had done, it was right, something completed for a human who had been my friend for many years. The statue came next; it wouldn't be as easy, only this time I knew someone would die.

Chapter 39

Cassandra

I got back from a walk along the beach, feet covered in sand and leaving tiny flecks on the black carpet. Beth had circled high above me in the form of an eagle, ever watchful, ever protective. Sarina had gone out. No note, no message, then there never was. I'd clean up the sand later. Walking into the bedroom, I noticed a difference immediately. The black world had changed slightly. The three large photos of Bela Lugosi were gone, his penetrating eyes no longer looking down over the bed. In their place hung a single large colour photograph, the frame gold and silver craze; modern.

There was Sarina and me shaking hands the first time we met. The photograph had been taken at the writers' fellowship meeting. How? Who? I sat on the bed, looking at the colours penetrating the room. Sarina's dark world had shifted in a way I didn't expect. Where had the picture come from? What did hanging it on the wall mean? It wasn't a hard guess or one that wasn't expected, Sarina loved me, so it was no surprise she was putting me in her life, incorporating my colour into her world. Emotionally there came a mess of conflicts all mixed with events that could readily destroy any relationship by themselves. Did the same feelings affect me? Did I see colour amongst all the black? Guessing about what was represented didn't help, being wrong lately had become the norm and the unexpected expected. We looked good together in the shot, our smiles genuine, our stances relaxed and mutually inviting. The picture displayed a comfortable unity over the hard darkness of the room. Should there be acceptance of this change? Could there be a mutual feeling in the photograph's representation? Tension still held tight, more so now with the suggestion on the wall. Even so, now wasn't the time for any of this. Maybe Sarina was making the point quickly because she knew my time was short.

The front door opened. I didn't know what to do, stay in the room, meet her in the hall. What?

"Do you like it?" She headed me off, coming straight into the room.

"It's a surprise," I said, being truthful.

"I like it, it's nice, and we both look good." She sat on the bed beside me, taking my hand. "I couldn't think of a better place to hang it."

"Who took the picture?"

"Blas."

"He was there?" The tension increased.

"He sent it yesterday. I had to wait for you to go out this morning to hang it."

"Why?"

"Hang it?"

"Send it?"

"I don't know why," she said, releasing my hand and pushing hair back from my shoulders. "Maybe a thank you for getting the book back."

I looked at the picture. It had been taken from one of the side rooms. "You believe that?"

"No, though it would be nice if true."

"He knew we'd meet," I said, a sinking feeling in my gut. "He already knew where the book was."

"He was following me. I doubt he knew who you were when he memorised this."

"Memorized?"

"He wouldn't have used a camera. Prelŭstitels don't handle technology; they access it through the dark web that blankets all things." I rubbed my brow. That was how he used the phone. "Cassandra, all he would need to do would be to touch a sheet of paper and this image would appear."

Sarina kissed my cheek. Her breath hot against my face, her smell sweet, fruity. The touch of lips soft. The distraction didn't last long. What was it all about? I turned my head to stare right into her face. I wanted to kiss her. I wanted her to tell me what this all meant.

"Why send this picture? And why now? He is going to kill me, Sarina, is he now playing with his food?"

"We'll never know," Sarina said. "Prelŭstitels don't work in the same way we do, and we don't think in the same fashion as humans. Who knows why he's doing this? He might not have even realised what he has done."

"Guess, I need something to help me understand."

"I think Blas might still have some remnant human feelings." She moved back a little, so we could see each other clearly. "I'm guessing, Cassandra. Prelŭstitels don't have feelings, real feelings. He wouldn't understand information in a linear fashion; it would just be pieces he'd put together, he would have only known why he had been at the meeting after the book had been returned."

"Is that possible?"

"The only explanation I would offer. I have to say we got lucky. If he did help us out of some remnant emotional state, I doubt it will be there in our next encounter."

We sat on the bed, holding hands and looking up at the picture. Sarina had said the change had to be made; she had to accept her Bela was gone and also accept something was happening in her life she liked. She didn't come out and state her feelings again, leaving me to accept them unsaid. I wanted to. Thought I could, only when the thoughts hit my head, taking the long road from the heart, confusion and doubt crammed it out. After what felt like half an hour, we both showered and changed, sharing time together under the water. We still had Aza'zel to deal with, and Blas wasn't completely out of the picture yet.

191

Sarina looked exhausted. I knew how she felt. Beth, pouring drinks for us, just stomped and swore. Our meeting generated nothing. My life still hung in the balance and Aza'zel still presented a large and real threat. Beth wasn't happy with going up against him to protect a human; me. She had her Goth life and enjoyed the people she'd met and killed. Her only contribution was to suggest giving the horseback. It meant little in the scheme of things. Why die for a symbol? And in the process why not hand me over as well; kill two problems with one gulp.

Marie just looked radiant, happy and relaxed. I'd told them about the book and how Blas had said he would take care of Samantha's crime. Marie looked truly pleased and hugged me at the news. I liked her; her refreshing manner gave nothing away of her age. She could only suggest that the three of them somehow protect me, shelter me from the threat until a solution could be found. Beth grunted.

"Waste of time," she said. "Bitch can drink herself to death for all I care."

"Beth," Sarina cut in. "For me, okay, do this for me."

"I get it," I said. "I didn't plan to get involved in any of this, you know?" Beth's place looked even more of a tip than usual. I didn't think you could get so much stuff stacked into a sink. It almost blocked out the window and the smell. Sweet woman body odour, sickly and pungent, the smell of rotting food; an overflowing compost bin sat on the bench. To think I confided in this woman, this creature. I thought she cared, listened to me quietly out of concern. She listened because she was my protector.

The day grew darker, and we'd made no headway with the problem. Sarina said something to Marie, the conversation animated but both women seemed to be agreeing on something.

"I have to dance tonight," Marie said breaking from the conversation, "Which means I need to feed."

"You can't leave me." Panic threatened, my heart jumped, "If you need light you can have some of mine."

"Thank you, Cassandra, but I need quite a bit, and the strip club allows me five or six takings at time. I have to go."

"And I need to eat." Beth's admission wasn't as easy to take on board. She had to kill someone gruesomely. "So, I'll leave you lovely ladies to your human for the evening."

Beth left for Goth Club while Sarina suggested we go with Marie, stay together. Being in a room with two Uttuku had to be safer than one. We took the limo down to the club, I had a few drinks for the trip and welcomed the seclusion behind the heavily tinted windows. Sarina had done my makeup, and I looked good but, in the reflection, I could see loss and black dog of depression sat quietly at my shoulder. He had grown bigger over the last couple of days, and my mood swings wouldn't have been out of place on any psych ward. I didn't want to talk, drink and think; only the thinking wasn't all that helpful, at every turn death waited. So, I would survive tonight, maybe tomorrow night but how long could I last? The women could protect me forever; they couldn't be with me every minute of every day for the rest of my life. The reflected dog got bigger, and I poured yet another drink. Was this how my crazy bitch mother felt all the time, if so, maybe how she was in my life did make sense. I wanted to believe that, I wanted to believe a lot of things.

At the club Marie sat with us for a while, she had some time before her first performance. It was hard to believe she was the one-time Queen of France. I watched how she held herself closely. The regal mannerisms remained the tilt of the head, the way she held her hands when speaking, even the way she walked when coming out on the stage. You could tell she had that special something, the many steps above the basic coarseness of the other girls. True she was an Uttuku, not human at all, but I could see she was no ordinary dancer. As she moved across the stage, up and down the pole I liked the overall feel of her presence, and I had to admit, Marie was very beautiful.

She danced and stripped to the cheers and jeers of a packed house. Sarina and I applauded, yet there wasn't joy in the offering, I had no joy left in me. Marie had been immediately called away for a lap dance in a shadowed corner of the room. We watched her personal attention, the closeness, the breast rub in the man's face. We watched as Marie leaned forward touched the top of the man's head. A tiny flash of light. His eyes flickered. In an instant, she'd just taken. She would need to feed several times before the night was out and the men wouldn't know. This kind of work suited the Uttuku, no questions about getting to close to the men and a management use to throwing out people who couldn't remember anything - perfect.

Another dancer took to the stage; she looked solid, big breasted. Her skills were limited, but the men didn't seem to notice or be overly bothered. Once naked it didn't matter what you did. Marie took a brief break to say she would finish early; she'd had enough energy. We could go someplace quieter, talk. She took to the stage, moving delicately about the lights, gliding up and down the pole like a gymnast. Her muscle tone, highlighted by the lights, gave her the vision of being an elite athlete. I found myself wishing I had such tone, was less of a girly girl in appearance. Then everything stopped.

Aza'zel dropped from the ceiling, his blackness dulling the lights. I shivered. The temperature dropped, I could see condensation as I breathed.

"You have come a long way," he said. "It was a pity I didn't get you last time."

"What do you want?" Marie stepped away from the pole. She walked off the stage, naked but defiant. With fists clenched she stood before Aza'zel. I guessed after all the abuse she received before her execution, facing him wasn't a big issue.

193

"You have lowered yourself to their level." His voice became a dull thud against my body.

"Why are you here?"

"For you of course."

I looked to Sarina who simply grabbed my wrist, holding me firmly at the table. Could he take an Uttuku? Sarina had suggested he couldn't.

"Idle threats do you little justice," Marie said, sitting on the table top that ran around the edge of the dance floor. "You might as well leave, now."

Aza'zel waved his hand, a wisp of blackness moving through the air. A man stepped out of the shadows; he wore jeans and a T-shirt, a scruffiness hung about him. I didn't recognise him though it was clear he was having difficulty standing and moving. Marie turned, her face lined with surprise.

"What is this?"

"You just fed from a Prelŭstitel." he laughed. Solid, painful, gut-wrenching. "Now the darkness within you is greater than the light." He shifted towards her. One hand outstretched. Marie looked to us. I could see fear in her eyes, pleading in her face. How could this be? A Prelŭstitel couldn't be in the presence of an Uttuku. Sarina had said so, that was why Blas didn't come for the statue directly.

"This won't get you the horse of Alexander," Sarina said. A weak defence of her friend.

"I know, but it will show your human friend there is no protection. I doubt Marie will have the courage to fight me, anyway."

Marie stood tall, steadied herself. "Courage! I have shown it for years; think you I shall lose it now when my sufferings are to end?"

Sarina's grip on my arm tightened further. I could feel her tension growing. This wasn't happening. She'd said we'd be protected, were safer together.

"You've said that before," he said. "Thought you could find something new by now."

Aza'zel plunged his hand through Marie's chest, between her breasts. The light faded from her eyes, and she collapsed. Aza'zel vanished, and so did the young man in jeans. Sarina released me, and we rushed to Marie's side. She felt cold.

"She's dead," I cried. "You said this couldn't happen! You said we were safe!" I stroked Marie's still face.

"Help me." Sarina slipped her arms under Marie's. "Take her legs."

"She's dead."

"She will be if you don't do as I ask. Now move!" We carried her out the back, through the girls' change rooms to the top of the back stairs. The world still hung in limbo; silence and stillness created a surreal scene. I put Marie's legs down. Sarina still held her shoulders. I wanted to cover her; it didn't feel right to be carrying Marie about naked.

194

"We don't have much time. Once everyone becomes reanimated, it will be minutes before security notices her missing." She hefted Marie over her shoulder. "Go out front, get a taxi and bring it around the back alley. Now!"

I ran through the club, everyone frozen in place like mannikins. I had to push a couple of guys over to get down the narrow staircase. Out front of the club, motion was still in play, the world moved on. There were some cabs ranked to the side, slapping my hands down on the hood of the lead taxi I got the attention of the driver immediately. The driver threw his hands up, giving me the 'You Crazy Woman' look. I climbed in back and ordered him into the back lot. It wasn't until I stuck my stiletto to his throat that he took me seriously. It felt like an age before we were behind the building. I didn't know where about Sarina would be. I made the driver switch on his high beam. Had the world in the strip club returned to normal? Had they found Sarina and the dead Marie?

Sarina stepped out in front of us, Marie draped over her shoulder wearing Sarina's long coat. Good, at least she wasn't naked. We pulled up, and I helped Sarina get her into the back seat. The cabbie protested, but Sarina threw a couple of hundreds at him, and he shut up.

"Venice Beach," she said, climbing in beside Marie. "Fast. Another five hundred on arrival."

The tyres squealed.

I unlocked the door while Sarina held Marie. We carried her inside, Sarina slamming the door closed with her foot. Marie looked pretty dead to me. The blue lips, grey skin. I hadn't known her long, but grief had set in. I felt numb. It took a long time to get back to her place, a long, long time.

"Leave her to me," Sarina said, dragging the body down the hallway. "Bring the horse. Hurry."

I ran across the room, picked up the horse and headed into the hallway. The only place to go was the kitchen. Why? At the end of the hall, where a black wall should have been was a rectangle of white light. Bright against the black of the walls. What was this? A hidden room?

"Hurry, Cassandra. I need the horse."

I ran into the light and a bright room of yellow furniture and colour pictures. A vase of yellow roses, bright, stood on a computer table beside a yellow computer screen. Marie lay on a bed, her pale body against a quilt of large sunflowers on blue. Sarina snatched the horse from me. I stared. The room came as a shock, a difference full of confrontation and sensory assault.

Sarina eased the head off the horse, putting its jet-black body on the yellow bedside table. She pinched out some of the ash.

"Help me, please."

I dropped beside the bed, close to Marie's head.

195

"Open her eyelids. Quickly, we don't have much time. I pried open one eyelid; she sprinkled a little of the ash over the dull eye. We repeated the action with the other. Sarina wiped the remaining powder on the inside of Marie's lips before standing.

"What did you just do?"

"Hopefully, saved her." Sarina eased the head back on the horse then sat on the bed beside her friend. She held her right hand, stroking the fingers as if trying to will the woman back to life.

I sat on the brilliant yellow, high backed office chair and watched. What had Sarina just done? What did this room mean? I thought I understood some of what was going on, even managed to help, but this... The yellow computer was an Apple, all modern design and beautiful. Above the desk stood a rack of books, coloured spines, titles I could read, some author's I knew. The story collection *Leaves of Blood*. Nothing of the Sarina I'd come to know existed in here. Nothing.

The quiet, the deathly quiet clung to us like a second skin. Sarina continued to hold the dead woman's hand, and like a doll with no one to play with, I sat and watched, hoping whatever Sarina had just done would work. She cried, I cried, for some reason the room required emotions. Marie remained lifeless, her skin grey. I thought of CPR, though I doubted it would do anything for someone already dead. If Marie were going to return to us, it would require magic, Uttuku magic and given what I'd seen these past few weeks I believed anything was possible. As I looked at the pretty slack face of a queen, I prayed to whatever gods accepted prayers that some magic would work now. A clock on the wall, a yellow sunflower, said we'd been sitting and waiting for over two hours. Whatever was meant to happen hadn't.

"She's dead," I whispered. "Let her go." Sarina didn't answer, didn't acknowledge I'd spoken. This was going to be hard. I got out of the chair and knelt beside the bed, looking up into her tear stained face. "She's gone."

"No, I won't let her."

"You've done all you can, I'm sorry."

"There's still time; there has to be more time." She begged as much as stated; she wanted to believe Marie still had a chance.

I placed my hand over hers, helped hold Marie. Her fingers were cold, cold.

"You have to let go." I tried to make eye contact with Sarina; she wouldn't look at me. She didn't want to acknowledge the truth.

"No, not yet. I can't let her down; I can't." He voice was so soft I almost didn't hear her.

I gripped the back of her hand, stopping the stroking down on Marie's fingers. I tried to ease the dead woman's hand from her grasp. She wouldn't let go. I didn't know what she expected the ash of a dead man to do. Was this another legend she'd heard and had to try? Not all legends were based on truth. I only had to think about Blas to know that.

I returned to the chair, my backside ached. I would sit here all night and all the next day if I had to. I wouldn't leave her side, not now. And as I thought about it, not ever.

The silence hung about us like a fog, the room too bright, too yellow for us in our blacks. Despite the colour my feeling of depression didn't ease, in fact, it felt like it was deepening. I thought I could hear the beating of my own heart.

"I don't feel so good," I heard Marie say.

"Marie, Marie," Sarina cried.

I fell to my knees, not sure of which God to thank if any. Sarina looked at me, face wet, eyes red weals, hair matted; gone was the constant lustre. She smiled with lifting grief.

"Cassandra?" Marie asked.

"I'm here." I moved to her side. Sarina put an arm about my shoulders.

"You have to do it," Marie said, looking at Sarina. "You have to." Her eyes closed. She'd drifted into sleep. I sat and watched the rise and fall of her chest. I'd just witnessed a miracle.

Sarina covered Marie with a blanket, and we retired to the front room. I rubbed at the tiredness stretching my face, pulled down on my hair in search of respite from the tension in my neck. The world of yellow had shocked my system as much as the death and resurrection of Marie. My world was in shattered pieces at my feet, and there were no King's horses and no King's men to put them all together again. We sat on the sofa, Sarina's face streaked black like a clown, her eyes tired.

"Now you know why I have the horse," Sarina said, as the first rays of the sun broke through the night. "This is the secret."

"Does Aza'zel know?"

"Only I know, well the three of us know. It's why I can't give it back."

We sat together on the sofa watching the sun spread across the sky — a new dawn in so many ways. I looked down the hallway, the yellow room, the white lights.

"That room?" I said.

"My escape. A secret place where I keep things of a more private nature."

"But yellow?"

"Yellow is only another form of black," she said. "It is one of your colours as well if my thinking is correct."

I understood my yellow, had lived with it and taken medication for it. Sarina's yellow, the brighter side of black, did it mean the same as mine?

"Mine's depression," I said.

"I have a yellow dog," she said. I hadn't known.

"The painting of sunflowers?" I'd seen one like it in the mental institution.

197

"Van Gogh," she said, "an original."

"How?"

"Dr Gachet, one of his doctors, was an Uttuku." She closed her eyes and tilted her head back, she sighed. "After Vincent's death he had a lesser artist paint a copy, he kept the original." The words came out in automatic as if Sarina was speaking to fill the silence. I knew that feeling. "He gave me the painting shortly before his death to Aza'zel. I've kept it ever since. If only Gachet knew what I knew now. Vincent might have been saved."

"Didn't he suicide?" I didn't know art or artists, but the sunflower was synonymous with depression.

"A sad story, Cassandra, and I don't want to tell it now," she said, sounding tired. "Another time, maybe. Let's just say the yellow room is the blackness I feel when I'm sad."

We shared far more than I realised. For some reason, this shared view of the world made a difference that went beyond love. She did know what it was to be on the dark side, the human dark side. I let the quiet of the room, the sounds of our breathing settle emotions and thoughts. At every turn, there had been a surprise, a shock just waiting to jump on my face, mess with my head. From the initial doubts and fears, the constant confrontations, I felt stronger and closer to anyone I'd ever felt before. I wasn't alone. Despite what happened in my brain, despite the mania that gripped me from time to time, I wasn't alone. I might soon be dead, but I wouldn't die thinking no one knew how I felt. Funny how such a small thought made such a whole world of difference.

The important object, the horse, needed some more explanation, I might be marked for deletion, but I still wanted to know the truth, it was only fair. Aza'zel didn't know what it represented, didn't know its power, and I didn't know what the hell I'd just witnessed. Marie had been dead, stone cold, empty-eyed, life gone dead. Now she slept in the yellow room as if she'd overcome a bout of the flu.

"So how does the ash work?"

Sarina sat up, rubbed her face, the questioning dragging her back from sleep. "Alexander," she sighed, "despite the darkness he brought to others, was a gleaming light, a brightness us Uttuku could aspire to; the ashes are the essence of this life; his light. The life light."

The explanation came between yawns, a tired voice mumbling over legend like honey over fresh bread. By applying the ash to the eyes of an Uttuku who has dropped into the *Abad* of Aza'zel, it became possible for them to use this light to find their way back, escape from the darkness. The only problem was that it had to be applied soon after death. The longer in the pit, the harder it was to leave. The light is only temporary, a brief glimmer. Sarina had only used it once before. One of our kind in England had stepped too close to the dark, taken from a Prelŭstitel by trickery, if they take the darkness of a lot of humans quickly or at the same time it can afford them a brief time in the presence of an Uttuku. Back then the Prelŭstitel had taken him, making the resurrection easier. They could only take you to the edge of the *Abad*. Aza'zel could thrust you into its depths. Sarina spoke slowly, sharing a secret she had kept since discovering the horse.

I helped her up and steered her to bed, where she dropped.

"The roses?"

"He's been sending them for years." She closed her eyes. "Used to get them on my human birthday, after his death, I started getting them once a month." She stared up at me, eyes vacant. "As a Prelŭstitel he wouldn't remember something like that, so I'm guessing he is using the cycle of the moon to remind him to send flowers." The last words came out as a whisper, a deep breath before sleep dropped over her. I covered her with a blanket I found in the foot of the wardrobe and headed back to the front room. A half bottle of George T. sat on the table. Kicking off my shoes I unscrewed the cap and took a swig. A death and resurrection all in the one-night talk about emotional chaos. Not knowing what would come next, I sat on the sofa and planned to empty the bottle.

The rose smell came from Blas. I watched the sky move through the colours of creation, the coming of new life with the morning. I drank from the bottle, just like my mother. In my escape from her, I had become like her. What did she see in life? What kind of pain drove her into the abyss? Wiping my eyes, I found I missed her, wished I'd had the chance to tell her how much I loved her. Another swig, another shudder, another memory. She died, but the feelings I'd had for her as a child died long before. I wanted so much for her to love me, to accept me as her child. I looked at the near empty bottle. This is what she saw — a life in ruin, a blur of thick glassy vision, distorted emotions. I tilted my head back, closed my eyes. I let the loneliness of the past catch up with the present. Now would be a good time to die.

"Cassandra." The voice, a feather touch. "Cassandra, wake up."

Marie was sitting on the floor by my head. She still looked grey. I tried to sit. My head throbbed. I let it rest back on the cushion.

"What time is it?"

"Eight am. You slept more than sixteen hours." She looked a little sad; then I suppose that could be expected when you'd died for the second time. "You aren't safe."

"Thanks," I said, this time managing to sit. My head thrummed like a bass guitar. "Any other good morning gems to share?" I sounded curt. She didn't deserve that. "Sorry."

She stood and waited for me to struggle to my feet. I didn't feel too good, which was odd, as I never suffered real hangovers. Neither did my mother come to think of it. If I'd felt better that might have bothered me.

"There is only one way to save you, Cassandra."

"Hide me in a thick cell?"

"Come with me." She led me to Sarina's bedroom. She still slept, curled into the blanket like a child. Marie sat on the bed and gently shook Sarina's shoulder. She opened her eyes, saw Marie and smiled.

"How do you feel?"

"A lot better thanks to you." She took one of Sarina's hands. "You can't wait any longer, Sarina, if he comes, he will take her and the horse. You will lose both."

"I know."

Marie looked at me. Sarina sheepishly offered her gaze. I think I knew what they were considering; was I ready? Did I want what they were about to offer? I'd seen enough to give me two choices, and one of those wasn't too good.

"It will hurt," Sarina said.

"What makes you think I want to?"

"You don't want to die. And I want you beside me. Please, it is the only real option we have."

I still didn't know. I wanted to be with her. I couldn't see the future without her, but eternity?

Marie stood, hugged me then left the room. This was between Sarina and me. So much had happened. We studied each other for a long time, neither of us wanting to speak first, say what had to be said.

"How will I change?"

"You'll look younger for a start." She laughed, a pleasant sound considering the moment. "Your body will change, your life light, natural light will fade away, and you'll have to take a little from others to survive." She sat up in bed. "You can be with me forever if you choose, or you could go your own way." She looked down at our hands.

"Anything else?"

"When you take your first, you may find you cannot stop, and you may kill them. I'm sorry, the light is powerful and sometimes the hunger so great you may not be able to stop at just a little."

"Anything else?" This didn't sound too bad. Not the killing part.

"More than I could possibly explain in the next few minutes. Blas is close, and Aza'zel will make his move. We can't stay in the apartment indefinitely. No food." Her face hardened, lips thinned. "Most of the changes are best learned through time." She wriggled her shoulders, getting kinks out of her muscles. "It is up to you, Cassandra. What do you want?"

That was the question she needed an answer for. Did I love her? Did I want to spend eternity with her? I didn't know. Was this how it felt when someone asked you to marry them? No wonder many couples didn't make it to the altar.

"How much will it hurt?"

"A lot." She patted the bed beside her, an offer to sit. "You might even die. Many conversions do."

"Choices?" I sat.

"You know the choices."

Death or possible death. "What do I do?"

She eased me down onto the bed, made me comfortable on my back, removing the pillow, so my neck was straight. Sarina held my right hand, gently stroking my fingers. I could see she had trouble taking this step.

"This time there will be no euphoria, I will be giving not taking this time, and my invasion of you will bring pain beyond belief."

"It's okay. I want to." I said it, but I still didn't know. Not really. I could have done with a drink to help me think, decide.

"There's so much I want to say to you. If, if..."

"I love you, Sarina." I meant it, believed it. She relaxed a little and squeezed my hand. "I think I loved you soon after we met, but all this craziness, my mania, I couldn't think. I suppose I wanted to be sure."

"I'll stay beside you the whole time," she said, pushing hair from my face. "You aren't alone, remember that. You aren't alone." She touched her fingers to my forehead. "I love you, Cassandra." Light flashed.

I screamed.

I stood on the beach watching the waves, feeling the breeze in my face.

Six days I'd spent in and out of consciousness, six days of pain, loss and incredible loneliness. I kept remembering Sarina's promise, yet I couldn't tell if she'd held to it. At least she was there when I opened my eyes and managed to keep them open. Moving hurt, thinking hurt, everything ached as if I'd been beaten over and over. I could smell me, the sweet stink of sweat, and something else I didn't want to think about.

Sarina helped me shower, washed my hair and dried me. All the time she kept me away from the mirror. I wanted to see.

"You are different," she said, readying me for the first look. "I guided you to this."

Sucking in a deep breath, enjoying the taste of the air, I investigated the mirror. The woman who looked back was me at twenty-five, a better looking twenty-five. The mole on my shoulder was gone, the lines around my mouth and eyes, even the appendix scar from when I was a child were gone. I started to cry. Sarina embraced me, held me close. I looked beautiful. So beautiful.

I let the waves wash over my feet, the sand tickling, settling between my toes. I not only survived the conversion, I also became untouchable to Aza'zel. I did wonder what Blas would say. I liked to think he would be pleased, happy I'd decided to stay with Sarina.

I needed help with my first taking, Sarina showing me how to gently touch and pull away quickly once I'd found the energy. I took the light of a man sleeping on the beach, he looked excited when two beautiful women offered to rub sunscreen into his back. Clumsily, after Sarina had touched his shoulder with a tiny light flash that sent him to sleep, I pressed my hand to his brow; the light, bright, moved through me with the same warmth a good port gives as it drives off cold. It didn't take much, two brief seconds and I felt invigorated, more alive than I'd ever felt. I had taken once more since then, Sarina again helping and telling me how to control the touch, how to make the moment quick definite. I felt the desire to take everything with a touch, the energy was addictive and hot and if it were not for Sarina's guiding hand, I felt sure that I would have taken a life; it would be so easy to do.

A walk was needed to help with the changes, to accept and, perhaps, to have some regrets. I heard Sarina coming down the beach from behind. Hearing also improved, so did eyesight, smell and taste. My senses were so alive. I felt overwhelmed the first time I'd ventured outside.

Sarina stood beside me and handed me a bottle of water and my morning pills. I still had to take the medication, over time the need would reduce; not entirely as even Uttuku suffer from depression. The sadness of loss over time. I took the pills and sipped water, keeping my eyes on the horizon. A tanker, a black smudge against the sky, headed out to deep water.

"Blas did what he promised," she said, handing me a newspaper.

The paper showed the arrest of Samantha, hands cuffed behind, hair a wild mess, mouth open, screaming at the camera. Uri got his justice. I handed the paper back with the feeling of relief and sadness.

"Will we see him again?"

"Often," she said. "I don't think he'll contact us though."

"The horse?"

"Aza'zel will probably send someone else."

I felt a little sad at the news. Oddly I liked the old general come Prelŭstitel. He held a dignity about him that belied his purpose. In a way, I had looked death square in the face and found he wasn't such a bad guy or was that just my mood talking?

"Marie has started work on a project for you." Sarina sounded pleased. "It will make up for the slow loss of your prominent career." She touched my shoulder, then my face. Her fingers were warm. "I knew the time might come, Cassandra, so I planned in advance, just in case."

"Thanks," I said. We still had some issues to sort out in our relationship, and trust to establish. It would take time; time we had a lot of. The sounds of waves breaking lured me back to the ocean, away from the immediate. Sarina and I would talk more later, for now, all I wanted was the peace of mind I felt to continue and to continue for a long time.

Chapter 40

The Prelŭstitel

He'd made his move without telling me. He'd killed Marie to panic Sarina, to pressure Cassandra with fear. It failed, and if he'd told me the plan, I could have explained why it would. Cassandra's conversion didn't come as a surprise. Uttuku do not convert humans often and even then, only under duress or out of love; Cassandra fit both categories.

He watched me, eyes bright, gleaming. I'd failed. He'd failed to get the horse. We stood together in the centre of 3rd St Promenade; the stores were closed, the funnel-like building causing the wind to blow hard and gust.

"This is where a lot of darkness comes," I told him as he ran his fingers over the trunk of a tree.

"Fitting," he said. "This has nothing to take, yet it lives." He moved about the tree, the leaves rustling in the breeze. "Do you feel complete?"

It was an odd question. "Why do you ask?" Cold touched me.

"Has the last of the human emotion for Uri been satisfied?"

"Yes." Is that why he thwarted some of my attempts?

"There must be no distractions for you Prelŭstitel. I have removed it, and you are free."

"You did all this so I would be a better hunter?"

"I did all this so you would have a better chance in succeeding with you task. It has worked so far." He sat on a bench, his darkness swallowing it like a shroud.

"I still have to retrieve the icon."

"Perhaps. Next time you won't be alone." I heard the cry of millions of lives as he said it. "You will lead him to them. He will do what you would not, and he will show you the way to the completeness."

"I understand." The new Prelŭstitel was already here, this I knew. He was the one who had tricked Marie. I know of him and know the great darkness that follows him.

"Do you?" He pressed into me. Mixed darkness with darkness. "He knows the full power of the mind; he knows how to take an Uttuku. He has done so before."

I did understand. I knew who they had taken, tricked into death and then resurrected from the *Abad*. An Uttuku-Prelŭstitel was rare and weak. For now, everything would continue forward for Sarina and Cassandra. They'd move, and I would move with them, keep them ready for the next attempt at the horse. I wondered if I would let the new Prelŭstitel take the women.

"Prelŭstitel," he said, a sound not unlike a train in a tunnel. "I will send him soon; you will do as he says."

"I will follow his commands."

"Should you not he will also remove you from the realm."

"But that is your right!"

"I have given it to him. It should keep you focused on the real task, don't you think?" Aza'zel dropped through the ground and was gone. Not for long I suspected. Until then I had to find a way to get the horse without killing the women. It was wrong to have let Sarina take it, but I owed her for saving me several times when I should have died. No, the human memories were not all gone, sometimes they did come back, the important ones and the ones to do with her.

I let myself be seen. Two officers approached, their lights bright, both within and without. They walked up to me, hands on guns. I tore their darkness free before they could speak. I let them scream, I let them feel the pain of darkness crush their lives. I squeezed and squeezed until they no longer drew breath.

When he came, I would need to be strong — needed to be prepared.

Chapter 41

Cassandra

I closed the front door. I wouldn't be coming back. Mariz was gone, crossed over, and Samantha would be doing time along with her lawyer, who was in on the scam and the murder. Sarina explained what Samantha had become in her time with him. A succubus. She sucked away his strength, his money and his will to live. I purchased a copy of Sissy Falloe's *A Whisper of Blood*. It helped me understand the type of person Samantha was and how lucky I had been not to get trapped in her web. Sarina wouldn't read the book, said she already knew enough about the subject to last too many lifetimes. I was saddened that my writing career would be limited. Even to me, Cassandra Whitehall had started to die.

In my hand was an invitation to a special dinner to be held in my honour. I was accepted back into the fold. I also had a letter from Amanda Debbs inviting me to apply for a new grant she was sure I would get. How quickly the tide can turn.

The house, now on the market, was the last of my old life. I didn't want to sell it. I had enjoyed my garden and the scents of the flowers. Staying wasn't an option. Sarina and I would spend a few months in the apartment before packing up and moving on. A new place, a new start of sorts.

I was now to step away from me. I would still write, still had contracts to honour, but eventually, works wouldn't be published under my old name. The agent Sarina had got from Li was ready to sign an unknown based on her recommendation, and this new writer would be me, a never seen anonymous person turning out books and hopefully best sellers. I could live with being a mystery and never having to face fans or interviews. Sarina had said in a way I would have to become less and less known, something she had become very good at over the centuries.

I walked to the front of my car, also to go up for sale, a laptop sat on the bonnet. I had an email to send to the auction place, telling them where the key was and giving them the all clear to start their job.

My mobile rang. "Hi, Marie." Her name on the call register.

"The guys at the agency just called." She sounded excited. "You on the net?"

"Checking email, why?"

"Go to www.CassandraWhitehall.com," she said. "It's all been set up. You will be able to use this for a while, maybe a few years at least."

I typed in the URL, and the site came up — a writing site for me. I could post stuff there until I was ready to give up my name completely and with the pseudonym writing, I would be able to write for years to come. Maybe the greatest love of my life would have to end with the greatest sadness of my life.

"It's brilliant."

"I'm glad you like it, Cassandra. It was the least we could do. The site owner is ready to list stuff by you now; when you are ready, of course."

"Thanks, Marie. Thanks for everything."

Life might have taken a new direction, a longer direction, and I was happy the one true passion I'd enjoyed as a human could remain with me as an Uttuku. Oh, the stories I could write.

I climbed into Sarina's limo out front and said my last goodbyes to the house and my past. I wasn't out of danger, not completely but now I wasn't defenceless, and the more I could learn from Sarina would make me less of a target to the Prelŭstitel.

Blas still watched from the shadows; he hadn't made contact since getting his book back. He will always be with Sarina and me. He wanted the horse; he was a Prelŭstitel, his way wouldn't change. We couldn't be sure he'd never contact us again. He remained a shadow, a peripheral entity.

Sarina thought he watched out of love. Roses still arrived, and Sarina continued to put them on the desk in the yellow room. We shared the room often, a private getaway within a private getaway. It became our island. Sometimes we went out wearing matching yellow dresses, a concession Sarina made for me. The new black, she'd laugh.

Aza'zel stopped stepping into our world once he discovered I'd been converted. We knew he'd be back someday. The horse would always be something he wanted to hold up against us. Just so long as he didn't know its real power, we would be safe. And with Beth, quite a nasty Bruxsa, always watching our backs, we didn't need to live under the weight of threat.

Today I was having lunch with Sarina. The web site was allowing me to write some short fiction and articles. As we headed back to the apartment on Venice Beach, I tore the invitation and application in two I didn't need anything the fellowship offered, and money wasn't going to be a problem. It felt good to be able to turn my back on it all and not feel guilty. Sarina had set up the agent with Big Gary so I didn't have to deal with anyone directly. I hated to admit that amongst all the madness Sarina had set me up to continue with what I loved.

The phone rang. I didn't know the number.

"Hello?"

"I am coming; I am coming for you." The phone clicked off.

Chapter 42

The Prelŭstitel

"He said you would be here."

I didn't need to turn to know who he'd sent; I just hoped he was alone. "And what makes you think you can take her any more than me?" I turned to face the man in black. His hair was a modern spiked cut, his eyes bright, blue and penetrating. Of course, he looked thirty years younger than he did in 1938 and without the moustache he was quite handsome.

"It is the other woman I'm here for, Blaz. She is weak in the way and will not know how to hold me back. She will make a mistake and then get what we want. All you need to do is keep Sarina busy."

Adolf had shifted to Aza'zel well after me, but he was strong, clever and well suited to the requirements of a Prelŭstitel. He'd already fed well in the second world war, and like Stalin, they shared the uncanny knack of finding the darkest parts of the world before they turned dark. I knew where Adolf had been for a long time. The Middle East was a perfect feeding ground for him, and he who use to be Stalin still fed on his people in Russia, so great is the darkness of history there.

"I called her you know?" Adolf turned his back to the building and rested against a pylon. "Let her know we are coming."

"Why?"

"In fear, mistakes are made, even you should know this." He folded his arms and amused gleam in his eyes. "But you do know all this, don't you? Fear is the mind killer. How much human remains in you Don Blas de Lezo? I hope it is significant. When you cannot do you task, it will be fulfilling to take your darkness."

"And I suppose you have a plan?"

"I haven't taken you yet, so yes, there is a plan." Adolph looked over at the distant building; the second story lights were on, the women were at home.

Sarina's limo had returned late afternoon, and Cassandra had run inside. I had wondered what had frightened her, now I knew, Adolph has set a new game in play, and this time it would be quick.

Chapter 43

Cassandra

Sarina was in the yellow room when I entered. She lost her smile as soon as I mentioned the call. It hadn't been Bas though the same 555 number had been displayed. Despite the changes in me I still felt the edge of panic, it wasn't as strong as when I was human, still a strange way to think of myself, but it was still there.

"They are coming," she said. "And if this is who I expect we have a real problem and one not even Beth could handle for us."

"Who and should I be feeling as afraid as I do already?" Sarina led me into the kitchen, a bottle of George T and the tumbler I used this morning was still on the table, if there was any time to have a drink now was good. Then anytime was good for a drink.

"Hitler."

"Fuck me!" I poured another, and another.

"We can't fight against this Prelŭstitel, especially if he also has the help of Blas, which I am expecting will be the case."

Going through the whole crazy arsed mess again wasn't pleasing me. I had hoped by becoming an Uttuku would at least give me some safety, some respite from the madness.

"You want one?" I poured yet another drink. Alcohol still affected me like it always did, only the effect wore off quick, and the definitely were no after effects.

"Come with me." She let me finish the whiskey before dragging me into the front room.

She picked up the horse and stared at me as if searching for something to do as if somewhere on my person I had the answer she needed. She clicked off the head.

"Get me a glass, a clean one." I picked the one up off the coffee table; I always kept one there just in case.

Sarina poured the ashes into the glass while I held it. The powder was fine, grey and easily filled the large glass. Sarina was going to give them the horse. Why didn't we think of this before? It seemed so simple and logical now. Sarina put the head back on the horse and put in on the table; she took the glass with the ash and took it down to the yellow room. In moments the room was sealed, and she was back, face pale, something in the look said this wasn't as easy as I was thinking.

"I don't think..."

I fell back against the sofa as something dark rushed through the window. No glass broke, but something came in. I went to stand, but again darkness pressed on me, keeping me down and momentarily blinded. Sarina gasped. She should have been a couple of feet to mu right. I reached out. The black eased away, and I saw here lying on the floor nearby, she was backing away, pushing up with her elbows. I crawled to her side as shadow, thick and murky shifted about the black room, the lights faded to red hallos in an impenetrable night.

"The horse will not be enough."

I turned to the voice. A man dressed unlike Blas stood by the window holding the horse. Beside him stood Blas, who was struggling to stand, he looked in pain.

"You have it, now leave." Sarina got to her feet. I joined her as the room grew increasingly cold. I'd felt the cold before, in the basement Goth party, in the strip club. Was Aza'zel going to appear as well? This wasn't going to be a happy get-together.

"I'll want the girl as well." The man stepped forward, but it was clear he was struggling.

"You don't have the strength, Adolph." Sarina stepped in close to me. The man didn't look anything like Hitler.

A rush of black knocked us into the wall. I heard air rush from Sarina's lungs. My head thudded into, and maybe even through the wallboard, I dropped to my backside, aching all over. I couldn't breathe, the blackness invaded me, sucked at my existence. In the distance amongst the deepening shadows, I saw a spiralling pit. The cold increased around me as the draw of the black maw pulled me closer, deeper into a sense of nothingness. I raised my hand to see light seeping through and away from my skin, particles of light bleeding off and disappearing into the growing hole getting closer.

The Abad. The pit of darkness Sarina had told me about. I was dying again. Adolph had somehow entered me and was taking me to Aza'zel. Then this was what total death was like. There was no feeling here, no fear or loss, as I drew closer, I felt less and less connected to myself. I was becoming nothing, nothing, nothing...

Light. Bright blinding slight hit me like a fist in the face. I knew I cried out, the scream echoed off the walls. The first thing to come into view was Sarina's face; she was staring at me from the other side of the room. She was speaking, but I could quite hear the words. She was kneeling beside someone, a man with one arm and one leg. Don Blas de Lezo? I crawled away from the wall and towards Sarina.

He lay breathing raggedly by Sarina's knees, he didn't look as young as before, and he was missing an eye as well as limbs.

"He took Adolph's attack." Sarina touched my hand; the man didn't have much left in him. "He sacrificed himself for us. Like he did in *the Battle of Cartagena de Indias*. He took on the odds."

"Can we help him?" She shook her head and by the look of him he way beyond anything I could do. "What about the ashes?"

She offered another head shake. She settled his head in her lap and stroked his long hair; he had short hair when he entered the apartment. From appearances, he'd reverted to what he'd been before becoming a Prelŭstitel. His breathing grew shallower with longer breaks between exhales. Sarina sobbed, I sobbed as we watched the man slip away. His last act was to save me and to save the woman he'd once loved. His breathing stilled and Sarina placed him carefully on the floor. She grabbed my hand, helped me to my feet and we moved away from the body, the air smelt strongly of roses, an invading smell that choked in my throat.

"Farewell *Mediohombre.*" Light grew outwards from the body, I felt it touch me, a gentle embrace, then it was gone, and so too was de Lezo.

"He loved you." I put my arm about her.

"I know."

I looked about the room; the horse was gone. Adolph had taken it. The horse without the ash was of no real use, couldn't be otherwise Sarina wouldn't have gone to all the effort of removing it.

"Is Adolph gone for good?" Sarina rested her head on my shoulder; I couldn't feel her anguish and loss.

"For now, but he'll be back, he has to come back."

"Why?" He had the statue.

"Because you are still alive because I'm still alive." She shifted away from me, taking both my hands in hers. "Blas has ensured we will be safe for a time, Cassandra. It's time we left Santa Monica for good."

The move inland was going to take a few months, Sarina had found a place, and we had to pack up the apartment. While packing away the photo album, Sarina confessed that the only time, she had ever spoken to Bela Lugosi was when he was a young soldier in Austria and he helped her get a cab for her and her cat. It wasn't a huge event in the scheme of events that surrounded her, a non-event really but one small act of kindness had influenced the life of the oldest woman in the world. I still had work to do on the Austrian connection in everything, but now I had plenty of time. I had a whole heap of time.

Chapter 44

The Prelŭstitel

"Why did you have him play this game?"

"Uri's death required human justice. He required human justice for him." A hint, the barest of hints in his tone. "Only this could remove the last traces of his human side, Prelŭstitel. Human revenge settled and then removed his last contact with what he once was. I had thought this would have been enough."

He was partly right. de Lezo needed to remove his last human trait, but it wasn't anything to do with Uri. I hadn't fully known this, Aza'zel had, and yet he still allowed the game to play out. I had the horse, and it was now returned to the *Abad* where it belonged. Don Blas had got in my way, and it will take time for me to recover the lost darkness.

"You could have just told me what was going on here," I said. I thought things could have been done in a simpler fashion. "I had retrieved the horse in less than a day."

"Then where would my plan be if you knew. No Prelŭstitel as is as I have seen and put into motion, you need only play your part."

"Which is?" There was a greater reason behind everything; there always was, such is the way of Aza'zel.

"Cassandra is still new; she will need to be taught and learn much about the Uttuku. She will lead us to where I want to go. This young Uttuku will be the death bringer to them all." He faded into the night and was gone.

Looking up I wondered when she would arrive. I could not just wait for the moment to come, and he knew I couldn't. He had ended the human trait within me; not the one that still influenced me the most. Trucks were coming and leaving the building; the women were moving. They could go nowhere without me knowing, the Uttuku cannot hide. Let him plan his plans, I still have something to settle with Sarina, and she will pay for what she has done.

Chapter 45

Cassandra

Standing in the forest was supposed to calm my nerves. I was still on medication the idea of being one of the undead troubled me beyond the effects of anti-depressants. I was an Uttuku for all that was worth, and I had to find the essence of life to feed from in order to survive. The gentle tickle of wind flicked my hair about my face, and I didn't care. Sarina had paid all the builders and decorators, and out new home was perfect. Perfectly black inside and out. Hidden at its heart was the yellow room and I was able to add pieces of my past life to its decorations, some books, a laptop with my last novel unfinished and some bottle of whisky I'd taken from the Goth bar the day we left the city.

"We need to show our faces," Sarina said from behind.

We'd been in the county less than six months, and already Sarina chair town hall meetings and the locals loved her. I loved her.

"I don't know anything about law enforcement," I said turning and staring into her beautiful face. "I'm too young in their eyes. I'm too young in my eyes."

She took my hands and squeezed, the rough warm and soft and pleasing. Without saying another word, she pulled me into an embrace, and I held her tight. Tears came, and I knew they were more than my constant depression.

"You'll do fine; the police station has plenty of deputies who will keep you in line, so follow their lead and listen to their advice." She pushed me back, her hands on my shoulders. "We need to establish a way to get what we need without causing suspicion. There's no Goth club out here."

"I'd prefer to own the bar," I said. "It wasn't like Goth club, but there was whisky, and with my new body, I could enjoy it without the old hangovers or messy mind.

We walked toward the house, she with one arm looped through mine. Amongst the greens and browns of the forest her all-black dress and fair skin made her more gothic that she appeared in Santa Monica. How could she not draw attention looking like that? At least in a police officer uniform, I would be out of black from some part of the day. I'd written enough about police actions in my fiction novels over the years, so I wasn't completely in the dark.

The house sat between two low hills, three large, black blocks with heavily tinted massive black windows. The original house on the property sat on top of a near hill and held the smarter vantage point, and the only reason we hadn't pulled it down was because the township believed we lived in the place. The black blocks were hidden from sight, though I knew in a small county everyone would know what was here. It was why I was more surprised by Sarina's easy acceptance on the town council and now my easy nomination for sheriff.

Sarina hadn't said Uttuku possess magic and I hadn't asked because I was still coming to terms with the notion of living forever provided, I wasn't hunted down and killed.

I wasn't alone anymore, and I felt good about the situation. Marie Antionette had also moved to the town under the guise of a psychiatrist, and naturally, I saw her every few weeks for an assessment. I didn't know if her qualifications were real, the qualification on the wall of her office looked real enough, it was just nice to be able to talk to someone my age. Well, someone who looked my age at least. She wrote prescriptions for the drug store and the town's people were quick to accept three young looking women into the fold. I'd already received a few requests for dates until I confessed my preferences and how Sarina and I were a couple. I thought that would cause some tension, though it didn't and in a way that caused a tension in me. Why?

"You take the Escalade into town, I'll follow a little later, I have something that needs my attention." Sarina steered me to the SUV. I would have preferred a little Saab 93 convertible, but they weren't made anymore, so I had to settled for the big, black and imposing GM monster.

"We need to feed," I said opening the driver's side door.

"After the meeting." She left me and went into the house.

Leaving out long drive to get on the tarmac into town I wished I'd put on something less formal and more in keeping with the relaxed nature of the town. My all black pantsuit was perfect for a corporate function but was it sheriff election night material.

"You are her weakness."

I slammed on the brakes. The wheels squealed as I slid to a stop. Sitting beside me was Adolph. I turned to my right, and he was there, sitting perfectly still in a neat grey suit with an orange tie over a blue shirt.

"What do you want?" I snapped, heart racing. Part of me wanted to open the door, jump out and run into the forest.

"Lilith." He smiled. A sight that was far from pleasing. "Then you. Eventually, I'll take you." He opened the passenger door and climbed out. "Blas might have been older, but he was also weak. I will not make the same mistakes." He gently closed the door and was gone.

I gripped the steering wheel tightly, struggling to control my breathing. Adolf had been in the car, been with me. How did he know where we were? How did he find us?

My phone rang. I snatched out of my jacket. It was Sarina.

"Adolph was here," I cried as soon as I heard her voice. "He was in the car with me."

"I know," she said.

"How? How did you know? It only just happened." My hands were shaking.

214

"He was here as well." She sounded calm, the always calm woman who'd seduced me, tricked me and then saved me.

"He said he wants Lilith." I closed my eyes. I had to calm my breathing.

"I know," she sighed. "Come back here, and I'll explain. It is time you knew the truth."

Epilogue

It had been raining for days, and I was getting sick of just sitting in the office taking calls about minor flooding in basements and lost pets. I wanted to be out investigating something, anything. I heard the front door close, so I stood and went to see who'd come into the station.

"Sherriff," Wesley Gowan, said when he saw me.

"What can I help you with Wes," I liked Wes, he ran the feed store at the end of Main and had helped with setting up my stable for my horse Beth.

"Been seein' some strange happening at the graveyard last few nights." He put his baseball cap on the counter, his big grey coat was dripping water everywhere, and his head was wet.

"What kind of things?" I thought of Sarina, I thought of Marie and how she conspired with Sarina to keep a secret I now didn't want to admit to knowing. This had to be Aza'zel. First Adolph a few months back, now this.

"It's nothing definite, like," he said," Just shadows moving about the headstones." He stared at me, and I could see the fear in his eyes. "Sometimes the show went into the grave, Sherriff. I know how it sounds, and I haven't touched a drop in a month like you asked. I saw what I saw, so I thought I'd better tell you."

"Thanks, Wes, I'll head out there now and have a look around for you." I stepped around the counter and rested my right hand on the grip of my gun. I still wasn't comfortable with carrying the weapon and I had nowhere to rest me hand with it sticking out from my side. "And good for you with the drinking. If you keep going maybe you and Rose can have a coffee, see about patching things up."

"You think?" He brightened.

"No promises, you keep off the booze and maybe she will agree to have a chat." I pointed to the door. "You better get back to the store while there's a break in the rain, I'll head out to check out the cemetery."

"Thanks sheriff, thanks for everything."

Once Wesley was out of the station, I called Sarina.

"Hi honey, how's work?" She answered

"He's here, Aza'zel is here." I expected it but part of me hoped this day wouldn't come. "And he has to know you are Lilith."

216

Source UK Ltd.
nes UK
950230622
00007B/126/J